AN ORDINARY SPY

BY THE SAME AUTHOR

10TH GRADE

AN

ORDINARY SPY

A NOVEL

JOSEPH WEISBERG

BLOOMSBURY

Published by Bloomsbury USA, New York
Distributed to the trade by Macmillan

All papers used by Bloomsbury USA are natural, recyclable products made from
wood grown in well-managed forests. The manufacturing processes
conform to the environmental regulations of the country of origin.

LIBRARY OF CONGRESS CATALOGING-IN-PUBLICATION DATA HAS BEEN APPLIED FOR.

ISBN-10 1-59691-376-2
ISBN-13 978-1-59691-376-9

First U.S. Edition 2008

1 3 5 7 9 10 8 6 4 2

Typeset by Westchester Book Group
Printed in the United States of America by Quebecor World Fairfield

For Ernest Batten, Robert Weisberg,
and Francis "Mac" MacDonald

PART ONE

1

Several months before I was scheduled to leave for ████, I was assigned to the ████ office in █ Division. Depending on scheduling and other bureaucratic considerations, new case officers ████ ████████████████████████████████. In my case, I was shipping out in August, so I would be in █ for most of the summer.

It was a busy time in ██████, but the officers running country desks liked to handle their own work. They'd give me an occasional name trace to run, or have me coordinate a cable with another division. But I wasn't busy. I'd read the morning traffic—cables from the stations in ████████████████████, and whatever ████████ traffic was coming in. I'd stop by my friends' offices throughout the building or meet them for coffee in the cafeteria. And one or two days a week, I'd take care of various tasks I had to accomplish before going abroad, like ████████████████████████████ and getting my final medical clearance.

Other than that, I spent a lot of time reading. I had a stack of books on my desk about the history and politics of ████, and I wanted to get through them all before I left. People at the Agency weren't really "book people," and when colleagues stopped by my cubicle and saw me reading, they'd usually chuckle or say, "Good for you," in a sort of half-admiring, half "I wonder if you really belong here" way. This was the same attitude I'd gotten from the Chief of ████ when I'd needed him to sign off on an ████████ course I wanted to take at the ████ Department. He'd said, "Nobody ever takes these," although after thinking about it for a few seconds he'd signed and said, "See if you get anything out of it."

One day, the Deputy Chief of ████, a bland, decent guy stuck at GS-13 or 14, called me into his office. There'd been some sort of routine request from Congress about ███████ and ████████████, and he wanted me to do a file review of all of the office's cases, active and inactive, going back five years, to find the information. He was apologetic about it, since even the words "file review" implied something wasteful and dull. But I didn't mind. I'd read a few case files while working on various matters, and they were an interesting window into the work I'd be doing once I went abroad.

The office's files were stored in long, low cabinets that ran the length of the wall between the Deputy Chief and the Chief's offices. There were probably about ███ of them, going back ten years. Inactive cases older than that were sent to Archives. ████████████████

██

██

████████████████████████████ labeled TRBALLOON, pronouncing both of the first two letters, and then the word. ████████████████████

██

██

██ either typed on a label or written directly on the folder. They varied in length, with the longer ones filling two or three of the orange folders.

Over the next few days, I'd grab an armful of files in the morning, read them, take them back to the file cabinets, and get another batch for the afternoon. I really could have just scanned them to get the information I needed, but as I said, I liked reading them, and nobody particularly cared, or even noticed, how much time I was taking with the assignment.

Like all CIA employees in the Directorate of Operations (DO), I had a Top Secret clearance, which meant that I was cleared to see almost anything. Certain types of information required a special ████████ clearance—████████████████████████████████████ ████████████████████████████████████. But if you were working on something where that clearance was required, your boss signed a slip, you handed it in to Security, and a day later you had the clearance. It wasn't really a big deal.

There was the idea of "need to know," which meant that you shouldn't see, hear, or read about anything you didn't need to know about in order to do your job. But this was largely ignored. If you were sitting with a friend from a different division at lunch, you'd tell each other about the cases you were working on. You might not do it at a table of five people, but if your boss knew you were talking to other officers about your cases, he almost certainly wouldn't care. He did it, too. The environment was surprisingly open within the Directorate. And in a sense, learning about a wide variety of cases would help you understand your job better, so you could even make an argument that you "sort of needed to know."

In any case, I had no real need to know about the details of these cases I was reading. But I was cleared for them, and they were within my division, and even my office, so I didn't hide the fact that I was reading them much more carefully than I needed to.

Each of the files contained the cable traffic ████████████ ██ ██████████████████████████████████. In a lot of the cases, it was determined after a few encounters that the target wasn't susceptible to recruitment, or didn't have access to useful, classified information. These were the thin files. In other cases, there were multiple meetings, and a relationship developed that often produced some intelligence, but the case never turned into a full-blown recruitment. These files were a little bit thicker. Finally, in some cases, an agent was recruited and either run for a period of time or was still being run. These files could be anywhere from ████ to ████████ pages, depending, presumably, on the Chief of Station (COS) and his attitude about Headquarters. Some COSs saw Headquarters as troublesome, bureaucratic, and meddlesome, and felt that only the broad outlines of a case should be reported. Others obviously encouraged their case officers (C/Os) to write in great detail about every aspect of a case, either because it forced the C/Os to be clear and rigorous in their thinking, or as a cover-your-ass maneuver in case something went wrong.

These more detailed files were, of course, the ones I liked reading the most. They were filled with cables that described operational meetings in great detail—what the target or agent was wearing, what their facial expressions were like, how they responded to what the case officer said and did. In just a few months, I'd be running meetings like this, and these real-world examples were an education in how much less formal and systematic the recruitment process was than the way it had been taught in training.

In addition to the operational cables, a file might or might not include intelligence reports. Unlike the other traffic, these ██████ ██. It was the information you were actually after when you recruited an agent in the first place. Whether there were a lot of them or just a few of them in the file depended on whether or not the officer at Headquarters in charge of the case was conscientious about putting them in. Most of the intel reports that were there were pretty dull, and it was hard to imagine them being that useful to an analyst. Friends in the Directorate of Intelligence (DI) had told me that the secret intelligence coming from the DO rarely had much of an impact on their analysis, and I could see why. On the other hand, there was an occasional nugget of information that seemed enormously important and useful.

2

About a week into the file review, I opened a folder labeled TDTRACER (all the cryptonyms, pseudonyms, and names in this book have been changed). The top cable was stamped ██████ ████████████████, which was a complete surprise. My heart started racing a little bit as soon as I saw it. ███████████████ ██████ cables were more compartmentalized than other traffic, and normally they wouldn't be in a regular file. I hadn't seen any of these since starting at the Agency, except to sign for their delivery to the office once or twice. I'd certainly never read one. Arguably, I shouldn't read this one without getting clearance, but here it was in front of me, and I was supposed to be doing the file review.

The cable had originated in ███████████, where I was going to begin serving in about a month. I was, obviously, particularly interested in cases that took place there, especially more recent ones where the agent might still be active. The cable was dated June 2000, so it was certainly possible that it dealt with an agent who was still being run (this was the summer of 2002). Under the date was the normal range of headers—██ ████████████████████████████ written by a C/O with the pseudonym Franklin D. McCelvoy and then the text of the cable, which ran more or less as follows (██ ████████████████)█

AS PART OF ONGOING EFFORT TO DETERMINE THE WHEREABOUTS OF STATION ASSET TDTRACER, C/O FRANKLIN D. MCCELVOY RAN A 48-HOUR HOT WATCH OF ████████ EMBASSY. WATCH BEGAN 6/19/00 AT 2200 ZULU. WHEN C/O MCCELVOY ARRIVED AT WATCH SITE 6/20/00 AT 0800 ZULU TO RELIEVE HEADQUARTERS SPECIAL PROJECTS TEAM MANAGER GRIMES, HE WAS DEPLOYED AT █████████████ IN CONTRAVENTION TO SPECIFIC INSTRUCTIONS GIVEN AT OUTSET OF OPERATION. VISUAL AND ███████ OBSERVATION GAVE NO SIGNS OF TEAM HAVING BEEN DETECTED.

FOR DURATION OF HOT WATCH, ALL PERSONNEL ENTERING AND EXITING EMBASSY WERE PROCESSED THROUGH ███████. ALL SUBJECTS WERE EMBASSY PERSONNEL OR FOREIGN NATIONALS WITH ESTABLISHED TIES TO EMBASSY.

████████ PICKED UP NO UNUSUAL ACTIVITY ON EMBASSY █████████ ████.

HOT WATCH PRODUCED NO INFORMATION ON TDTRACER.

WHILE CONSIDERING FURTHER POSSIBLE COURSES OF ACTION, C/O MCCELVOY AND STATION BELIEVE A PROBABLE LIST OF EXPLANATIONS FOR TDTRACER'S STATUS INCLUDE: ACTION BY ██████ AS DIRECTED BY ██████████████████, INDEPENDENT ACTION TAKEN BY ██████, OR

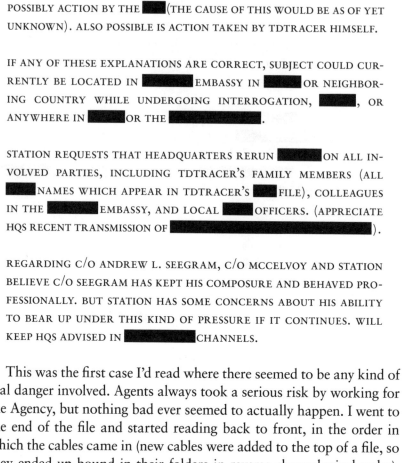

POSSIBLY ACTION BY THE ████(THE CAUSE OF THIS WOULD BE AS OF YET UNKNOWN). ALSO POSSIBLE IS ACTION TAKEN BY TDTRACER HIMSELF.

IF ANY OF THESE EXPLANATIONS ARE CORRECT, SUBJECT COULD CUR-RENTLY BE LOCATED IN ████████ EMBASSY IN ██████ OR NEIGHBOR-ING COUNTRY WHILE UNDERGOING INTERROGATION, ██████, OR ANYWHERE IN ██████ OR THE ██████████████.

STATION REQUESTS THAT HEADQUARTERS RERUN ████████ ON ALL IN-VOLVED PARTIES, INCLUDING TDTRACER'S FAMILY MEMBERS (ALL ██████ NAMES WHICH APPEAR IN TDTRACER'S ██████ FILE), COLLEAGUES IN THE ████████ EMBASSY, AND LOCAL ██████ OFFICERS. (APPRECIATE HQS RECENT TRANSMISSION OF ██████████████████████).

REGARDING C/O ANDREW L. SEEGRAM, C/O MCCELVOY AND STATION BELIEVE C/O SEEGRAM HAS KEPT HIS COMPOSURE AND BEHAVED PRO-FESSIONALLY. BUT STATION HAS SOME CONCERNS ABOUT HIS ABILITY TO BEAR UP UNDER THIS KIND OF PRESSURE IF IT CONTINUES. WILL KEEP HQS ADVISED IN ████████ CHANNELS.

This was the first case I'd read where there seemed to be any kind of real danger involved. Agents always took a serious risk by working for the Agency, but nothing bad ever seemed to actually happen. I went to the end of the file and started reading back to front, in the order in which the cables came in (new cables were added to the top of a file, so they ended up bound in their folders in reverse chronological order). TDTRACER was a ██████ national, working as a ██████████ at the embassy in ██████. A C/O with the pseudonym Andrew L. Seegram had met him at a conference the ██████ government had set up on for-eign investment. He'd written TDTRACER up as a target with primary access to information on ██████ economic policy. But he'd also writ-ten that TRACER might develop into a source on terrorism (which was a hot-button issue at the time, even before September 11). ██████ was fighting a separatist movement in ██████████, and their intel service, the ████, collected extensively on worldwide terrorism. The hope was that TRACER might have, or might develop, intelligence service contacts within the embassy, or come across some information simply by virtue of being in the embassy. It might have been a bit of a stretch, but adding terrorism to the targets a potential agent might work against helped ensure Headquarters' approval for pursuing a recruitment.

Seegram initially suggested to TRACER that they get together to discuss their respective countries' interest in a trade pact with ████. They had lunch, and when it went well, Seegram suggested they get together again. Over the course of several more meetings, they became quite friendly. TRACER was guarded when discussing ████ and his work at the embassy, but that was to be expected. Seegram was concerned that TRACER might be an intelligence agent himself, developing Seegram for recruitment. Likewise, there was a possibility that TRACER might have been a double agent the ███ was dangling. But these were always potential concerns, and as Seegram and TRACER spent more time together—primarily lunches and dinners at local restaurants—Seegram became increasingly convinced TRACER was neither an intel officer nor a double agent. Much of this was based on intuition, which is not considered a reliable guide in intelligence. But especially in the early stages of a recruitment, there often isn't much else to go on.

The cables went into less and less detail as the development of TRACER went on. Presumably, Seegram started to ask more and more questions about ██████ policy and what went on at the embassy, and TRACER responded. In a textbook case, TRACER would eventually cross a line where he was revealing things he should not have been. Seegram would continue to gently guide him down this path. Eventually a formal recruitment would take place.

However it did progress, a cable in December said that TDTRACER had been formally recruited. Subsequent cables ticked off the C/O's standard work at this point. Seegram moved their relationship into a fully clandestine mode, moving all meetings to secure locations. He trained TDTRACER in the fundamentals of tradecraft, including ███ ███████████████████████. A form of payment was set up, █████ ███████████████████████ by the case officer.

The operational cables now began to be interspersed with intelligence reports. There were three or four of them on ██████ economic policy, none spectacularly interesting but one or two containing information that seemed like it would have been of interest to analysts working on ███.

Seegram and TRACER had had five or six meetings since his recruitment, over the course ████████, when the cable traffic written by Seegram suddenly stopped. Seegram's last cable detailed a fairly ordinary meeting at which ████████████████████████████ ██████████████████████. Then came McCelvoy's ████████████████ cable, dated two weeks later, in which he reported that TDTRACER was still missing and that the station was losing confidence in the case officer with the pseudonym "Seegram."

I went back to the file cabinet to see if there was another TDTRACER folder. Sometimes folders were misfiled, so I looked all through the cabinets, but there was nothing else there.

Back at my desk, I turned to McCelvoy's cable again. I found the line that was sticking in my head: "SUBJECT COULD CURRENTLY BE LOCATED IN ███████ EMBASSY IN █████ OR NEIGHBORING COUNTRY WHILE UNDERGOING INTERROGATION, █████, OR ANYWHERE IN █████ OR THE ██████████." It was quite a list of possibilities.

3

There was a contractor working in ████ named William. There were a fair number of these guys around, retired case officers who got bored in retirement and came back to work desks in their old Divisions. William was more impressive than most of them. He was probably as close as there was to a George Smiley at the Agency, meaning he was extremely smart and highly compassionate. He also looked the part of the wise old hand, with white hair and square, chunky glasses.

William had taken me under his wing as soon as I'd arrived in the office. Everyone at the Agency was friendly—you called your bosses by their first names, and even the Chief of the Division knew my name. It was a requirement of the culture that you be nice, and people knew how to do it. But William's kindness felt more genuine. He asked questions about my personal life and talked to me about things that had nothing to do with the Agency. He went down to the cafeteria with me for lunch at least once a week. He even invited me to his house for an anniversary party where there were only eight or nine guests. Several of them were very high-ranking Agency officers, and William introduced me to them as "an extremely promising young C/O."

I was also fortunate because William's final tour before retirement had been as Chief of Station in ███████. I asked him endless questions about the operational environment and the people and the customs, and I felt the things I was learning would allow me to hit the ground running when I got there.

The day after I read the TRACER file, I went over to William's cubicle. He turned away from his computer and motioned for me to sit down.

"I'm working on the file review," I said.

"How's it coming?" he asked.

"Not bad. I'm getting there. I ran into this case—TDTRACER."

William nodded slightly.

"You remember it?" I said.

"Bobby Goldstein's case."

"He was the C/O?"

"Yup," William said.

"Andrew L. Seegram?"

"I think that was his pseudonym. It sounds right."

"You were COS then?"

William nodded.

"It's funny, the last cable is ██████████████. And it's by a different C/O. From the way it was written, I thought it might be from the DCOS"—Deputy Chief of Station—"or something. I hope it was okay that I read it."

"If it was in the file, I wouldn't worry about it."

"Why's a ███████████████ in with the regular file?"

"Probably just misfiled."

"And the whole thing just kind of stops in the middle. Where are the rest of the cables?"

"Probably all got kicked into ██████████ at that point," William said. "Or maybe turned over to ████, I can't remember."

"Why would it go into ████████████████?"

"Sometimes when things start going south they move it into ████████████████."

I nodded.

"Seegram . . . what did you say his true name was, Goldstein? He wrote a good cable. I got really caught up in the story."

"Bobby was a fine young man," William said. "One of my favorites. You remind me of him quite a bit."

"How so?" I asked.

"Very bright. Good sense of humor, which you don't see enough of around here. People thought he was going to do great things. Jewish kid, too."

"Huh," I said, nodding to indicate that William's foray into my ethnicity was perfectly all right with me.

"He was a good kid."

"He still around?"

"No, no. I think he's up in New England somewhere now."

I looked at the blank gray wall of the cubicle for a few seconds. Then I turned back to William.

"So what happened?"

William rested his chin in his hand and thought for a few seconds.

"I don't think you want to know that story. Not when you're heading out on your first assignment. Come see me in a few years, I'll tell you about it. That and his other one. LXMALIBU. All we talked about around here for a while."

This was obviously the final word.

Later, when William was out of the office, I looked through the cabinets for an LXMALIBU file. But there was nothing there.

For several days, I couldn't stop thinking about TDTRACER. It was horrible—an agent had gone missing and was possibly being "interrogated" by his home country's intel service. Terrible as it was, though, there was no denying that it was the closest thing I'd seen yet to what I'd expected to find when I came to the Agency.

4

On one of my last weekends, I went up to Boston College to see Professor Wolfgang Lang. Lang was a renowned political scientist and had more or less shaped my worldview over the course of five classes I'd taken with him during college. He had also been the only professor I ever had any kind of a personal relationship with. I'd spent many Saturday nights during my junior and senior years at his apartment, where he hosted a kind of salon for students, professors, and visiting government ministers and intellectuals from all over the world.

Lang was also, in a roundabout way, the reason I was at the CIA. Four or five years after I'd graduated from college, I was working at a small think tank in D.C. that specialized in U.S.-Russian relations. Lang had come through town for a conference, and we'd had lunch. When I told him I was getting bored at the think tank, he suggested I try intelligence work. I'd certainly thought of this before, but somehow the idea had never seemed serious until Lang said it. I told him I was definitely interested. I'd actually thought at the time that he was recruiting me, and I spent months after that waiting for the phone to ring. When it didn't, I sent in a résumé to the CIA.

Three years had passed since then. Getting into the Agency had taken a year and a half—an endless series of tests, interviews, psychological evaluations, a polygraph, a security check where officers posing as ███████████████████████ interviewed my friends, relatives, and former employers. Then another year and a half of training, split between Headquarters and the Farm.

Now, before my first tour abroad, I wanted to say good-bye to

Professor Lang. I hadn't spoken to him since that lunch, although I'd seen him on TV and read about him in the papers quite frequently over the previous year. Lang had been in great demand since September 11, because it was easy to spin his no-nonsense view of the world's dangers as somehow predictive of the events to come.

I met him in his office, which I was upset about after coming all the way from D.C. We chatted about world events and drank tea from a small samovar. The Lang I had known had a certain joie de vivre and a cutting sense of humor. These traits had apparently disappeared. He had a slightly wild look in his eyes now, as if he'd come a bit unmoored. He spoke as if everything he'd ever said had been vindicated, and he came off as pompous. But his considerable charisma was still there, and somehow it was even enhanced by his new sourness.

Eventually, Lang got quiet, and I said, "I wanted to say goodbye, because I'm about to go abroad on my first tour with the ███████████."

"You decided not to go into intelligence?" he said.

"It didn't seem quite right for me."

He looked down at his tea. At first, I couldn't believe he'd accepted my cover so easily. Then I decided he knew perfectly well what the truth was, but he understood the proper response was to play dumb. This almost professional attitude made me wonder if he did have some connection to the Agency after all.

5

The final few weeks before my PCS (permanent change of station) to ███ involved packing, shipping my car and household goods overseas, and dealing with various other logistical matters. Officers on their way abroad usually checked into a hotel for the last week or two before they left, since their apartments were packed up or leased out by then. But I moved into William's house. William and I drove to Headquarters together every morning, and he used the car rides to give me last-minute pieces of advice on everything from tradecraft to dealing with the slightly difficult woman who was going to be my COS.

William's wife offered to make a big breakfast for anyone I wanted to have over on my last morning. My friends Suzette and Danny from my training class came, and an older officer I worked with on the ████ desk named Finn. I didn't invite Lenny, my college roommate who was also living in D.C. at the time. Lenny, like some of my other old friends, refused to believe my cover and constantly insisted that I worked at the CIA. This would have been too awkward around my Agency friends, who would have felt like their own covers were being jeopardized.

After the breakfast, William drove me to Dulles. He parked in an airline-employees-only lot close to the terminal, flashing an ID at the guard. He flashed the ID again at security and went with me to the gate. Instead of saying anything when we got there, he squeezed my shoulder, nodded, and walked away.

I slept on and off during the first part of the flight, then woke up with a jolt when we touched down in ████████████. During the second leg, my mouth was dry and I couldn't get back to sleep. I checked my watch over and over again. It felt like entire days were passing. When we finally arrived in ██████, I was disoriented and not as alert as I wanted to be.

An Agency admin officer named Phil met me at the gate and hustled me past customs with a wave to an army officer. The half-air-conditioned airport terminal was sticky and suffocating, but nothing compared to what hit me when we walked outside. It felt like diving into a pool of heat. My clothes were soaked by the end of the ten-second walk to the car.

Phil drove me to my house in a leafy, almost Mediterranean neighborhood called ██████████Hill. Two ████████ guards stood in front of the gate, rifles slung over their shoulders. They pulled the gate open and gave a friendly wave as we drove past. Set back behind a few ████ trees was a two-story white house, with a well-tended flower garden along one side. My car, a blue Dodge Dart, was sitting in the driveway on the other side of the house. I'd bought that car because I assumed it would look bad to have a foreign-made car at the CIA. Then the first day I'd driven it to Headquarters, I saw that the enormous Agency parking lot was filled with Hondas and Toyotas. My Dart looked more at home here in ███████.

6

After showing me around the house, Phil took me to the den at the back of the first floor and talked about security arrangements. The den was designated as a safe room. He showed me how to trigger the mechanism that brought a ██████████ out of the wall, which swooped in a ███████████ and locked on the other end.

"Couldn't they still shoot you through that?" I asked.

"The █████ is designed to protect you against kidnapping," he said. "They can't get to you in there. Food, water █████ the ███████████. You can go three days in here without a problem."

"But what if they want to shoot you?"

"Well, then, I guess you're gonna get shot."

"Wouldn't it be a better idea, then, if there were some sort of attack, or unrest, to just flee? Get out into the yard, go over the back fence? Just get out?"

"We recommend you use the safe room. This is where we'll come looking for you."

7

The next morning, I spent a few hours unpacking, then I did a trial drive to the embassy to make sure I knew how to get there and how much time it took. In the afternoon, I went down to the ████

District. When you see a photograph that's trying to conjure ██████,
it's probably ███. The crowded, dusty streets, with brightly col-
ored ████ hanging from windows, are somehow repulsive and appealing at the same time. Men in sweat-stained shirts, women in
██████████████, and the occasional animal stream down the main
thoroughfare in both directions. In American cities, large groups of
people divide naturally into lanes to facilitate getting down a crowded
street. Here, two masses just pushed forward, bumping and weaving
as they went.

I couldn't help thinking the controlled chaos was the perfect meta-
phor for ██████. After all my reading, I knew the broad outlines of the
history and political fissures that had shaped, and also oppressed, the
country. After the ██
██
██
██
██
██
██
██
██
██
██

There was really no good explanation for ████████████████████
██
██
██████████████████ Just human frailty, I suppose.
It may have been overly idealistic, but I thought that if the ████████
██
██
████████████████████████████████████

8

Monday morning, a secretary met me downstairs at the ███ and took me ██ to the Station. The DCOS came out to meet me and gave me a hearty handshake. He was a small man with meaty hands and a slightly oversized mustache. He led me back to his office, where we sat and talked for a few minutes, mostly him asking me questions about my background and how I'd liked my training. He seemed like an agreeable guy, not instantly recognizable as either an up-and-comer or a young officer peaking at the DCOS level. Something about the mustache, though, was slightly uncomfortable, hinting that the odds were against him.

After we finished chatting, the DCOS took me around and introduced me to whoever was in the office. Most of the case officers were already at their ████ jobs, so the place was half empty, but I met the admin and support personnel. Almost all of them said, "Let me know if you need anything," before I moved on to the next person.

After we finished making the rounds, the DCOS took me into the COS's office, introduced me, and left.

Adrienne Tiner was one of the few female COSs at the Agency. She was in her mid-forties, was extremely thin, and had prematurely white hair. Somehow I had expected her to be plain or even unattractive, but she was pretty in a composed, angular way. I'd heard that she was a "smart, capable manager," which was obviously a put-down, or possibly a synonym for "woman." Male COSs were described as "fearless," "innovative," "great guys," or "total shits." Even "total shit" had more of a ring of respect to it than "capable manager."

"I received a cable about you from William," she said.

"Really?"

"He said you're good."

"William's a great guy," I said. "He really helped me out in ██████."

"He's a good manager," she said. "I served under him in ██████."

"Yeah, he told me. He said you were a great officer."

He hadn't said this, and it was also possibly inappropriate for me to be relaying a compliment to a COS, but she smiled.

"Well, I think you'll like it here. It's an important time, obviously. Needless to say, we're very focused on the terrorism target now. That's a good thing for a new officer. There's a lot of work to do."

I told her I was ready to get to work. Then I said two or three sentences about the history of ██████, showing off my knowledge of the country.

"Yes, good," she said. "I like an informed case officer. But you do know we're here to spy?"

"Of course," I said, smiling.

"I had a case I was keeping for you, a ████████████████████ Jodie Ross recruited about a year ago. But the intel was getting so low-grade I had her terminate before she left. Wasn't worth keeping just to give you some practice running SDRs [surveillance detection routes]. You'll be fine. Just get out there. You know what to do. And keep your eyes open on the visa line. It's mostly garbage, but I once recruited a guy off the visa line who gave us the whole order of battle of the ██████ army."

"Really?" I said, smiling appreciatively.

"There's some good intel out there," she said.

We talked for a few more minutes. She asked the same questions about my background and experiences in training that the DCOS had. She talked about how, when she was at the Farm, you still had to strangle a rabbit with your bare hands as part of the paramilitary program, a requirement that had since been dropped.

Then she walked me back over to the DCOS's office, shook my hand, and said, "We'll be seeing a lot of each other."

The DCOS gave me the schedule of weekly meetings, then told me I'd be starting my cover job immediately. He took me downstairs to the office of the Chief of the ██████ Section, who stood up behind his desk, gave me a quick handshake, then turned me over to his secretary. He obviously wasn't going to waste any time with an Agency officer. The secretary took me to a First Secretary in the ███████ Section, who frowned, got up, and gave me two big, white notebooks marked "███████" and "███████." Then he took me down to the ██████. On the way he said, "Have you read ████████'s *History and Culture of* ██████?"

"Yeah," I said.

He turned and looked me in the eye for the first time.

"Really?"

"Yes, really," I said.

"Well, you're the first one."

"It's a great book. Don't see how you could understand ██████ without it."

"Tell your colleagues that," he said.

The visa line was a long, narrow room with a row of open booths stretching from one end to the other. The First Secretary brought me over to one of the booths and introduced me to Evelyn, an officious-looking woman in a dark blue pantsuit. The first thing she said to me was, "The last one of you I had down here had terrible handwriting. How's your handwriting?"

Before I could answer, a woman in a ██████ and long ███████ sat down on the other side of the booth. She was nervous and fidgeted constantly as Evelyn asked about her family, education, and financial situation. The woman was in her fifties, was married to a man who owned a laundry, and wanted to go to the States to visit her nephew. When the interview was over, Evelyn told her that she'd receive a response by mail within three weeks.

After the woman left, Evelyn said, "What do you think?"

"I'm guessing no?"

"No it is. You won't find this in the book"—she pointed to the two white notebooks I'd put on the floor—"but here's how it works. If you're ███████, you're not getting a visa. If you're ███████, you're also not getting a visa, because that would be unfair to the ███████ and the ████████. So, if you live in this country, you're not coming to America. Unless you're rich, your relatives in America get a congressman to call for you, and you're willing to leave your baby or your left leg behind. Probably both, actually. Then you get a security review. But the security guys will turn you down for anything. If you've ever stepped foot in a ████, they'll turn you down."

"So, it's pretty much all no's?" I said.

"Pretty much all no's."

9

After observing Evelyn for a week, I started handling my own visa applicants. On the ████████████████████████████ ████████████████████████████. Each one required filling out almost twenty different sheets of paper, mostly checking boxes and entering basic information. Mistakes could come back to haunt you, so you had to be careful, even fastidious. I also took extra time with my handwriting to keep Evelyn happy.

Back at the Station, there were staff meetings twice a week. At the Monday meeting, all of the case officers would update the COS on what they were working on. The Thursday meeting was a briefing by the DCOS on what was going on at Headquarters, anything big that had happened at other Stations we should know about, and any new tasking requirements from Headquarters (this might mean that an analytic group, or even a single analyst, had requested information on a specific topic, and we were supposed to see if we could get relevant information from any of our sources).

I was expected to lay low for a while, above all not attracting any attention from the ████████ intel service, the ███. So I kept up on traffic, studied maps of ████████, and got used to the long, heartbreaking interviews with visa applicants. To gain the respect of my colleagues at the Station, I kept my mouth shut most of the time, while to get along at the ████████, I asked a lot of questions and sought advice on complicated visa cases.

As for my social life, the Station people mostly stayed away from each other outside of the office. This way, if an officer was compromised, you wouldn't be too closely associated with him and therefore suspected of working for the Agency yourself. I did make a few friends from my cover job in the ███████████████ and went to occasional dinner parties and barbecues at their houses. They were a nice enough group, smart and deeply engaged in the world. But they knew what I did—███████ officers could easily tell who the Station officers were—and they always seemed a little awkward and uncomfortable around me because of it.

Most nights after work, I'd either go to official functions or head straight home. I had a cook who came in four days a week—this was unbelievably cheap in ██████, and most ██████████ had a cook and a full-time maid. ███████ had been recommended by a ██████████ in the ████████, and after some initial reluctance, she started making me traditional ██████ meals. I'd eat by myself in the dining room because ██████ didn't seem to want me in the kitchen when she was cleaning up.

On weekends, I took long walks and drives, studying ██████████ nooks and crannies, always on the lookout for duck blinds (██████████ ███ ██████████████████████████), drop zones, and the rest of the urban geography that would allow me to do my job once I started recruiting people. ██████████ was an unusual city, part ██████████████ and part ghetto. It was exceptionally crowded, which was a benefit and a problem. It was easier to get lost in a crowd, in certain ways easier to make or collect a drop amid the tumult. On the other hand, you never knew who was watching you. We'd been warned constantly not to underestimate the ██████, who might well employ an army of beggars and street people to follow you all day long. You'd have a hell of a time picking it up with the teeming crowds all around you. So I looked for more isolated pockets in and around the city to work in, but in those places a Westerner obviously stood out more. It was, as the DCOS was fond of saying, a "challenging environment." The only real advice for dealing with it was to "hold your breath and trust your training."

10

By the end of my second month, I was attending two or three diplomatic functions a week, some Station-assigned, some from invitations that circulated around the ████████. Most were cocktail parties or, if you were lucky, dinners to honor visiting dignitaries, celebrate a mission's home country's holidays, bestow awards, and the like. I'd march up to anyone I saw standing alone at these parties, introduce myself, and start talking. By nature, I wasn't quite this outgoing, but it was the type of thing that got much easier after you'd done it just three or four times.

My goal in these conversations was to find out who I was talking to, find out what they did, and establish enough of a rapport that I could call them for lunch later if I wanted to. Since cards were routinely exchanged in the diplomatic community, I'd always walk away with a phone number.

The day after a party, I'd tell the DCOS who I'd met, then send ████████ request cable to Headquarters. ████████████████████ ██ I'd report this to the DCOS, who would tell me to wait and see if I ran into them again. This was partly because none of the people I'd met were compelling enough targets to go after hard, and partly because if I was going to go after them, it would raise fewer flags to do it after meeting them socially a few times rather than just once.

At the weekly meetings, I'd listen as the more experienced C/Os talked about cases they were running and targets they were going after. There was a third-tour named Rob Lyle who'd been running a ████████████████████ for over a year. He'd gleefully recount their obscenity-filled debates over who the best-looking American actresses were, occasionally looking over at Adrienne with a shrug that conveyed, "I get to talk this way because that's how he talks." Adrienne never returned his smirks, but she never stopped him, either. It was possible that she didn't care as long as the operation was going smoothly, but it was also possible that she'd destroy him for it in his end-of-tour evaluation.

A second-tour named Tim Dorring was developing a ███████████ ████████████████████████. At least the fiction was maintained at the meetings that Dorring was developing him. From his own stories of their random encounters at official functions and their dull, stilted conversations, it hardly sounded like it was going anywhere. Dorring had a flat demeanor and was out of place in the Agency, though he didn't show any signs of knowing it. There was something grating about his cluelessness.

As for me, when my turn came to talk, I'd mention whoever I'd recently met, that the name traces hadn't turned anything up, and that I was waiting to see them again. It was more or less what was expected of a new officer, and I tried to convey in my tone that I knew this and that I felt good about how things were going.

11

I finally got permission to pursue my first target after I had several encounters with a low-ranking secretary from the ████████ Embassy. I first met him at a party at the ███████ Ambassador's house, then I ran into him again on the street outside the ███████ Foreign Ministry. At the party, we had a brief, stilted chat and traded cards. Outside the Foreign Ministry, we spoke for several minutes about a meeting he'd just had there. He was a serious man, with a dark, bald head fringed by a half circle of neatly trimmed hair. He reminded me of a Latin instructor I'd had in high school, a very formal Frenchman who didn't seem to like anybody. ███████ wasn't the most important country in the world, but stations worldwide had been tasked to come up with reporting on a recent shake-up in their armed forces, and even though a military attaché would have been vastly preferable, any of their diplomats might know something about it. Furthermore, a ███████ diplomat might be valuable over the long term, reporting not just on ██████, but conceivably serving as an access agent to virtually anyone on the diplomatic circuit.

Before calling him for lunch, I went over to the ██████ neighborhood, where the ████████ Embassy was. I walked around for several hours trying to find an appropriate restaurant—not so crowded that we'd be seen together, not so out of the way that it would look like we were trying not to be seen together if we were seen. In a tangle of side streets off ████ Road I found a small ████████ restaurant that looked right.

The next day, I called. He seemed slightly taken aback, but agreed to meet for lunch at the restaurant I suggested.

On the day of our lunch, I pulled out of the ████████ parking lot and headed toward the restaurant. I watched for surveillance, although I wouldn't have broken off even if I'd detected any. If I was being followed, it would have been a routine ████████, and it was perfectly normal for two ████████ to have lunch. I didn't ████████████████ or ████████████, since any counter-surveillance techniques ran the risk of being recognized as counter-surveillance techniques and giving you away as a CIA officer. So I just ████████ and watched my rearview mirror. I didn't see anything, but I understood why one of my instructors at the Farm had said his sixth sense told him he was being watched for the entire two years of his first tour. It was an almost sickening feeling, and I bounced in and out of its grip every few seconds.

When I walked into the restaurant, I saw him sitting at a table against the wall. The room was dark, and at first all I noticed was how straight his back was. But as I approached the table he looked up, and I instantly realized the lunch had been a mistake. His posture, the perfect crispness of his suit and tie, the non-expression on his face—he was offended. Maybe calling after meeting him only twice was too friendly, or too presumptuous. He was more formal than that. And he was older than me, so perhaps I'd come off as a

young, brash American. Or maybe a lunch invitation from a junior ██████ officer was too odd. My duties didn't include anything substantive, politically or economically, so what official business was there to discuss at such a lunch? ████████████████████████████
██
███████████████████████. I still laugh when I think of that.

Of course, I also wondered if he suspected what I was doing there. Every country's counterintelligence service briefs its diplomats on the ways in which CIA officers in the field will go after them. But he obviously couldn't have known anything about me in particular—there was no way I could have blown my cover yet—and it seemed unlikely he would behave this way toward any U.S. diplomat. It seemed, instead, personal.

I sat down and tried to smile my way out of trouble. I thanked him for coming, told him how important it was for me to learn about diplomacy from those more experienced than me. He didn't so much as nod.

After we ordered, I tried some friendly questions. When I asked where he'd grown up, he said simply, "████," and when I asked what part, he said, "████████." I tried some questions about the educational system in ████, but he said simply, "We have a traditional educational system in our country."

Once the food came, I tried my life. I talked about growing up in Chicago, told stories about my parents. I moved, somewhat awkwardly, into the subjects I'd studied in college and how my education had led me to join the ████████████. He looked back and forth between me and his food. It was as if he were trying to show me how offended he was to even be there by wiping all traces of the offense from his expression.

Finally, I shut up. We ate silently for a while. This was actually less uncomfortable, but I couldn't help myself, and I launched into another series of questions about adjusting to life in ████. He gave two-word answers to everything.

12

The next afternoon was a meeting day at the Station, so I didn't get to make my report privately to the DCOS. I'd spent half the night trying to decide how to present the case. As we went around the table, I kept rehearsing what I was going to say over and over again in my head. When my turn finally came, I worried that I was sweating too much. It was so hot in ████████ that my sweat glands seemed permanently turned on, even after I'd gone into an air-conditioned room. I gave a brief description of who the target was and why I'd met with him. Then I said, "There wasn't much there. He didn't want to talk about work at all. He was just a very reserved guy."

One of the other C/Os said, "Might have suspected," and I nodded slightly to indicate that I recognized that as a possibility. Adrienne said, "Keep looking," and then we continued around the table.

13

My parents called every few weeks, and I dreaded our conversations, which were long and uncomfortable. They knew where I worked, and I'd given them careful instructions on what they could and could not say on the phone. But the pressure of having to talk so carefully, and the possibility that someone was listening in, obviously upset them. My mother, who was normally very chatty, spoke quietly and in short sentences. My father was practically morose.

I didn't get many other calls at home, so I was surprised one night when I picked up the phone in my den, expecting it to be my parents, and heard Lenny on the other end. I'd never given him my phone number here—when I was still in D.C., I told him I didn't have it yet, and I never called or e-mailed with it once I got to ████. He must have gotten it from my parents.

As soon as he started talking, I was nervous he was going to launch into one of his routines about how I really worked for the CIA, which I didn't want on the open line. To keep this from happening, I kept cutting him off and changing the subject every time he seemed like he could possibly go in that direction.

He'd say, "So how's your job? Do you . . ."

I'd jump in with, "Everything's great. I'm enjoying it. And this country is intense. The people here . . ."

The whole conversation was awkward and strained. Lenny finally said, "Are you on speed?"

When we said good-bye, he had a tone in his voice like I'd gone insane.

14

The conference room got quiet when everyone sensed Adrienne was about to begin the meeting.

"Item number one," she said. "General ████'s party."

Most of the other officers in the room started smiling, and a few laughed. After a few seconds, I realized they were all looking at me. I didn't say anything, but I tried to smile gamely.

"Do you know who he is?" Adrienne asked me.

"Deputy ████████ of the ████Army," I said. (Their command structure is somewhat different from ours, despite being modeled on the ████████, and this would roughly correspond to our vice chairman of the Joint Chiefs of Staff.)

"That is correct," Adrienne said. "He is also the most well-connected man in the ██████ armed forces. Really the only officer who bridges the divide between the branches. He also knows as much about the ██████ nuclear program as anyone in the country, including the head of the ████." She paused, then she added, "Unfortunately, he's unrecruitable."

"Oh, Adrienne, nobody's unrecruitable," said Rob, smirking.

"A few C/Os have gotten close to him," the DCOS said. "I think someone even pitched him back in the eighties. But that's about it."

"He is unrecruitable," said Adrienne. "But good targets are always swirling around him. He throws two or three big parties a year, lavish events. The ██████ just got invitations to his fall shindig, and a few came our way. We always like to send the first-tours."

She still had a serious expression on her face, though she was obviously having fun with me.

"Okay," I said. "I can't wait. But what's the big deal?"

"We call it the James Bond party," said Rob. "The closest thing. It's on a beautiful estate. The women are gorgeous. The food is fantastic. They're probably playing baccarat in the back somewhere."

"You'll enjoy it," Adrienne said. From her slightly softened expression it was clear the joke was over—they were actually sending me to a good party, and just teasing me a little bit about it. "You'll meet the General," she went on. "He greets all his guests. Just say hello, be careful with your cover. He's very sly. And see who else you meet there."

15

The party was on a Friday night. When I got home from work, ██████ had dinner ready for me, and I had to apologize for forgetting to tell her that I wouldn't be home. She said not to worry, but she looked slightly irritated.

I changed into a linen suit and more casual shoes. One of the ██████ contractors who guarded the gatehouse happened to be walking down the driveway as I went to my car, and he smiled at my outfit and said, "You have good time, sir."

When I drove through the gate to the General's estate, I was surprised by the scene in front of me. The grounds had a British feel, with sweeping, manicured lawns dipping down to a lake in the back. Torches were lit from one end of the property to the other, and some sort of honor guard on horseback was trotting around the inside perimeter of the stone wall. I couldn't tell if they were just for show or if they were actually on patrol.

The house looked like an ████████ castle. As I went inside and across the elaborate foyer to the ballroom, I thought that this was exactly what I'd expected when I'd joined the Agency. Warm, dark nights, beautiful women, people in uniforms, cocktails on balconies overlooking torch-lit lawns.

I walked through the party, looking for important-looking men. I sipped at a glass of wine and tried to look comfortable even though I wasn't talking to anybody. Occasionally, I stopped and stood by myself in various rooms, then moved on to other rooms. I knew I had to go up and introduce myself to people, but I felt like putting it off and just taking in the atmosphere of the party for a while longer.

About an hour passed. I was standing in the main ballroom, finally about to approach an elderly man talking to his wife, when I heard an authoritative voice behind me.

"I don't believe I've had the pleasure."

I turned around to see a surprisingly unimposing figure in an ████ ██. He was pot-bellied and had patchy hair.

"Mark Ruttenberg," I said. "████████████████ at the U.S. ████████." (Agency officers use their real name 99 percent of the time, including any time they're using their official cover, which is of course tied to their real name.)

"General ████. Very pleased to meet you."

"And I you," I said, accidentally over-mirroring his speech patterns.

"How are you enjoying your tour in ████?"

"Very much," I said. "And your party is lovely. Thank you for your hospitality."

"Of course, of course. Tell me, Mr. Ruttenberg, are you acquainted with a Mr. Bobby Goldstein?"

Bobby Goldstein was the officer who'd recruited and run TDTRACER, the missing agent whose file had made such an impression on me at Headquarters. My head got slightly foggy. I had to answer immediately, but what was the answer? There was an answer—there had been a whole lesson at the Farm on how to respond to questions like this. But this one was a little bit different, and I couldn't figure out how to handle it.

"Goldstein?" I said.

"Yes."

"No, I don't think so."

"I thought you might. He was here with the American ███████ several years ago. Perhaps a colleague of yours, perhaps not. I do not know. If so, I thought you might be acquainted. I would be curious for information about him."

"No, sorry," I said.

The General and I parted, and I decided I'd given the right answer. Whether or not he knew Goldstein's affiliation, and whichever affiliation I had, it was perfectly probable that I wouldn't know him.

But why on earth was he asking about him? He certainly sounded like he suspected, or knew, Goldstein was Agency. Could the General have been somehow connected to TDTRACER? Then I remembered there was some other case of Goldstein's that William had mentioned to me as well—it took me half a second, then I remembered the crypt. LXMALIBU. I hadn't found any file at all for him in the office at Headquarters—the whole thing must have been █████████████████ ██████████. Could the General be connected to that case? I didn't think he could be LXMALIBU, because Adrienne had said he was unrecruitable. Although you never knew—maybe she was lying, or maybe there was something she didn't know.

The next day, I told the DCOS that the General had asked about Goldstein.

"That was all before I got here," he said. "It's over and closed now. Just forget about it."

16

A few weeks later, which was three months into my ▮▮▮, I went to
a native ▮▮▮▮ dance exhibition hosted by the local ▮▮▮▮ International Friendship Committee for foreigners in ▮▮▮. It wasn't
likely to be a target-rich environment, but there was nothing else going on that night, and I felt like being around people instead of sitting
in my house by myself. I also had some vague sense that possibly I
liked dance.

The ▮▮▮▮ Cultural Center was on ▮▮▮ Road, a small street that
curved downward off of ▮▮▮ Park. It was a concrete building with a
domed top. Inside, it was sort of dilapidated-historical, with faded
floors and peeling paint but beautiful murals and gold inlays high up
on the walls.

I took a seat in the main hall at the back. The French windows leading out to the courtyard and the gilded windows high up on the walls
were all open, but it was hot, and I was quickly covered in a gloss of
sweat. A small band with native instruments I'd never even seen before
came onstage. After they'd been clanging away for a few minutes,
about twenty ▮▮▮▮ dancers from the ▮▮▮▮▮ Province came
down the aisles and went up onto the stage. Their costumes were
somehow muted and colorful at the same time, and both the men and
the women wore necklaces and bracelets. For the next hour, they bent
and twisted and gyrated to the music. The whole thing had that strange
feeling ethnic dancing always does when it's transplanted into a city and
put on for foreigners, like it's hovering in some ether of falseness.

After the performance, everyone gathered in the courtyard for
drinks and ▮▮▮▮▮. Torches were burning, and a flower-scented
breeze was moving silently through the guests. I felt like I was in Hawaii, or somewhere more familiar than ▮▮▮.

I took a glass of wine from a passing waiter and then went over to the buffet. As I piled my plate with ▇ and ▇▇▇▇▇, I heard a woman's voice with a muted British accent say, "You are hungry?"

Standing next to me, holding a plate with only two pieces of ▇▇▇ on it, was a dark-skinned woman a few years older than me. She had on glasses that may have been a bit too big for her face, and she was wearing a lilac-colored pantsuit that looked like something you would have seen on the first generation of American working women. As is often the case with non-British people with British accents, she had the vague aura about her of being a walking historical artifact.

"Who can resist ▇▇▇▇▇▇?" I said.

"I think many Americans do not like this."

"Well, we like hamburgers," I said.

We introduced ourselves—I'll call her Daisy—and walked over to a quiet corner of the courtyard, her following me or me following her, it wasn't quite clear. Our conversation quickly led to the fact that I was an American ▇▇▇▇▇, and she seemed very impressed by this.

"What do you do?" I asked.

"I'm a secretary at the ▇▇▇▇▇ Embassy."

My body filled with . . . not quite adrenaline, but with something that sped up my brain and shifted it into a new relationship with everything around me. ▇▇▇▇ was a high-priority target country, partly because of its general geopolitical significance, and partly because its own homegrown terrorist networks were known to have at least informal connections to Al-Qaeda.

A secretary (and she had clearly used the word in the sense of doing secretarial work, not of being a diplomatic secretary) could go either way as a potential recruitment target. Most secretaries wouldn't have access to that much classified information. But the secretary to an ambassador or a high-ranking military attaché could be a very valuable agent. And something about this woman's bearing, both her confidence and her relatively strong command of English, suggested at least the possibility that she could be the secretary to someone high-ranking.

My opening position, furthermore, was almost ideal. She had approached me, which was good for my cover. The same suspicions would not be aroused as if I had approached her. Also, she was a secretary, so it was very unlikely that she was an intelligence agent (although you never knew).

I asked her how she liked her job, and she said, "The work is quite dull, and the people in the embassy are not very agreeable. But I have served in ███████ and ████, and this opportunity to travel and see the world has been wonderful. I always wanted to do this. Since I was a small girl."

The people in the embassy were not very agreeable. Disaffection.

We chatted a bit about the dance exhibition. She found it exciting and compared it to some of the traditional dancing in her own country. I said that I had liked the costumes, and I made a few lame jokes about disco dancing. Crumbs from my ██████ kept showering down around me every time I took a bite, but we both smiled each time it happened.

Finally, I said that I had to go home. I handed her my card, and she apologized for not having one herself, but wrote her office number on the back of another one of my cards. I said I hoped we'd see each other again, and then, worried that it sounded too much like I was hitting on her, babbled something about being interested in ██████ and wanting to learn more about it. I immediately realized, of course, that this probably made it sound even more like I was hitting on her.

17

I ran a name trace, and when it came back, it showed that Daisy had been met a few years earlier by a C/O in ███████. She was working as a secretary in the cultural section of the ███████ Embassy then, and the C/O hadn't pursued it any further. This was neither here nor there in terms of her suitability as a target now, but since it was the first trace I'd ever gotten back with anything on it other than "NO RECORDS ON SUBJECT" or a few tiny pieces of information, I was excited.

I went in to see the DCOS.

"Hmm," he said. "This could be good. You sure she didn't think you were hitting on her?"

"No, she might have."

"Well, that's okay. It's hard to pursue female targets, there are always those issues. Just be careful."

We chatted a little more about my general impressions of her, and I mentioned what she had said about not liking the people at her embassy. Finally, he said, "Have Headquarters assign a crypt."

This took another day for the cables to go back and forth. The crypt Headquarters assigned was CSHELICOPTER. Somebody from my training class, or somebody who knew somebody from my training class, was obviously on the ███ desk. Crypts were a combination of a coded two-letter prefix indicating the country of origin of the agent followed by a supposedly random word. But officers at headquarters sometimes got a little bit clever with the "random" words. When I was at the ██████████████████████████ (SOTC), I'd thrown up during a helicopter ride that was part of an escape-and-evasion exercise. It wasn't from motion sickness; I'd been sick with a stomach flu for days. But I'd taken a lot of ribbing for it. On balance, even though I didn't like it, I had to admit this latest joke was one of the better ones.

18

I tried to come up with a pretense for calling her that wouldn't sound like I was pursuing her romantically. But due to the circumstances of our initial meeting, there was really no good way. The best I could do was check ████████████████████████ out of the ███ library and read the whole thing. When I called, I said that I had been reading███████████████████████████, and that I was anxious to talk about it with someone from ███. Before she could stop herself, she laughed gently.

We met for lunch at a Chinese restaurant off the central ███████ that another C/O had recommended to me. During training, we'd learned that you had to find places for developmental meetings that were out of the way but not obviously so, that you never went to the same place twice, and that you didn't use locations that other C/Os had used. But I'd also been warned in my training that local conditions could make it hard to follow basic procedures, and I'd heard from experienced case officers that a lot of security precautions simply went out the window once you were abroad. The truth was, there weren't an unlimited number of restaurants or other places to meet, or an unlimited amount of time to look for them. Furthermore, case officers and potential recruits liked good food. The C/O who had recommended this restaurant to me had done so in front of the DCOS and two other officers, and no one had blinked.

She was waiting for me when I got to the restaurant, and as I sat down, I noticed for the first time that she had a little series of pockmarks rutted into each of her cheeks. Maybe they'd been concealed by makeup, or the night, the first time we'd met. She was wearing a modern gray dress, or at least modern for ████, and a silver necklace with little purple jewels in it that hung down not quite provocatively, but decidedly between her breasts.

After we said hello, I said, "Do you like Chinese food?" feeling stupid that I hadn't asked this when we spoke on the phone.

"Yes, of course," she said.

We talked about the weather and how oppressive it was. Her whole demeanor instantly relieved all my fears about repeating the fiasco from my lunch with the second secretary. I felt so at ease with her that I almost showed her the sweat stains in my underarms as we discussed the heat, but I stopped myself in time.

There was a brief lull in the conversation, and I picked up my menu a bit too quickly. She followed suit. After we ordered, I started talking about ████████████████████████████████. When I mentioned the fall of the ████ government, she said that ██████ had misunderstood the cause, and proceeded to explain how the ██████ and the ████████████ had become disenfranchised and set

everything in motion through the influence of ██████████████.
She was extremely bright and articulate, and I was certain she would
not have been a secretary had she grown up in the United States.

When the food came, she ate carefully, dealing with the noodles in
a way that felt almost professional. But she wasn't stiff. She laughed
easily, if not heartily. When I spoke, she looked me in the eye in a focused and comfortable manner.

We continued to talk about the history and politics of ████. She
nodded or raised her eyebrows whenever I made a point. When we got
to the current government, she smiled wryly and said, "Dragoons."

"Dragoons?" I said.

"Maybe this is not the right word. I mean—well, you know. Not
real people."

Disaffection, again. Things were going extremely well. I felt that
I was working effectively and efficiently, and that we were getting
along with each other. But there was also a specific piece of information that I wanted to get—who she worked for—and I realized it was
time to try to elicit it.

Eliciting information was a major theme in my training. The idea
was that unless you were dealing with an agent you had already recruited, you didn't want to ask specific questions. It certainly would
have been awkward, and maybe even rude, had I said simply, "Who's
your boss?" It could also raise red flags, either for the developmental
or for security personnel in their embassy. (Once you recruited someone, you asked them about any conversations they'd had about you.
Were Daisy to mention to people in her embassy, for example, that
she'd had lunch with someone from the ████████ Embassy, it would
be important to know that. And if, specifically, she mentioned that
the person had asked, "Who's your boss?" that would certainly raise
suspicions if it got back to counterintelligence personnel.)

To avoid this, you elicited information by talking about yourself,
which usually leads to another person talking about themselves. During training, this had seemed rather obvious to me. It was a conversational tool I used already in various circumstances. But now, it
suddenly felt like a precise tool. I began to talk about my work

███████████. I told her about my daily routine on the ███ line and how frustrating and sad it was to turn virtually everyone down. I spoke about the injustices of the global economy and how I saw America's place in it. (Nothing wrong with showing some thoughtfulness or even skepticism about my own country with someone I might ask to betray hers.) When I finished, she nodded sympathetically and wiped her mouth with her napkin. But she didn't say anything.

"How about you?" I prodded gently.

"Oh, every day is much the same. I answer the telephone, I type many documents. I work for a colonel, so everything is very—how would you say it—regimented? Right on the buttons? No mistakes, please."

Bingo. Apparently, elicitation really did work. And the response couldn't have been much better. If he was a colonel, considering the size of their embassy in ███████, he was probably the chief military attaché. In any case, I could find out easily by checking the diplomatic rolls. It wasn't quite the Ambassador, but in many ways it could be even better.

I wanted to show that I agreed with her perception of military officers, so I started talking about the military attachés ███████████ and how stiff and difficult I found them. (This wasn't true—the two or three military guys I'd had contact with ████████████ were pleasant and easygoing.) Then I wanted to get off the topic while I was ahead. Soon, we were talking about traditional dance again, and this time she was making jokes about the costumes of the dancers we had seen.

19

"Write it up," the DCOS said after I gave him my report. "And trace the colonel."

Before the cable went out, he cut my three-page description of the meeting with CSHELICOPTER down to one paragraph. The next day, the one-line response came from Headquarters: SUBJECT IS OF INTEREST.

The day after that, the name trace on the colonel came back. It showed that he'd attended the ███████████████████ Military Academy in ████, had served seven years in the ███ Division as a staff officer, and was a cousin of the defense minister.

20

The incredible, dense heat that assaulted ███████ from the sky and the ground simultaneously had been turning into something more watery and bearable. It left me clammy instead of burning up on the inside, which was actually an improvement. It had also started to rain once or twice a week, a lush, warm rain that would have been pleasant if you weren't wearing a suit. The first light spray that always came before a downpour started to sweep across the air just as Daisy came up to me at the entrance to the ████████████████████ Gardens, where I'd invited her to join me at an outdoor concert of traditional ████ music.

We went and stood near the trunk of a ████ tree, its broad, low canopy protecting us as the rain intensified. It was too loud to actually talk to each other, so we just pointed occasional facial expressions at each other that indicated "This is quite a rain storm" or "I wonder when it will end."

But it didn't end, and I was starting to feel that it was a real problem. Somehow, I was screwing up here. But when I increased the number of "I'm sorry" faces I showed her, her "It's not your fault" faces became more and more intense, until they seemed almost strident.

When the rain finally ended, not tapering off but simply ceasing in an instant, we walked into the gardens and found a place to sit along a low stone wall. The band, featuring a ████ and a group of ████, was setting up on the damp grass. My forehead started to sweat, and I wished I'd gotten wetter in order to disguise it. I made an operational note to myself that it would be a good idea to hide sweat with rain. Daisy produced a handkerchief and offered it to me.

The music was dull but hypnotic. I heard Daisy sigh several times, but I couldn't tell if it was out of boredom or because she found the music beautiful. I stared off at the ████ trees and beds of ████ around us and imagined a time when the ████ had strolled here in their ████ and ████.

After the concert, we walked through the gardens and came out the back way, then strolled down ████ Street until we found a little Italian restaurant. I used some sort of combination of body language and grunting to steer the hostess toward a table in the back, and I stepped around Daisy to get the seat facing the front of the restaurant. This was more important in a situation where somebody might come in and shoot you, but in all cases, it was a good idea to be able to see who was coming in and out of the restaurant, and at the very least know who had seen you. We ordered pasta and wine, and I felt myself finally cooling off in the dark room.

After speaking about the concert and other things, I decided to push a little.

"How's work?" I asked.

"Oh, fine. As usual."

"Yeah?"

"Yes."

I watched as she mechanically twirled a small bite of pasta around her fork. After eating it, she said, "There is a woman in our consular section, an administrative aide. Whenever she sees me she stops and talks to me. She thinks we are friends. But she is very silly and unmannered. Today, she decided to make a list for me of all the men she notices in the embassy and say which of them are very attractive to her and which are not. I stand there, but I don't know what to do. How I can get this woman away from me?"

"You don't like gossip?"

"No, no, gossip is okay. I don't like her. She is so silly, like a young girl. And this is bad for her reputation. Although perhaps a woman like her is quite happy, yes? Perhaps she will go on in her life and never have any problems."

"Everyone has problems."

"Of course you are right. But I wonder about a person like this and what she wants in her life. Simply to be an administrative aide? In ████, many are satisfied like this. There is no need to do many things. We are not like the Americans."

"Yes, nobody's like us Americans. We're a little crazy. About . . . ambition and things like that."

"Perhaps a bit."

"So what do you want to do?"

She smiled and twirled another small bite of pasta.

"I want simply to learn. To see the world. To make a family one day. Simple things, but not always so simple."

"No, not so simple."

I took a sip of wine and made a move.

"I think it's important for people to help their countries to get along better. To help countries understand each other in the way only people can."

"Yes?"

"Yes. I mean, not only people can. Countries can understand each other, too."

"Yes?"

"Sure. It seems important to me, for example, that our two countries understand each other."

"Oh, certainly. All countries."

"There are so many problems today."

"Very many."

I stopped here. I could have said, "For example, your country knows things about Islamic radicalism that would help both our countries to fight against this problem," but of course that would have been too much.

21

I wrote it up—this time I kept things to one paragraph—waited another week, and called her again. We made a dinner plan for the following Wednesday. I tried to speak on the phone with a lightness and bonhomie that would indicate a good-hearted ██████ working to improve relations with another country, but really there was no getting around the fact that she was a secretary, and as far from responsible for her country's relationships as a goat herder on ████████████████████.

Figuring he must have been in similar situations, I asked Rob how to handle the fact that it probably looked more and more to Daisy like I was trying to date her.

"Is she hot?" he asked.

"I don't know," I said. "I mean, she's got a nice figure."

"Figure?"

"Okay, okay, she's got a good body. But she's very prim."

"Prim? Librarian? That's the best. You take the glasses off, BOOM!"

I felt like I was starting to become responsible for what Rob said just because I was in the conversation with him. I was afraid that Adrienne would hear about it somehow and take me down, too, in her end-of-tour eval.

"Anyway, just don't give off any romantic vibes," Rob said.

"I'm just interested in her operational utility."

"You're just interested in her operational utility? That's quite a sentence. Sounds like you're totally fucking in love with her."

"Fuck off," I said.

We met at a restaurant she suggested this time, a crowded, centrally located ██████████. This made me uncomfortable, but once we were there, it felt extremely unlikely that anyone was noticing us.

Plates clattered, groups of men played ████████, there were even the noises of ████████████████ that I hoped weren't coming from the kitchen.

I was having a good time at dinner, in a way. Something about Daisy's company was enormously pleasant. One felt that she was, in a sense, completely in favor of you. This was obviously connected to ████████ culture and the fact that ████████ women were subservient to men. But in her somewhat modern version of it, it just felt like a quiet desire to make sure I was all right, at all times.

Unfortunately, nothing was happening. The few forays I made into work produced more of the same mild complaints about coworkers that she'd made the last time we were together. Partly, she just seemed to want to talk about other things. But she also seemed to have a very specific line she didn't want to even approach in discussing her work. She probably knew she wasn't supposed to discuss what she did in detail, and she didn't.

Theoretically, over time, a developmental lets their guard down and starts revealing more and more to you as they come to trust you and like you better. It's not that this was necessarily supposed to happen this early in a relationship, but somehow I couldn't help feeling that she'd never cross any of those lines with me. There was an almost buttoned-down, corporate solidity to her that felt impenetrable. And in any case, I was going to run out of reasons to keep making plans with her unless we really were dating. Had she been a man—if we were becoming friends—this wouldn't have even been a problem.

At staff the next day, I reported on the evening's events. I'd become more comfortable in these meetings as I'd gotten to know everyone better, and I was fairly straightforward about the fact that nothing too interesting had happened at my meeting. I also discussed my concerns about my relationship with Daisy veering too far toward dating. Rob said, "Sounds like you *are* dating," and everyone laughed. Adrienne said, "Why don't you let it cool off for a little while. Then maybe see if you run into each other again. Or even call her in a few months to see if anything's changed."

I was surprised, but I nodded gamely.

22

A month passed. I was stamping ███ applications, going to parties, talking at the staff meetings about people I met at the parties. But I hadn't gotten a single solid developmental going. The DCOS told me not to worry, this was perfectly normal. Rob said, "It's like getting laid. It's hard the first time, then it's easy." And a middle-aged admin officer named Becky, who seemed to know more about what was going on in the Station than I did, said, "Every case officer goes through this."

The heat had simmered down to a moderately blazing boil, and the rains had become routine and untroublesome. I went to sleep alone each night in my four-poster bed, the air conditioner blasting and a down comforter pulled over me. For some reason, I was feeling less energetic and excited about things, and I particularly noticed it when I went to bed at night. I thought that it might have been the heat. It could have been having a cumulative effect on my psyche, slowly draining something—and specifically something American—out of my life force. I saw signs of this in a few of the first-tour ███ guys as well, who looked almost like they were aging by the day. But it didn't seem to be happening to any of the Agency people. I particularly noticed how dry and solid Dorring always looked, marching comfortably around the Station as if he weren't in a foreign country at all, much less such a hot one.

Every few weeks since I'd arrived, William and I had e-mailed back and forth. (There was a secure link for this, although any detailed operational matters had to go in cable traffic.) Mostly, he just asked how I was doing, and I always responded that things were going well. But now, I wrote and hinted at the fact that I felt a little stuck. He wrote back that he'd started his career feeling the same way, and so did almost everyone else he respected. He said that it was important to make things happen in this job, not wait for them to happen, and the best thing was to go out and create opportunities.

This was when I started thinking about CSHELICOPTER again. Her access to the ███ military attaché was a big deal—she would be a very solid recruit for a first-tour. Really, if the access turned into good intel, she'd be a solid recruit for anyone. Adrienne had said I could try calling her again in a few months, but she didn't sound like she even necessarily thought that would be a good idea. She may have said it simply to let me down easily from the case.

Still, if I did want to see her again, should I just call? There was a trick they'd told us about in training for when you wanted to meet somebody. You ██ ████████. That, of course, was a bit too extreme here. But I thought about it happening and wondered if she'd be glad to see me under those circumstances.

23

One night in early January, there was a party at the Russian Embassy to celebrate the birthday of Czar Alexander I. It was obviously some sort of joke, the full nuance of which was lost on me. I wouldn't normally have gone. The Russian Embassy was not a comfortable environment to search for targets. Their intel service was every bit as capable and sophisticated as the KGB had been in its day, and God only knew how many people, cameras, and possibly even microphones would be following you around the embassy. On the other hand, a bunch of the Station guys were going. And I remembered Daisy telling me she had a friend who worked there who she'd met in ████. Maybe Daisy would be there.

The Russian Embassy was large and stately, something from a previous era and, stylistically, a very different country from ████. There were, of course, American embassies like this as well, but they were usually redecorated into something more modern on the inside. Certainly the American Embassy in ███ was ████████████████. At the Russian Embassy, the interior and exterior matched. There were candelabras with actual lit candles in them on the walls. Old but elegant curtains covered the windows in the main ballroom.

Much of the embassy staff had dressed up for the occasion, wearing officer's tunics from the nineteenth century, peaked caps, and in a few cases, swords. Somewhat disturbingly, a few of them had dressed up as Cossacks. On the bright side, there were enormous glass bowls filled with caviar, and all sorts of delicious eggs and pickles and salads. Waiters with silver trays moved through the crowd offering shot glasses of vodka.

I walked around, staying away from the other Station officers and looking for Daisy. The party spilled out of the main ballroom and into two other halls on the same floor, and I went from room to room over and over again, only stopping occasionally to fill up my plate at the buffet. I didn't see Daisy anywhere, but I kept looking. I felt like I was in high school, desperate to catch sight of a girl at a dance.

I was out on the veranda when I saw General ████ turn away from a group of officers and slide a piece of toast with caviar into his mouth. I hadn't seen him since his own party several months earlier, but his name came up frequently at staff meetings, since one C/O or another was always running into him at a function and coming back with a story to tell about the interaction. He was like the Holy Grail of the Station, a source everyone knew would never be tapped but who all the C/Os dreamed wistfully of recruiting.

I didn't feel like dealing with him myself just then, and I was about to move away when he looked up and saw me.

"General," I said, striding over and extending my hand.

"The man who does not know Bobby Goldstein!"

"You're very interested in this Goldstein," I said.

"Yes, yes, it is true."

"What is it about him?" I asked, wondering if I should drop the subject instead.

"If you do not know, I cannot tell you," the General said.

"Ah," I said.

"A Jewish name, is it not, Goldstein?"

"Sounds like it."

"You are Jewish as well, if I am not mistaken?"

"Yes."

"A very fine people. I never understand what all the fuss is about."

"Thank you."

The General looked around, nodding approvingly.

"A beautiful evening, yes?"

"Indeed," I said.

"Carry on, then," said the General with a smile.

He may have winked at me—I wasn't sure in the dark—then he walked away.

I went back inside. It was getting late, and I'd had two shots of vodka, which was enough to make me tipsy. I hadn't spoken to anyone other than the General all night. A waiter approached and put his tray in front of me, and I took another drink. Then I heard, "The Russian vodka is very famous."

She was standing with her arms at her sides, looking more sullen than her comment indicated.

"Daisy, there you are," I said.

"You were looking for me?"

"Well, I thought you might be here."

"I see."

She was stern and cold, the first time her manner had matched the natural sharpness of her face and body.

"Yes, I've been wondering how you are."

"One way in which people find this information out is to call them and ask," she said.

"I'm sorry," I said, "things have been so busy ▉▉▉▉▉▉. The ▉▉▉ line has gone crazy. Terribly backed up. I've been wanting to call, it's just been . . . I haven't had time."

"Yes, I'm sure the work is very much."

And with this she shrugged, turned, and walked off across the ballroom.

I stood still, drunk and confused. There was something in the snap of Daisy's body as she turned away from me that caught me off guard. I had an impulse to rush after her, grab her arm, and spin her back around. But I didn't know what I'd do after that.

Did I want to kiss her? I'd always found Daisy attractive on an almost abstract level—I would have described her as an appealing woman. But I'd wanted to recruit her, not sleep with her. And after all the time and effort I'd put into this case, I did need to recruit her, or at least get some good intel out of her. But I suddenly felt like I'd missed something. She obviously liked me—why else would she be so angry that I hadn't called? And there was something about that turn—the hips first, the body following.

I finished my vodka and looked around for a waiter with a tray of drinks. I was sure that when I sobered up, the passion would go back to its rightful place in the background.

24

The next day, I told the DCOS that I'd seen Daisy at the party, and that there had been no significant developments.

"Time to let this one go," he said. "She's not budging. You gave it a shot. Most of the time this is how it goes."

I wanted to argue with him, but he was right. The case wasn't going anywhere.

As for something more, I'd blown that, too. It was almost impossible to get clearance to have a relationship with any kind of foreigner at all. One you'd been developing was out of the question.

"Should I write it up?" I asked.

"No details, just 'Terminating development of CSHELICOP-TER.'"

25

A few days later, Dorring recruited the ████████████████████████.
It would probably be fair to say that everyone in the Station was
shocked. We'd been following the ████████████ development since the
beginning, and it just didn't sound like it was going anywhere. Adrienne
had even told Dorring he shouldn't spend too much more time on it.

Dorring himself hardly seemed capable of a recruitment. He certainly didn't have the typical C/O personality. He wasn't outgoing, or
socially impressive, or even very smart. In fact, he was quiet to the
point that you barely even knew if he had a personality. After the recruitment was announced at staff, he of course understood that he
had to maintain a sense of modesty and seriousness, in effect pretending that what had happened was no big deal. This was necessary
both to demonstrate your professionalism and imperturbability and
to insulate yourself from charges of overconfidence in case anything
went wrong. But Dorring, while saying and doing all the right things,
couldn't help smiling whenever he talked to you now. And it didn't
fade after a few days, either. He had undergone a real transformation.
It was so simple you could hardly begrudge it. He was happy.

26

With CSHELICOPTER out of the picture for good, I became
increasingly worried. I'd been in-country for eight months now,
and it was starting to seem likely that my entire first tour would be a

bust. I hadn't met anyone new and interesting in a long time. William's admonition to go out and make things happen wasn't going to lead anywhere except to the same string of cocktail parties and useless meetings with governmental nobodies. And on top of it all, I felt restless and bored, which seemed ridiculous since I was in ███, working for the CIA.

One night, I had security duty for the first time at the Station. This involved waiting until everyone else had left the Station, then securing the various vaults, closing down the ██████████, and signing the security register.

Adrienne left at around seven o'clock, the DCOS about ten minutes later, and the last case officer at eight thirty. I was ████████ ███

anyway, so I wasn't in a hurry, but I finished around nine o'clock and started to get ready to leave. I looked over the security checklist one last time, and was about to shut the inner vault when I stopped. This was the first time I'd even been alone in the Station. I thought about everything that had gone on in here over the years. The meetings that had taken place when ██████████████ was bounced out. The operations against ████████████████. And Bobby Goldstein, walking back and forth across these floors, moving fast in the middle of whatever crisis he'd been in the middle of.

I went back into the vault and walked over to the line of metal file cabinets against the wall next to where most of us had our desks. I opened T–V and ticked across the folder tabs until I found TDTRACER. When I opened the folder, there was a single cable inside, simply reporting to Headquarters that they were deactivating the file.

That was pretty much that. I was never going to find out what had happened to TDTRACER. Did they find him? Was he killed? Did they ever figure out how he'd been blown, if he had in fact been blown?

This left the other case of Goldstein's, the one I didn't know anything about at all. I opened the L–M drawer. ██████████████████ ██████ cables weren't separated out in the field the same way they were at Headquarters, so I might find something. I fingered through the L tabs until I got to LX. There was just one file there. LXMALIBU.

I suddenly had an overpowering feeling that I was somewhere I shouldn't be, and reflexively, I turned and looked behind me. But the Station was dead quiet.

I pulled out the file, which was very thin. When I opened it, it was empty. On the inside of the hard plastic folder, someone had written in black marker, "BURNED—DIR 1429 4/19/01."

27

A few weeks later, I came home late and slightly tipsy one night after a party at the Thai Embassy for some holiday I couldn't quite make sense of. I was sitting in my den staring out the window at the house next door when my phone rang. It was Daisy. She asked me to meet her for a drink at a bar on ██████ Street in the ██ Quarter.

As I drove down ██████████, the little washes of rain that meant the bigger rain was coming clouded my windshield. It was dark, and the dusty buildings of the ██████ District looked creepy and forlorn. I turned onto ██████, where the streets and buildings were more modern, and the only people out were diplomats on their way home. Finally, I turned onto ████████, where the young, hip ████████ nightlife was centered. I turned off again onto a little side street to park, then walked by two drunk ██████ men who stared at me as I went by.

Daisy was waiting in the bar, sitting at a banquette against the wall. She was wearing a black blouse with a scooped-out neck—obviously she'd changed after work—and the same purple jeweled necklace that she'd had on when we went to the Chinese restaurant. Her hair was pulled back into a long, tight ponytail. In the shadowy room, she seemed as sharp and angular as the tables and chairs.

As I sat down she gave me a rueful smile.

"Well," she said, "thank you for coming."

"Of course," I said.

"Yes? Of course? I was not sure if you wanted to see me."

"I always like to see you."

"Ah. I see."

My elbows were on the table with my hands loosely clasped. Daisy reached across and put her hand over one of mine. I let my arm drop slowly to the table, our fingers lacing together. I stared at her, hardly shocked at what was happening, but surprised all the same, as if I'd finally walked into a room I'd been looking into for a long time.

I got up and sat down next to her on the banquette. Our hands, with mine still in hers, came to rest on my leg. Daisy took a sip of wine, then leaned over and put her lips on mine. I hadn't kissed a woman in almost a year. The slow movement of her lips, and her wine-breath, were overpowering. But there was a tremendous clattering in another part of my brain, trying hard to ruin the lips. This wasn't a good idea. It couldn't be. Fooling around with an agent, or a developmental, was obviously completely wrong. But she wasn't an agent, or even a developmental. The development had terminated. It had been officially ended. With Headquarters being informed and everything. So I was kissing an ex-developmental. Again, that couldn't possibly be a good idea. But it might not be fatal.

I struggled desperately to sort it out as we kissed. I wouldn't have to report her as a foreign contact since I had already reported all about her. I would be expected to tell the DCOS what had happened, but I might get away without doing that. I could simply claim later, when the truth inevitably came out on my next polygraph, that she was no longer a developmental, and this was my personal life. It would be a bit of a sketchy claim, but as long as this was a one-time thing and not a long-term relationship, it would probably work out all right. After all, I couldn't possibly be the first person to have this problem. A lot of Agency officers slept with foreigners. Or did they? I wasn't really sure. One way or another, I knew it was a terrible idea. But Daisy put a hand on my side, and somehow that one hand won the battle for my attention. One simple hand on my side settled it.

28

We drove back to her apartment in the ██ District. ██ was a fully ██ neighborhood, and tradecraft aside, I felt almost invisible as we walked down the narrow street from the car to her building. Going up the dimly lit staircase, the smell of ██ cooking intensified a feeling of being in a more real ██ now.

Daisy's front door opened into a clean but run-down eat-in kitchen. We stepped through it into a boxy little bedroom with a single window overlooking ██ Street. Daisy closed the bedroom door, and by the faint light coming in through the window, we undressed.

I don't know exactly what to say about our lovemaking. The whole time, she was obviously more concerned with me than with herself. It was almost like her pleasure had to be hidden. She'd look at me, see that I was happy, then look away quickly. But every few minutes, her stomach muscles flexed and quivered so much it seemed like they were restraining something incredible inside. And whenever I looked at her face, her mouth was wide open, even though no sound ever came out of it.

I slept strangely. I was aware of the damp sheets and smell of sweat close to my face, even though I was asleep. I was aware of being in a foreign country, in a foreign bed. With somebody. And there seemed to be some sort of dome arcing over me, keeping its own atmosphere inside. But there was something pricking at the air too, sharp little flickers of light, just a few inches away from my body.

29

Daisy was sitting on the side of the bed, already half dressed, when she woke me.

"I must go," she said.

I rolled onto my side.

"The colonel has a meeting today with the ███████████████████ attaché," she said, pulling on her shoes. "Such an ass! And I must make six, six!, typed copies of the list of this garbage they are buying. Beasts, they become such beasts with the money and the guns." She stood up. "You can close the door when you go out, it will lock itself."

I was startled by her tone, which seemed more distracted, or unguarded, than at any time since I'd met her. But while I wanted to concentrate on that, I also knew instantly that I was, more or less, screwed.

I heard the front door close, and I sat in her bed for a few minutes and tried to sort it all out. She had just, indisputably, provided me with a serious piece of intel. As far as I knew, no one knew of any arms transfers between ████ and ████████. The very fact that the deal was being hammered out in ██████ indicated that the respective governments were trying to keep it secret. But how could I report it? It didn't matter. I had to report it. To fail to report intel was far and away the most serious mistake I could make. I would never pass the poly with that on my conscience, and if I did it and then admitted I'd done it, I would definitely be fired.

So I had to report it. For that matter, it was good intel. It would be good for my career to report it. It would, arguably, even be good for the United States government to know it. But if I reported it and explained how I'd gotten it, I would be sleeping with an agent. Or at least with a developmental. I could argue that she wasn't a developmental anymore when I slept with her, and then she just happened to turn back into one. But going into the DCOS and saying that as soon as the development of CSHELICOPTER had officially ended, I'd felt free to sleep with her, really wasn't a possibility. I might or might not be fired, but it would be tantamount to admitting that I was the biggest idiot who had ever set foot in a CIA station.

So report the intel. Don't report the sex. That was the only way. I would undoubtedly have to admit the sex on my next poly. Otherwise I'd almost certainly fail. But that probably wouldn't be until after my second tour. Four years from now. I would have had a long time to compile a track record. To make myself someone that the Agency wouldn't want to fire. All of that would be taken into account.

And I had heard stories of officers doing worse—or at least doing comparable things—and surviving. One C/O in ▮▮▮▮ had allegedly slept with an agent of the COS's when he was filling in for him at an emergency meeting. He'd only gotten a reprimand (though he had apparently stalled out at GS-13 as a result). A female C/O I'd actually met at Headquarters was rumored to have slept with an agent she'd recruited for the entire two years she was running him. She hadn't been fired, I'd heard, because the intel was so good.

Again, as long as I reported the intel, I would have reported the intel. That would be the most important thing. The rest of it would look bad. But it was survivable. Maybe.

I did, for just a moment, consider the possibility that being fired wouldn't be the end of the world. If I'd had some promise at this job, I wasn't living up to it. At least not yet. And I wasn't exactly enjoying my tour so far—I had no close friends, and nothing to do except go to parties. But I knew I was kidding myself—being fired was unthinkable. What would I do next? I couldn't go back to a think tank. I had no other real interests that I could turn into a job. This was it. And besides, if there was one thing I believed in, it was the importance of making a difference in the world. Professor Lang had always said, "Devote yourself to the world, or ask nothing of it." This was still my chance to devote myself to the world, whether it was working out yet or not.

I was already late for work, but I couldn't show up in the same clothes I'd been wearing the day before. I hurried out of Daisy's apartment and back to my house, running the conversation I was going to have with the DCOS over and over again in my head. I'd tell him that she'd called and we'd gotten together. And to my surprise, she had produced this piece of intel. And that would be that. I wouldn't affirmatively lie. I just wouldn't mention the sex part. And hopefully he wouldn't ask for too many details about the meeting.

30

The DCOS's eyebrows shot up when I told him the intel.

"Write it up. Maybe we"—by which he meant Adrienne—"were too hasty on this."

He didn't ask for any operational details about the meeting.

Two days after my cable went out, Headquarters responded that they were very interested in arms transfers between ▮▮▮ and ▮▮▮▮▮. At the staff meeting, Adrienne mentioned it, setting off a round of positive head shakes from the other C/Os. After the meeting, Rob slapped me on the back and said, "Ah, I remember my first piece of solid intel. I found out that the ▮▮▮▮▮▮▮▮▮▮▮▮▮ was banging the ▮▮▮▮▮▮▮ Ambassador's daughter. Way to go." Dorring came up and said, "Nice work," which I both appreciated and which made me want to punch him.

31

I saw Daisy again the following week. Now that she was affirmatively supplying intel, I had to start running SDRs (surveillance detection routes) on the way to meet her. Doing it sooner would have aroused suspicions if anyone was watching, and there hadn't really been anything to hide. Now there was something to hide.

I left ████████ before we were supposed to meet, and ███████████ ███ ██████████████. On the second leg, I saw a blue sedan with ████████████ about four cars behind me in traffic on ███ Street. The car passed me a few blocks later, and I ████████████ to see the driver's face. Nothing about this worried me. But twenty minutes later, stopped at a ████████████, I saw a similar blue sedan parked in front of the ███████████████████████. The license plate was different, and there must have been a lot of cars like this one all over ████████. Changing the plates wasn't the most likely move for an urban surveillance team in this situation. But it wasn't impossible.

Standing next to the car was a man eating a ███████. He had a mustache, a wide face, and a disinterested expression. He looked a lot like the guy I'd seen in traffic. But the shirt was different. Again, a clothes change was possible, but was it likely here? For that matter, why wouldn't he have ██? ████████ had certain features that could make it hard to distinguish between two men who looked similar if you didn't get a long look. It probably—almost definitely—wasn't him.

But my heart was racing now. I pressed my ████████████ and checked the ████████████, trying to remember to stay calm and follow procedures. I added an extra leg to my SDR, which would make me late but give me a better chance of discovering surveillance

if it was there. I turned onto ██████████ and went ███████████████
██
██. I didn't see
anything else. You couldn't break off over something like this, at
least not at this stage with an early developmental. It was, almost
certainly, nothing.

I arrived at the ███████ and saw Daisy waiting at the entrance. We
hugged each other, then went in and took a stroll around the water. It
was the first cool night I'd experienced in ██████████, and I actually
kept my suit jacket on without sweating. I was still wound up from
the SDR, and I tried to look behind me on ███████, but every time I
looked at Daisy, I forgot about ████████████████ and found myself
wondering if she was pretty. She wasn't one of those women who men
stopped and looked at on the street. On the other hand, I kept pictur-
ing her rocking back and forth on top of me, and her stern, angular
face suddenly took on a different quality. Not exactly pretty. But
somehow animal-like, and feminine.

After we'd spent several minutes discussing the coolness of the
night, the latest brouhaha in the Foreign Affairs Ministry, and a bombing that morning in Indonesia, I decided to make my move. When I
had initially realized the fix that I was in, I thought I'd just stop asking Daisy about work and hope no more intel came up. But I quickly
realized that wouldn't fly on the poly. If I wasn't affirmatively pursuing whatever information she had, I was in trouble. So I had to continue nudging her toward work-related questions and then just hope
she didn't take the bait. I would, in fact, be something close to reverse
case-officering her. It was the opposite of everything I'd been trained
to do, and as I started, my pulse began racing much faster than it ever
had during a proper elicitation.

"Everything go okay with your six copies?" I asked.

"Oh yes, it was fine. Just a lot of typing."

Stop there, Daisy, I thought.

She did.

We walked twice around the lake, and then, without anyone saying anything, we got in my car and went back to her apartment. I had
told myself many times over the previous week that it would get

worse if we did it again, but I hadn't exactly resolved not to. Now I drove toward her apartment like it was the only possible choice.

We undressed in her little bedroom and went through the same motions, at the same pace, as we had the last time. It was like we wanted to repeat something that deserved repeating, to revisit the exact movements in a way that would mix our memory of what had happened with the new moment of doing it again. She was contained in the same way, too, but with that intensity that felt like she had a bomb inside her body that she was barely preventing from going off.

We lay in bed afterward with her head tucked into my neck. After a while, I said, "Listen. I've got a little problem. I'm supposed to report you ███████ as a foreign contact. We're required to do that. But it always makes problems. They're very difficult about it."

"Yes," she said, "I have the same problem."

"You have to report your foreign contacts?"

"Oh yes. They are very worried about this."

"So did you report it?"

"No, no. It is the same thing. They might insist that I do not go on spending time with you."

"I'm not sure what to do," I said.

I really was good at this. I could have written down her response almost word for word before she said it.

"Perhaps we should keep this as something only between us."

"Well . . . but what if someone sees us?" I asked.

"I don't know."

She thought for a minute, and I kept quiet. Then she said, "We can go only to places where nobody we know goes to. I think we must not tell anyone."

"Even my house might be a problem," I said. "There are guards there, and they work for the ██████. I don't think they would tell anybody, but who knows?"

"We can go only to my apartment," she said.

As carefully as I was following this conversation, there were two parallel streams of words and ideas racing alongside it in my head. In the first, I was considering the possibility that she was a double agent. After all, she'd gone along very easily with what I wanted, and needed, here. Yes, I'd steered her well. But you could never be sure that you were steering instead of being steered. I found it exceptionally unlikely that Daisy was a foreign intelligence officer. The ███████ intel service didn't have many women in their ranks, and probably wouldn't use a secretary to a military attaché as cover. Of course, that's exactly what would make it good cover. But overall, it didn't feel right. Much more likely was that she had reported the contact with me, and the ███████ intel service had decided to use her against me. The goals here could be getting me in trouble and then trying to turn me, or more likely, letting me recruit her and then using her as a conduit of bad information. These types of operations were run all the time. So it was possible. But the odds of Daisy, if she wasn't an intel officer, being such a good actor, were slim. All things considered, then, I thought it was extremely unlikely that she was a double. But you always had to worry, and wonder, about it.

In the other stream of thought, I was trying to figure out how much worse sleeping with Daisy twice was than doing it once, and how much worse doing it more times would be than doing it twice, and simultaneously realizing that I should be stopping it instead of planning it. But I also knew that, whatever I was thinking, it was the conversation we were having now that was going to determine what happened. My awareness that it was a bad idea felt abstract and increasingly distant. It was as if my judgment, which had never in my life had any competition in deciding what I did, had simply fallen by the wayside. Of course, I was in this job, more than any other reason, because this didn't happen to me. Other people exercised poor judgment. Not me. But now it was me, too.

Daisy had stopped talking. I stared down at the tops of her breasts and at her pinprick of a belly button. I kissed her, then we went to sleep.

32

I started seeing Daisy once during the week and once on the weekend. I'd report the weekday meetings at staff, always opening by saying I'd seen her but hadn't gotten any more intel. I'd repeat, in slightly different words each time, that I thought more intel would come slowly—that what she'd given me at first had slipped out, and we'd either have to wait for more to slip out or wait for the relationship to develop to the point where she was ready to give it on purpose. The DCOS would say, in slightly different words each time, to move toward formal recruitment very slowly with her. He thought that it might take a year, and that this was fine. At one meeting where he made this point, one of the C/Os asked how long the tours were for secretaries in the ■■■ Embassy. Embarrassed, I said that I didn't know, but that she hadn't said anything about leaving.

As for the weekend meetings, I never told anyone about them. We ate at out-of-the-way restaurants and visited parts of the city that foreigners didn't frequent. All in all, we practiced fairly good tradecraft. In fact, we were probably doing exactly what I'd want us to be doing if I were actually developing CSHELICOPTER for recruitment.

33

After we were doing whatever it was we were doing for about a month, Daisy and I stayed up very late one night, drinking tea in her kitchen and talking about ourselves and our families. Daisy had grown up in a ███, something she described as a cross between a small city and a village. The center of town was almost modern, and teeming with commerce. But you could turn any corner and find yourself on a street of dilapidated shacks with animals roaming freely. Fields and farms ringed the town, and through some miracle of urban coincidence, rather than good planning, the closest factory was several miles away. Unless the wind was blowing directly toward the town, the stink and pollution that hovered over so much of ██████ wasn't a problem.

Daisy's father was a middle school teacher, and her mother worked at a variety of odd jobs over the years, from butcher's assistant to bakery manager to truck mechanic. Although her work was hard and dull, Daisy's mother was full of wit and energy. Her father, on the other hand, was a quiet man. He was enormously popular with his students, which Daisy never fully understood. Most of them left school by the equivalent of seventh grade, but for years afterward they would stop by their old teacher's apartment to sit and talk about their lives. As a little girl, Daisy found them incredibly glamorous and exciting, even the ones who showed up with grease on their faces and necks, wearing near-rags. They would sit on a chair across from her father and tell him about their work, their marriages, their children. He never did much except nod at them, but they always left in a great show of respect and admiration, bowing and smiling and thanking.

When Daisy was fourteen, the ███████ government launched a program called ██████████████████████. The idea was to take talented schoolchildren from the provinces and give them a better education in ██████. Daisy was brought to a boarding school in ██████, where she no doubt acquired the plain but refined manners that she still had. She never felt close to the other girls, and school was a hard place for her. But the government sent her home four times a year, including summers. When she would arrive back at the apartment her father would always break into a wide grin, virtually the only time she ever saw him smile. Her mother would bake a cake and fuss over her for days until things returned to a normal routine.

Somehow, I found my own life almost impossible to discuss after hearing about Daisy's. I don't know why my history would have seemed any stranger to her than hers did to me, but somehow my recitation of my private school education, my modest success at most undertakings, and my struggles to make choices amidst an almost limitless set of opportunities felt absurd. But Daisy was fascinated. She asked about small details, like what kind of clothes my mother wore and which books my father read to me as a child, things I could hardly remember well enough to answer.

When she asked about how I'd decided to join the ████████████, I gave a disjointed answer about growing up in the upper middle class, ways in which my parents had shielded me, Professor Lang opening my eyes to the world, and needing to spend time away from the country I'd grown up in. I think I might have even mentioned religion. Obviously, she didn't know where I really worked, and so I couldn't tell her the true story. But when you lied, you were supposed to stay as close to the truth as you possibly could, and the rambling version of my life that came out felt both accurate and surprising to me. I recognized the story I was telling, but I didn't know exactly where the words were coming from.

By the time we finished talking, it was three in the morning. We got a little sleep before work, and decided before parting that we'd celebrate her birthday that weekend at a ████████.

34

I felt like I was living in the shadow of the poly. I'd lie in bed, or drive my car, mentally preparing for the questions I would be asked. My next exam was almost four years away, but I couldn't stop thinking about it.

At the beginning of the poly, they ask you if there's anything you want to say before the questioning begins. This is the time where you have to let out any secrets you're holding. If you don't, once you're hooked up to the machine, you may get deceptive results even on questions where you're telling the truth. So this was where I'd have to explain about CSHELICOPTER.

I decided that I would admit straight out that we'd had a sexual relationship. And that I hadn't reported it. I'd justify this by explaining exactly what had happened. How she was no longer a developmental, then she unexpectedly produced some intel. I'd stress that I reported all the intel she provided. And that I'd tried to keep it flowing by asking questions about her work and her boss. It wasn't my fault that she didn't give up any more useful information.

It was going to be rough, and of course all of it was going to be reported to my Division. I'd undoubtedly raise some eyebrows and get in some trouble. But again, the goal was just to survive it.

Of course, I'd also have to admit that I'd been planning for the poly for the entire four years between now and then. That I'd been worried about it, and had thought constantly about what to say. That type of meta-thinking actually seemed to go okay with the examiners. I'd had plenty of it on my previous two polys, the first when I was applying to the Agency, and the second right before the final phase of my training. But the fact that this was going to be crowding my brain for four years was an unpleasant thought.

During one of my initial training classes, I'd gone for a walk one night at the Farm with a woman who worked as a polygrapher. She was married, but her husband didn't work at the Agency. The Agency felt like a different universe from the rest of the world, and the Farm felt like a different universe within the Agency, so he was two universes removed from us that night. The road we were walking down wound through a cluster of corrugated-iron, World War II–era barracks, then past a dusty parade ground, and finally veered into the woods, where the tree canopies hanging overhead made it feel like a tunnel. The distant fences ringing the Farm added a safe feeling to the night that it doesn't have in nonsecure locations. That, and the feeling at the Farm that you were simultaneously in the 1940s and the present, and the husband's nonexistence in this world, made walking with her feel flirtatious and heavy with usually impossible possibilities.

We started talking about her work. I'd heard all sorts of theories about the polygraph since coming to the Agency, and I asked her if it was true that the whole key to the test was to make people so scared of the machine that they admitted everything in the pre-test interview. She smiled and said, "I can't really talk about it."

I can't really talk about it. I was just coming to realize that a polygrapher, or a security officer, or even an analyst were all more likely to say "I can't talk about it" than a case officer. They were more likely to follow the rules to the letter than those in the thick of it, those surrounded by so many secrets that if you couldn't talk about them you couldn't talk about anything.

In any case, I was sure that what I'd heard was true. It made sense that everything important came out on the pre-test interview. Because the test itself obviously didn't work. Or didn't always work. But if it worked sometimes, people like me couldn't take any chances. We had to let everything out in the pre-test interview. Of course, I hadn't really had anything to hide on my first two polygraphs. But what if you did have something to hide? You'd just have to cross your fingers and hope the machine blinked. You can't actually ███████████████████████ or ███████████████████ to throw off the machine. These techniques are easily discovered by a trained polygrapher.

They must have really celebrated at the KGB when Aldrich Ames passed his poly. They couldn't have known that he would. In fact, they probably saw the odds as heavily against him. But they crossed their fingers and won.

Ultimately, it probably depends on someone having a sick enough mind not to feel a reaction when they're lying.

35

Dorring brought a sandwich over to my cubicle at lunch, opened it on my desk, and started to talk.

"How's the ▮▮ line?"

"Dull. I didn't join the Agency to ▮▮▮▮▮▮▮▮▮▮"

"I know. Next tour, you'll probably get into a ▮▮▮▮▮▮▮ slot. You're an intellectual guy. You'll like it better."

He ate his sandwich quietly for a minute. Normally, I would never have let this much time pass without making conversation. But somehow, with Dorring, I enjoyed not taking responsibility for the flow of our words.

Finally, still chewing, Dorring said, "How's HELICOPTER?"

"Going okay."

"Y'know, I think that could be a good case. Really. A lot of potential."

"Yeah, I'm just trying not to push it."

"That's good. Y'know, I don't think it all has to be so perfectly planned. You go about your business, get closer. Kind of let it run its own course. Then it almost surprises you. One day, you're ready. You can feel it."

I felt like saying, "You are a stupid, stupid man. Dull witted and slow." But really, who was I to say it? ▮▮▮▮▮▮▮▮▮▮ was producing highly graded intel, and Dorring was definitely going to get promoted in the next cycle.

36

received an e-mail from William with the subject "Sad News." It read:

Mark—

I'm afraid I have some bad news. I know that you were close with Professor Wolfgang Lang. I'm sorry to tell you that he was killed this morning when a helicopter he was riding in was shot down in Sri Lanka. Lang was there advising the government on counterinsurgency policy. I had the good fortune to meet Lang a few times and was a great admirer of his. He will be missed, both by friends and by a nation that relied on his brilliance.

I sat still in my chair for a long time after reading the e-mail. I pictured Lang smoking cigars and making subtle jokes at his salon. I thought about my last meeting with him, and how serious he'd become. I wondered if William knew him better than he was saying, and if, after all, Lang had recommended me for this job. Perhaps directly to William.

For the rest of the day, I hardly said a word to anyone. And then that night, sitting alone in my living room, I decided it was time to rededicate myself to my work. I had allowed myself to slip, to lose focus. As a former student of Lang's, I should have known better. I should have realized the world couldn't afford slips. Decent, dedicated people had to work tirelessly to protect and promote freedom, or all was lost. That's what Professor Lang believed, and I did, too.

I knew where to start. I needed to cut out the romance and get back to actually trying to recruit CSHELICOPTER. If I could get a steady stream of intel about the ████ Attaché, it might not change the world in a huge way, but it would be a good start.

It would also save my tour. Because if I didn't recruit anybody at all, I'd be sinking fast into mediocrity by the time I got to my second post.

37

And so, on the night of Daisy's thirty-second birthday, I headed off to meet her with the idea of gradually moving our relationship back onto a professional footing. It was her birthday, so I wouldn't do anything drastic. But drastic wouldn't be the way to handle this anyway.

I left my house at ████ and ran a ████████ SDR. I didn't see anything. The streets were unusually quiet around ████████████, and I opened my window and enjoyed the flowery air that blew across the neighborhood gardens, picking up their scents as it went. Turning onto ██████, much more unmistakably ██████, I watched groups of boys dragging sticks and clumping together more closely in the night as they wandered the ████████████.

Daisy was standing against an earthen wall outside the ████████. There were two red lanterns hanging from the restaurant awning, and the prick of a ██████ being played somewhere in the distance. For some reason, it made me think of Mexico.

I wished her a happy birthday, and we kissed. When we broke away, we smiled and then started to kiss again, more slowly. She was wearing a white dress with a purple flower print, and my hand slid a patch of the rough-textured silk up and down against her back.

Inside the ████████, we sat close to each other at a round table big enough for ten. ████████ were my favorite thing about ██████. Waiters covered your table with enormous silver bowls of every imaginable kind of ▮▮▮▮, including combinations you'd never order, or never even eat if you knew what they were. About half the dishes were so spicy that I'd usually be pouring sweat after just a few minutes, but I didn't really care. With hands moving constantly from bowl to bowl, and arms getting tangled up with each other, dinners were almost like exercise anyway.

While we were waiting for our food, Daisy started to talk about a woman who had been stoned to death that week in Pakistan. She mentioned that her boss had made a joke about it, which she found insulting and cruel. My work for the night was done. Although I wouldn't be reporting on this meeting, I could use that as the information gleaned from our next meeting. It showed disaffection and, perhaps, a future willingness to screw her boss.

Obviously, whenever I was with Daisy, there was a part of me observing our surroundings, rehearsing cover stories in case someone saw us, and even planning escape routes from restaurants and neighborhoods, although there was virtually no scenario in which that would be necessary. All of this simultaneous brain activity made me feel like I was in several different places at the same time. Sometimes, I'd notice Daisy staring at me as if something was wrong, and I'd realize I'd drifted into one of the other worlds of thought and left her and our conversation behind. Then I'd smile and say, "Sorry, I just got distracted by something"—which was true—and I'd reenter the conversation. Being a C/O was obviously going to require being able to manage all these simultaneous trains of thought without dropping the ball on any of them.

I actually managed this most of the time, but that night I stopped listening to her for several straight minutes as I thought about all the things I had to think about. I came back into the conversation just as Daisy was saying, ". . . so we sat and ate the cake on the floor. In a little circle, each with our fork. My father did not care about his pants. I stopped crying. It was a very delicious cake, too. I think the best one I have eaten."

I wish there was some sort of cliché for what happened to me at that moment, but none of them quite seem to fit. Maybe it was most like that thing that happens when you get a vision test, and you think you're seeing the letters clearly, but then the lens you're looking through slides out, everything blurs, a new one slides in, and suddenly everything is in much sharper focus. I looked at Daisy's face next to me, and suddenly I saw the face of someone I loved. It didn't make any sense to me at first. I stopped chewing my █████, and I'm afraid my expression may have contorted into something almost disdainful. I thought quickly of the old formula that had been popular in high school, whereby you could love somebody without being in love with them. The truth was, I'd told myself that about every woman I'd been involved with since high school. But now, I couldn't see the difference. Daisy looked quizzically back at me. I managed a smile and said, "Spicy."

"Oh, here, have some water," she said, handing me my own glass.

38

I spent the next day wandering around my house, and the day after that barely paying attention to my interviews on the ██ line. For the first time in my life, I felt incapable of organizing or keeping up with all the thoughts in my head. Cover stories, escape routes, love, intel, Daisy's pretty blouse draped across her breasts, polygraph, DCOS . . . I couldn't zero in on any of them.

I kept spinning out plans, all versions of each other that would seem to work one minute and fall apart the next. As long as Daisy didn't provide any more intel, I'd never be expected to recruit her. And then, in seven or eight months, the development might be terminated again. Then, near the end of my tour, I could report that we'd run into each other again, and if romantic "feelings" developed, I could plead surprise, but ask for permission to date her. Which I might get. Again, C/Os did this. They came home with foreign brides.

But the very fact that I had just planned all of that meant I could never get it by the poly. I'd have to admit that I'd planned it.

And besides, now I was suddenly going to marry her? And what, take her around the world with me from now on? Did she even want that? I knew she liked me, but there was no real reason to think she loved me. And yet, I was almost sure she loved me.

But what if we weren't in love and this whole thing was misguided, which seemed, at least when I thought about it in a removed way, like a real possibility. In that case, Daisy and I would no longer have a relationship by the time I left ████ anyway. I could keep quiet about it and go back to the first plan, sliding it by as a stupid but forgivable transgression on my next poly. Or in that case, maybe I still needed to move this toward a recruitment. Was it possible that she would allow me to end the romantic part of the relationship and still be interested in working as an agent? That seemed ridiculous. But if she loved me, maybe she'd do it. But did I want her to do it for that reason? I couldn't sort it all out.

39

On a Tuesday afternoon, I was sitting at my desk trying to read the day's traffic, and waiting for staff to begin, when my ████ line rang. It was Adrienne's secretary.

"She wants to see you."

"On my way," I said.

I hadn't met with Adrienne alone since my first day at the Station. I saw her in meetings, said "Hi, Adrienne" to her in the halls, and that was about it. She spent most of her time in her office, with the DCOS and Section chiefs coming in and out. She also went ████ to the Ambassador's office with some frequency, and left the building several times a week to meet with ██████████████.

Her secretary nodded toward the door to indicate that I should go in. Adrienne looked up from her desk and motioned with her hand for me to sit down in a chair across from her.

She stared at me for a moment, then she said, "Are you sleeping with CSHELICOPTER?"

For the first time in my life, words completely deserted me. Any answer I spit out would prove itself wrong before I finished saying it. In my head, sentences kept starting to form—"What happened was," "It wasn't really"—but they didn't go anywhere.

"Yes," I finally managed. "I . . . I . . ."

"Pack your bags," she said.

She picked up some papers on her desk and started to read them.

"I couldn't . . ."

She looked up at me, then back down at the papers.

As I went through the outer office, the secretary said, "See the DCOS."

In the hallway, I walked straight past Rob, who was on his way into Adrienne's office. He gave me one of his sly winks. I wasn't sure if it meant that he knew what I'd done, or if it was just his way of saying hello.

I went to the DCOS's office, where he stood up before I could sit down.

"You're flying out tomorrow morning," he said. "They'll be waiting for you at Headquarters. Don't call her."

"My things?"

"We'll take care of it."

40

At the house, I took off my suit and tossed it into a corner of the bedroom closet. I put on shorts and a T-shirt, then got a glass of iced tea from the fridge and went into the den.

There were two immediate questions: what was going to happen when I reported to Headquarters, and should I or shouldn't I call Daisy? The Headquarters question seemed simpler. I was going to be fired. I was being sent home from my first assignment for lying, or at least for not telling the whole truth. It was an integrity issue. You got fired for those.

Although I had seen a couple of C/Os who'd been sent back to Headquarters and not fired. I was never sure exactly what they were sent back for, but one of them moved over to the Directorate of Intelligence and worked as an analyst, and the other one was working a desk in ██████ while I was there. I had some sense he was waiting for the outcome of an investigation into some sort of financial question—whether or not he'd stolen money or something like that. This meant that even if they thought you'd stolen money, you didn't necessarily get fired right away. Although I doubted you'd have much of a chance of ever being sent abroad again. In any case, there wasn't really anything to investigate in this situation. I'd lied. Or not been forthcoming with the truth. I'd admitted it to the COS. I was done.

Or was I? I wasn't absolutely positive. The CIA probably didn't like to fire people when they had a choice. After all, Agency officers knew a lot of secrets, and it was probably considered more risky to fire them than not to. Maybe they evaluated how many secrets you knew before deciding what to do with you if you committed an offense. How many sources or operations you could blow if you decided to blow them.

How many secrets did I know? I was inside—I knew a lot—but I certainly wasn't in the inner sanctum. On the other hand, did the CIA really have an inner sanctum? Certainly the Division Chief knew a lot more than I did, but didn't he know mostly more of the same kinds of things? I wasn't really sure.

So maybe there was some chance they'd offer me a job in the DI, or somewhere else. Which I had no idea if I'd take or not. But probably I would, for the short term.

I also had to figure out what to say. Because certainly I'd be asked a lot of questions when I got back to Headquarters. Probably in a fairly hostile way.

And what would I say to William? Would I even see William, or would I just be hustled into a room in Security, interrogated, and kicked out onto the streets of suburban Virginia?

I couldn't come up with answers for anything, and nothing could be done about any of it now anyway. But Daisy . . . that I had to figure out in the next few hours. Should I call her? I wanted to talk to her. To tell her, at least, that I was leaving, and that I almost definitely wasn't coming back. But that we could stay in touch, and maybe plan to see each other again someday, somewhere.

But could we? What could I really say if I called her? And why did they tell me not to call her? Why did they care? Were they just punishing me?

Maybe they were actually looking out for her. Maybe her embassy knew about us, and she was under suspicion, and it would get worse if I called. In other words, maybe Daisy was in trouble. Because of me. After all, how did Adrienne know about me and Daisy? Maybe she'd found out from the ███████. That was improbable, on many different levels. But was it impossible?

This was the real question. How did the Station find out? I had no idea. And if I couldn't figure it out—and early indications were I couldn't—it was possible that I'd never know.

I also didn't know if anyone would even know if I called her. Were my calls being monitored? Maybe they monitored all new C/Os as a security precaution. More likely, now that I was in trouble I was being kept tabs on. Or maybe . . . maybe . . . There were too many maybes. How had I gotten into this position? I'd never been screwed up like this before in my life. I'd never been screwed up at all before in my life. I'd certainly never been fired from anything. Never even really been unsuccessful at anything.

I didn't decide not to call her. But I didn't.

41

The next morning, as my plane climbed, I watched ███████ get smaller and browner beneath me. The city took on a certain kind of symmetry and sense from above that it totally lacked when you were inside of it. I pictured Daisy as a little dot down there now, a tiny bulb of light that pulsed on and off.

At cruising altitude, I started to feel strangely disoriented. I wasn't sure if I was departing or returning, or if I wanted this time in the cloudless sky to go on or end immediately. I always wondered what was wrong with people who had panic attacks—I wondered what a panic attack even was—but I thought I was getting some little inkling of it now.

There was a stopover in ████████, and I spent a few hours in the airport before changing planes. The antiseptic, well-organized terminal, though hardly American, felt familiar, and I grew a little steadier. On the second leg of the flight, the low hum of the plane's engine and the gradual melting away of the light dropped me into a stupor, and after a few hours, I fell asleep.

I'd flown into Washington many times, and I always felt a rush of excitement and unbridled patriotism as I saw the Washington Monument and the Capitol out the window. This time, I awoke with a jolt as the plane touched down at Dulles. My mind flew into a state of frantic activity. I'd meant to figure everything out on the plane, but I'd be at Headquarters in an hour, as unsure of everything as I'd been when I left ██████.

With my one bag slung over my shoulder, and accusations and explanations racing through my head, I took a cab to Headquarters. (You could say "CIA" to any taxi driver in Washington and they knew how to get there.) At the gatehouse, I handed over my driver's

license ████████████████████████████████, then checked in
at the security desk in the main building. I was handed an "Escort
Only" badge, which pretty much settled it. I was fired.

Along with my escort, I went up to ██ Division, where the secretary sent me to HR. Chief HR for ██ had changed since I'd left, but
was just another fifty-year-old GS-14 who hadn't accomplished
enough in Operations to become a COS anywhere. I sat across from
him while he looked through some papers, then he said, "Well, this is
obviously an integrity issue, as well as a very compromising operational misjudgment. You're being discharged. Chief ██ didn't think
there was any reason to have the review board look at it."

I nodded.

"You'll be processed out this morning. Any questions?"

"Not really," I said. I was surprised he didn't have any questions,
but maybe that would come later.

Chief HR stood up, and I did too. He didn't offer a handshake.

"Can I say good-bye to William?" I asked.

"That's your next stop."

The escort led me out and then over to ███████. The vault door was
closed, and I didn't remember the code. It felt strange to knock, but
Patsy, the secretary, let me in and gave me a big smile. I wondered if
she knew what was going on. I walked over to William's cubicle, where
he was working at the computer.

"Hi," I said.

He swiveled around, frowned at me, then stood up.

"What the hell?" he said.

"I don't know," I said.

"I'll say," he said.

Words started streaming into my head, but like with Adrienne,
they didn't connect with other words and go somewhere.

"First Bobby Goldstein, then you," William said. "I don't understand it."

"Sorry," I said.

"Maybe it's this place. Something about it."

"Hard to blame anyone but me here," I said.

"True enough."

William put his hand out.

"Thanks for everything," I said, shaking it. "Really."

My escort brought me down to a windowless office in Security, where a guy in shirtsleeves and a tie was sitting behind a messy desk. He could have been a low-level bureaucrat anywhere. I sat down, and he handed me a large brown envelope.

"This packet contains information on extending your health insurance coverage through COBRA, instructions for transferring your IRA and Thrift accounts, and contact numbers should you need to reach the Agency in the future. If you'll remove the contents of the package, I'll walk you through it step-by-step."

For the next twenty minutes, he talked and I tried to keep the right piece of paper in front of me even though I wasn't listening. Was this really the whole thing? Nobody was going to ask me anything about what had happened? I was a highly trained operative, full of secrets, potentially a threat to the Agency if I was angry. Wasn't I? Or was I, but this was a clever sort of reverse psychology, their way of trying to convince me that I really didn't matter to them at all?

When we'd finally worked our way through the entire packet, he asked me what address I wanted to have my car and personal belongings from ██████ shipped to. He wrote the address on two separate forms and had me initial them. Then he pulled a single piece of paper out of a manila folder on his desk and slid it across to me.

"This is your secrecy agreement," he said. "Please review it and sign at the bottom."

I read the page, which stated that I'd never reveal any classified information, that I understood release of such information was a crime, that I wouldn't publish anything about intelligence matters without submitting it to the CIA first for review, and that I wouldn't grant interviews or discuss intelligence matters publicly without prior approval from the CIA. My signature was already at the bottom, from when I'd been hired, and now another signature line had been added under it, with "Exit Review" next to it in parentheses. I signed.

"Do you currently have any classified material in your possession?" he asked.

"No."

"Do you have any CIA documentation, such as agency credentials, parking permits, or ███ identification, in your possession?"

"I left that all at the Station."

"Do you have any further questions about your status, legal responsibilities, or health insurance?"

"No."

"All right. Your escort will take you out to your car."

"Thanks," I said. It came out the same way it would to a cashier at McDonald's who had just handed me a burger and fries.

PART TWO

1

I flew home to Chicago the next day. I had about $5,000 I'd taken out of my credit union account, and the one bag of clothing I'd brought from ██████.

The night before I'd called my parents to tell them I was coming—before that they hadn't even known I was back from ██████—and as soon as I got home, we sat down at the kitchen table. They looked terribly worried. Now, all I offered them was, "It just wasn't for me." It felt awful to lie to them, especially when they were the only two people who knew the truth about where I'd been working. But I couldn't tell them I'd been fired. I'd stretched them to their limit just by joining the CIA, which made no sense to them in terms of how they saw me or themselves. To fail at it—and to fail because I'd slept with someone I shouldn't have—would have been one awful twist too many.

The first few weeks at home were strange but somehow calming. I went through the dresser drawers in my old bedroom a lot, turning over the various artifacts that had been building up there since I was a little kid. I sat at the kitchen table for breakfast with my father while he read the newspaper. A few of my high school friends were still in Chicago, and we stayed out late and got drunk at the same bars we'd snuck into as teenagers. They, of course, all thought that I'd been in the ██████ Service. I told them I'd quit because I couldn't deal with the injustice of the ████ line, where race and class determined whether or not you were admitted to our country. Not only didn't anyone question this explanation, everyone seemed to admire me for it.

2

My favorite teacher in high school was Mr. Treadwell. I can't remember anything specific that he taught me about U.S. or European history. The dates, the movements, the reasons for things—they're all gone. What remains is a powerful impression of him. Tall, bearded, forever not working on the Ph.D. he couldn't seem to finish. Endlessly, seriously engaged with his students.

Treadwell was also my adviser, and I'd felt very close to him. We'd stayed in touch after I'd gone to college, but by the time I got back to Chicago post-██████, we hadn't spoken in years. I e-mailed him and invited him to lunch at the Corned Beef House, a dingy deli near school.

I got there first, reflexively took a seat against the wall near the back, and waited. When he arrived, I was immediately struck by the fact that he'd put on weight and his beard had gone completely gray. But as soon as he sat down, his eyes started sparkling with the old intensity and interest. He was surprised that I'd left the ██████ Service so soon, and when I fed him my line about the immorality of the ████ process, I had a strong sense that he didn't believe me. Still, he spoke for a few minutes about people who had taken unpopular moral stands throughout history and the role they had played in forcing change.

Finally, he asked me what I was going to do.

"I don't know," I said. "I want to find something in Chicago for now. But I'm not sure what."

"Dyson's been pretty sick this year," he said. "Do you want to do some subbing?"

Mr. Dyson was another history teacher, and he'd been having health problems ever since I was in high school. Every year, he'd miss more and more days, but the school was too bighearted to fire him. I hadn't even known for certain if he was still around, but I'd figured that if he was, my conversation with Treadwell would go exactly like this. Even back in high school, he'd told me he thought I'd be a good teacher.

I paused for a moment, looking out the window as if it were a new idea.

"Yeah," I said, "that sounds interesting. I think . . . well, I think I could be a pretty good teacher."

3

I was half tempted to stay at my parents', but at my age, it felt too ridiculous. I rented a studio apartment a few miles west of their house in a neighborhood called Roscoe Village. I liked it because it had a Bavarian feel. There were three different old-world bakeries within a few blocks of my apartment, selling doughy pastries and terrible coffee. Fat women carrying heavy bags wobbled in and out of an Orthodox church on one of the corners. And a circular cul-de-sac at the end of the neighborhood's main street kept traffic down and gave everything a private feel.

The apartment itself was nothing but a room and a tiny kitchen, but I bought a mattress and moved in a dresser and an old desk from my parents' basement, and I was comfortable enough.

I started teaching two to three days a week. Dyson had two different classes he was missing, one on the history of the British Empire and one somewhat clunkily called "Literature and Its Adherents in Twentieth-Century Central Europe." I didn't know much about either topic, and I'd often have to answer questions by saying, "I'll have to research that." But by staying ahead in the reading, and focusing more on "idea discussions" than facts, I was able to teach the classes without too much trouble.

4

I was surprised by how much I missed the routines at the Agency. The morning commute along the George Washington Parkway, speeding around the curves with the feeling that I was going somewhere that was important and always awake. The crappy lunches in the cafeteria with my friends. The new training classes every few months. The habit of lying about my days and my whereabouts, which I had gotten used to so quickly.

In ██████, it was different—going to the Station each morning had been like heading to a secret closet instead of the secret mansion of Headquarters—but it felt even more vital. And I'd had my own house, bigger than anything I'd ever have here. Even the SDRs, and the constant fear of surveillance, and the unending tension—part of me missed it now, if it was possible to miss something that was partly a sickness in your stomach.

I thought about William almost every day. I wanted to call him or e-mail him, but I just couldn't. I felt like I'd let him down worse than anyone ever could. Except, maybe, for Bobby Goldstein. "First Bobby Goldstein, then you," was what William had said when we parted. Weird, that he'd said the full name, I thought. Just slightly out of rhythm. It should have been, "First Bobby, then you." But I knew I was being silly.

Still, I thought about Goldstein a lot. I wondered if he had ever found his missing agent, TDTRACER, and who LXMALIBU was, his other agent with the burn order in his file. And why the General, who'd asked me twice if I knew Goldstein, had been so curious about him.

The answers to those questions existed, but in a world I was no longer a part of. That was what I had to get used to. The secret world was going about its business, and I was as far outside it as if I'd never been inside.

5

I put it off for a few weeks, but I finally called Lenny.

"I'm back," I said when he answered the phone.

There was a long silence, then he said, "What the hell's the matter with you?"

"I just got so busy over there," I said.

"Oh, please. You blew me off all the time in D.C., too. Then you wouldn't even talk to me when you were in ███. I know you were busy and everything, but not a single phone call? A postcard, maybe?"

I was half tempted to just tell him everything, but I was supposed to maintain my cover, even now.

"Lenny," I said, "I'm sorry. It's nothing personal."

"It's all personal," he said.

I tried to make a little small talk, but he didn't bite.

6

I went on a few dates, one with a girl I'd gone to high school with, another with the daughter of a friend of my mother's. I particularly liked the girl from high school, Nellie. We hadn't been friends as teenagers. I was more bookish and straitlaced back then, and she was one of those girls who, even if they didn't actually take drugs, always seemed like they did. Over the intervening years, although something of her sallow, depressed affect remained, she had grown up into a bright and thoughtful young woman. Probably she always had been one.

During the few times that we went out, we seemed to take a kind of mutual pleasure from remembering, but at the same time leaving behind, our high school selves. Or perhaps it was the shared recognition that we were different people now that created a bond between us. Either way, and despite the fact that I found her physically attractive, I couldn't stop thinking about Daisy when we were together. It wasn't that I hadn't been thinking of Daisy constantly since returning from ████. But mostly, I ran through the details of our meetings, looking for some mistake that would explain how we'd been found out. When I was with Nellie, it was Daisy herself—an actual picture of her—that I couldn't get out of my head. And though it wasn't fair, the thought I kept having was that Nellie wasn't really a woman compared to her. She didn't have the same solidity, or grace, or confidence.

I never kissed Nellie. After each of our dates, I went back to my apartment, flopped down on the bed, and turned on a lamp with a blue lightbulb that I'd bought at the hardware store. I liked something about the weak blue light that only rose halfway up the wall. Until I fell asleep, I'd lie there with my eyes open, the bottom of the room blue and the top black, and wonder where Daisy was.

7

I'd been in Chicago for a little over a month when a letter arrived for me at my parents' house. It didn't have a return address on it, but it was postmarked Falls Church, Virginia. Inside the envelope was a small white card. It read:

14 Stone's Throw Hill
Beekridge, NH

Falls Church was Agency territory. I turned it over and looked at the back. Nothing there. I looked at the envelope again. It was addressed to me, care of my parents. The address on the envelope was written neatly, in blue ink. It occurred to me, somewhat absurdly, that there might be something else written on the note in invisible ink. But I didn't have ███, so it obviously wouldn't make sense for somebody to try to convey information to me that way.

Either the postmark made me think of William, or the address itself reminded me that William had said Goldstein lived somewhere in the Northeast. Maybe both happened at once. But I thought that this could be Bobby Goldstein's address, and that William might have sent it to me.

If that was right, I didn't know why William had sent it, or why he had sent it in such an oblique way. Obviously, for some reason, he wanted me to find Goldstein. But if that was the case, why didn't he include the name and phone number, and put in a note to me? My first thought was that it had to do with the poly. William was protecting himself for his next test. He was making this information as unclassified as possible by not including the name of an ex-Agency officer and whatever other information would make it all relevant.

But that didn't make a lot of sense. Sending it this way wouldn't be any better, really, than sending the full name and address. And who knew if William was even worried about the poly? Theoretically, Agency employees take one every ███████████████, but in reality, the polygraph office is always backed up, and an older contractor like William, who had already passed God knows how many polys in his life, probably went to the back of the line. He might never have to take one again. Or he might be planning on retiring before he took his next one. Or he might have already retired, since I'd left. Or he might simply not be concerned about the poly one way or another.

My next thought was that it was some sort of an ops test. Ops tests were almost like little games you set up to determine if an agent was telling you the truth. For example, you might ████████████ ██ ██ ██ ████. As long as an agent didn't know that this was an ops test, you could get a pretty good read from it on whether or not he was being forthright with you. Of course, a double agent might be expecting such a test and be able to pass it anyway. But generally speaking, they were considered useful operational tools.

In this case, the ops test wouldn't be to determine my fidelity, strictly speaking. It would be a different kind of test, maybe one designed to test my operational sense. Specifically, did I remember the time William had told me that TDTRACER's case officer lived in New England. And did I remember the two times William had mentioned his name. I did. The first time was when I originally approached him with questions about TDTRACER. And the second time was when I'd said good-bye to William after being fired, and he'd said, "First Bobby Goldstein, then you." Maybe I'd been right, there was something odd about his use of the full name. He'd wanted me to remember it.

If this was what was going on, what was the point of it? Why would William want to test my operational sense? I didn't know. Maybe it was a sign of respect. That he knew I'd pass. That I'd figure it out. And he was trying to tell me, "You would have been good at this job if you'd stayed in it." (Was there some chance I was being recruited back into the job? That William wanted me for something special, maybe in some part of the Agency I didn't even know about? That would have been a reason to test me, but it seemed more like something from the movies than from the CIA I knew.)

Also, if this was an ops test, it wasn't serious enough for him to drive to another state to keep from having a Falls Church postmark. For that matter, what would the point of that have been? He was sending this card, so he wanted me to figure it out.

Of course, the real question was why William wanted me to find Goldstein. Could he have just wanted me to meet him? Because he thought we'd like each other? Or could he have been making good on his promise to let me know someday what had happened with TDTRACER? He couldn't tell me himself, because I didn't have a security clearance anymore. It would be a crime to directly release classified information to me. Whereas if I heard it from Goldstein, it would be okay. Then again, it wasn't clear that this would be much better in terms of William's potential transgression. But maybe it was. I just didn't know.

None of these explanations felt really satisfying anyway.

In any case, I had the address. I knew what William wanted me to do with it. Assuming that this was Bobby Goldstein's address, and that William had sent it.

8

That night, I was drinking stale coffee and eating a chocolate stefanka at the New Warsaw bakery when another, more troubling possibility occurred to me.

What if this was, in fact, an ops test about fidelity? What if the Agency used ops tests for all its ex-officers? What if they were always worried that separating employees might do some sort of damage to them, so they tested them? If that was the case, I couldn't for the life of me figure out how this one worked. Of course, it would have to be designed for officers who knew about ops tests, and therefore would have to be almost impossible to figure out. In any case, I didn't know how to pass or fail it. Maybe I was just supposed to ignore the letter?

If it was this type of ops test, would William actually participate in this? He was supposed to be my friend. But he was also supposed to be a loyal Agency employee. As much as I liked him, and believed that he liked me, I just didn't know if he was someone who would or wouldn't do this, whether he would be loyal to me or to the Agency first.

9

For several days, I went back and forth over the possibilities. Could there be some other, much more complicated reason for all of this? No matter how much I thought about it, I couldn't come up with what it might be.

During class, it felt almost as if I were manually using my hands to grab my brain and move it over to another place. The British . . . the British . . . the British idea of empire was . . . let's discuss empire. I was not firmly in the classroom, and my students sensed it. A few of them even asked me if I was all right.

During lunch breaks, at home in bed, at the New Warsaw— William, Goldstein, TDTRACER, me, New Hampshire, LXMALIBU— and finally, what did I want? Did I actually want to meet Goldstein? Of course I did. I wanted to meet him, I wanted to know why William wanted me to meet him, I wanted to know what had happened to TDTRACER and who LXMALIBU was. For some reason, even gone from the CIA, I wanted desperately to know these things.

10

About a week after I'd gotten the card, my belongings arrived from ███. My blue Dart, my clothes, a few pieces of furniture that had taken a round-trip to ███ that must have cost many times more than the furniture itself. Suddenly, my sparse little studio was overcrowded, with clothes stuffing the closets and chairs crowding the previously almost empty floor.

11

On a Saturday morning, I got on the train and, after two transfers, got off in Wicker Park. Coming down the staircase to the street, I ███████████████. It was a classic ██████. I walked around for a few minutes, and ██.

I picked a pay phone on Hoyne Street. If this was an ops test, and I was supposed to contact Goldstein—or if I wasn't supposed to contact Goldstein—a letter was no good, because you didn't want anything in writing. On the other hand, if I called, they would either follow me and use a ████████████████ to pick up my voice, or tap Goldstein's line (or whatever line it was). Of the two, obviously the second would be much simpler. In either case, using a pay phone wouldn't help. That would only make a difference if they were tapping my phone, which wouldn't make sense because I might use a pay phone. (Unless there were budget issues involved, and they routinely only tapped an ex-C/O's home phone.)

In any case, I just couldn't call from home. I had to follow some modicum of tradecraft. Although, if this were an ops test, the odds of my beating it with the Agency's own tradecraft were extremely poor.

I got the Beekridge, New Hampshire (not the real town, not the real state, but close enough), area code and called information, but Goldstein wasn't listed.

He lived in a small town. I could easily get the number of some business there where they would know his number, then talk them into giving it to me. The risk of this was that in a small town, he would probably hear about it. So what business would have his number but wouldn't be likely to see him anytime soon and mention that someone had been looking for him? I couldn't think of anything that fulfilled that requirement.

At a coffee shop with an Internet connection, I found the number of a dry cleaner in Beekridge. At a new phone, I called. I told the woman who answered that I was a college friend of Goldstein's, but that I couldn't find his number. She told me Beekridge Dry Cleaners had a strict confidentiality policy and couldn't give out anyone's phone number.

I tried Beekridge City Hall the next morning, and then an auto mechanic and a local restaurant over the next two days. I went to pay phones in different neighborhoods each time. I couldn't really see the advantage of going to different neighborhoods, but I did it anyway. On each trip, I ██████████████████████████████████████ ████████████████████████. I never did a full SDR, but I did ████████ ████████████████. It felt silly and unnecessary, and I never saw anything.

On the fourth night after I'd started trying to get Goldstein's number, I was at home reading a book when my phone rang. I picked up and said, "Hello."

"Hello," a voice said.

There was a pause.

"Who's this?" the voice said.

"Who's this?" I said.

Another pause.

"Are you from a place where there are a lot of people with secrets?" the voice said.

"Um, yes, are you?" I said.

"Ex," he said.

"Me too."

"Long ex."

"I'm short ex," I said.

"Why are you . . . why am I calling you?"

"I don't know."

"Do you know who I am?"

"I think maybe," I said.

"Well, who are you? I don't know who you are."

"I don't know if . . . did you know a W?"

"There? At the place?"

"Yes."

"Yes."

"He was a friend of yours, right?" I asked.

"I wondered if he might have something to do with this."

"With what?"

"I got a card in the mail a few weeks ago with nothing but this phone number on it. It could have been some sort of sales thing, but I thought it was probably from W."

"I got one, too," I said. "With just an address. You live in Beekridge?"

"Yes. What's going on here? Why did you get the card?"

"Well, I don't know for sure, but I think Will . . . W maybe wants us to meet. I was a friend of his, too."

"Why?"

"Why meet? I don't really know. I think maybe he just wants us to meet each other. To . . . I'm not sure. Maybe we shouldn't discuss it too much on the phone."

That was a possible mistake. If Goldstein was out of this world long enough, not saying things on the phone could sound ridiculous. On the other hand, maybe that stuck with you forever, at least if you were talking to someone somehow affiliated with the Agency. And he was saying W instead of William, although I'd started that.

"I haven't talked to him in a long time," Goldstein said.

"It's easy to lose touch, I guess."

He didn't say anything.

"Do you think we should meet?" I said.

"I'm inclined not to."

"Right."

"Don't want to get mixed up in something of W's at this point."

"No, but . . . well, I trust W."

"That's good that you still trust people."

Desperate to show that I wasn't too trusting, I said, "I mean, could this . . . could it be some sort of . . . special test of some kind?"

"An ops test? Can't think of why. Or how."

"No, I guess that's crazy."

"How is W, assuming you've seen him more recently than I have?"

"He's good."

"It's been a long time."

"He's doing well," I said. "I think."

"He didn't say anything to you about why he wanted us to meet?"

"I told you, he didn't say anything at all. I just got this card. I've been trying to call you for days, but I couldn't get your number."

After a long silence, Goldstein said, "Where are you?"

"Chicago."

"Chicago?"

"I could come to you."

"You want to come all this way?"

"Sure, why not."

"Weird, with the card . . ."

There was another long pause, then I tried, "What would be a good time for you?"

"I don't know." A few very long seconds passed. Then Goldstein said, "What are you doing next week?"

"That's perfect. I'm teaching, and we've got spring break." (I felt the fact that I was now a teacher would send an unthreatening message.) "So . . . if I drive Saturday, Sunday . . . what is it from Chicago, two days?"

"I don't know."

"Well, let's say Monday, to be safe. I'll figure it out."

He gave me directions for the last part of the trip, and I said I'd call him from the road.

From the conversation, even though he'd been brusque, I liked him. Of course. He was a case officer. But even knowing it was a personality type, it still had its effect.

Nevertheless, I couldn't discount the possibility that, if this was an ops test, he was a part of it. That was enormously far-fetched. I didn't even think this was an ops test. So the odds of it being an ops test, and him being involved, were slim. But odds being slim didn't mean you could dismiss them.

12

The first cross-country drive I ever took was from Chicago to Massachusetts, on my way to college to begin my freshman year. I was driving with my friend Andy, in the Chevy Nova he'd received from his parents as a high school graduation present. I'd only gotten my driver's license a few weeks before, and I didn't have a good sense for the road yet. In the middle of the night, I was going ninety miles an hour on a dark and empty interstate, with Andy asleep next to me. Somewhere in central Ohio, the road curved, and as I turned the wheel, I felt the car slipping out from under me. I braked hard, and the car suddenly felt like it was going backward. Just as it seemed about to start spinning in circles, it somehow righted itself. After I was back in control, Andy shifted around in his seat, but didn't wake up.

I was on the same highway now, hardly ever drifting over seventy. I thought about Daisy while I drove, running again through each of our meetings. After a few hours, to stop myself from thinking about Daisy, I started thinking about one of my students, a kid named Eric, whose mother had just died. He was a simple, straightforward thinker, perfectly competent at memorization and rudimentary analysis, but lacking any kind of special spark. He'd barely attracted my attention before. But since his mother had died, he'd slowed down, shuffling in and out of the classroom like an old man and never speaking. I felt like I should do something for him, but I didn't know what. I imagined conversation after conversation with him where I was trying to say something soothing and helpful, but all the words kept coming out weak and transparently useless.

I stopped for dinner somewhere in eastern Pennsylvania. It was dark out when I finished, and when I pulled back onto the highway, I suddenly felt like I was getting very close to Goldstein. I didn't feel at all prepared for our meeting. He was obviously suspicious of me. Why wouldn't he be? So would he ask a lot of questions to establish my bona fides? And would he feel that I was interrupting his life, in which he'd moved on from the Agency years ago? For that matter, I was—or at least I should have been—suspicious of him. But I was having trouble feeling that way, as much as I knew I should have. Possibly because he was somehow suppressing it in me, on purpose?

I pictured him handsome and alone, if not a hermit something close to it, living in a little cabin on a New Hampshire mountaintop.

The dark highway went on and on. I did three more hours, then slept at a Quality Inn. In the morning, I called Goldstein and said I'd be there in the late afternoon.

13

He did, in fact, live on a mountain. Or at least a very big hill. The road up was paved, but cracked and narrow, with houses tucked intermittently into the woods on either side. At the very top of the hill, Goldstein's white cottage stood on a small, flat piece of land, surrounded by trees.

As soon as I turned off the ignition, he came out of the house. Not only wasn't he handsome, he was actually, I thought, ugly. He had a rectangular head, not quite Frankenstein-like, but close. He was tall and thin, but too thin for the head. His black hair rose just a little bit higher than a marine crew cut.

We shook hands, and he motioned me through the screen door into the kitchen. We sat down at a table in the middle of the room, and he poured us both iced tea from a pitcher.

"Well," he said.

"Yeah, how about this?" I said.

I was trying to act like our meeting was casual and a bit funny, but Goldstein didn't bite.

"That's the card," he said, looking down at a postcard on the table.

"I . . . I didn't bring mine. I'm sorry. I didn't think of it."

"Same handwriting?"

I picked it up and looked at it.

"I think so."

"Is it William's? I don't remember his handwriting at all."

"I don't know," I said. "I'm not sure I ever actually saw his hand-writing. Computers and all."

I could tell Goldstein was watching me analytically. Not necessarily for facial deceit markers, which I was as well-trained in avoiding as he was, but rather to see if he could pick up any kind of general feeling about whether or not I was a fake.

"How was your drive?" he asked.

"I hadn't gone cross-country since college," I said. "I think I'm too old for it now. I get stiff." (I immediately realized this wasn't true—I'd driven cross-country when I moved to Washington to join the Agency.)

"Is that considered cross-country? Chicago to here?"

"Well, if you're from Chicago. I mean, you never end up driving all the way coast to coast, because you're in the middle. So we almost consider Milwaukee cross-country."

I was trying too hard.

We sat quietly for a few seconds, then he said, "So how's William?"

"I think he's doing pretty well. You know, not that young any-more. But doing pretty good."

"Where'd you work with him?"

"████."

"That's where I first met him, too."

"Good office, I thought."

Goldstein shrugged noncommittally.

"And you're gone now?" he asked.

"Yes."

I asked him a few questions about living in New Hampshire. He started staring at me less as soon as we moved off of William and the CIA. It turned out he was a teacher, too, working at a public school in a nearby town. He taught seventh and eighth grade English, and coached the soccer team.

As we talked, I tried to figure out what to do next. I knew I might only have an hour or so with him, and if I wanted to find out about TDTRACER and LXMALIBU, I couldn't stay off the topic of the Agency for too long. It actually occurred to me to just ask him directly about them. Maybe he'd respect my forthrightness. But of course, I had to move more carefully.

When we hit our next silence, I said, "Weird to be out of the Agency. You get so used to it there, you know? After a while?"

"Yeah," he said.

"Things were so weird for me at the end."

"How so?"

"Oh, I don't know. I had kind of a bad experience."

Goldstein nodded, but more to himself, it seemed, than to me.

I started talking about Daisy. I had known, of course, that I would tell him about her. My story of screwing up would pave the way for his story of something going wrong. Because something had obviously gone wrong with TDTRACER, and maybe with LXMALIBU, too. But I had no idea I'd go on for so long. I told him about our first meeting, then about every subsequent contact. I described the patchy unfolding of the tradecraft. He was mostly silent, though he interrupted now and then to ask about operational details.

The whole pitcher of iced tea was empty; somehow Goldstein served dinner and we ate at the table, all without my stopping. I knew I was creating a sense for him of being my confessor, and I also knew that he might be aware I was hoping to elicit a confession from him in return. But the fact that we both knew about elicitation somehow neutralized the feeling of elicitation, and made telling him about Daisy feel like something close to total honesty.

When I finally finished, the kitchen was dark except for the squares of gray light coming in through the windows. We sat quietly for a minute, then Goldstein said, "Let's take a walk."

It was cool out, and more crickets were chirping than I'd ever heard before in my life. We walked down the same road that I'd driven up, and then, about halfway down, we turned off onto a logging road.

"I don't know what to do," I finally said.

We discussed the possibilities. I could write or call her, but there was a risk. I had no idea, and probably never would, how the Station had found out about us. If they knew, there was the possibility her embassy knew, too. That meant she could be in trouble—even if they didn't know my Agency affiliation, she still should have reported her contact with me. If I wrote or called her, I could make things worse. And if her embassy didn't know about us, writing or calling could alert them. Neither Goldstein nor I had any idea if the ███████ security service regularly checked embassy employees' calls and mail from abroad, but it was a definite possibility. Of course, there was also a good chance they didn't know about Daisy and me and wouldn't intercept calls or mail. But could I take that risk on her behalf?

"So what, I . . . I just never talk to her again?" I said.

"She could write you."

"My government e-mail's off. She doesn't know my address."

"You listed?"

"Yes."

"Wouldn't take a genius to get it, then."

"But why should she write me? I disappeared without telling her a word. She probably hates me."

"Occupational hazard," Goldstein said.

"But if we're meant to be . . ." I felt queer saying this, afraid that I sounded like a teenager.

"I don't know what else you can do, except wait and see if she finds you."

"I wouldn't, if I were her."

"Probably not. But you never know."

When we got back to his house, he asked me if I wanted to come for lunch the next day. He said he didn't have an extra bed, but there was a B and B in town, if I wanted to stay.

14

I caught these this morning," Goldstein said, standing over a skillet of fish when I came in the next afternoon.

"You fish?"

"You wouldn't believe the things you turn into up here. Bird-watcher. Fisherman. I got up at five thirty this morning to sit in the middle of a lake and wait for trout."

"Sounds boring."

"Not really. Well . . . it is boring. But in a good way."

His whole affect was startlingly different from the day before. By the time we'd parted the previous evening, there was some palpable sense that we'd come to like each other, so maybe it made perfect sense that he should be friendlier the next day. But on the other hand, it felt too quick. I had the uneasy feeling that I was being case officered. For some reason, Goldstein had decided that I should like him, and now he was making sure that I did.

But then again, the thing about case officers is that most of them are, deep down, extremely friendly and likable. They don't have to fake that part. So maybe this was just Goldstein deciding he could trust me and being more like the real Goldstein.

We sat at the kitchen table, eating the fish and talking about teaching. Goldstein sat with his chair turned slightly to the side and his legs crossed, waving around his fork, usually with a piece of fish on it, when he spoke. He had a lot to say about the psychological development of adolescents. He talked about Erik Erikson and a Swiss guy named Piaget, and told stories about his own students that he thought supported their theories. I felt embarrassed by how little I knew about the subject and muttered that I was teaching "more by feel."

"That can work, too," Goldstein said.

"What'd you think of the instructors at the Farm?" I asked.

Too obvious, too eager to discuss the Agency. Something about him was throwing me off. But Goldstein went along.

"The FTC guys were okay. I thought the SOTC guys were actually better."

Trainees do two main stints at the Farm, the first early in the training program when they take a ▆▆ week ▆▆▆▆▆▆▆ course known as SOTC (▆▆▆▆▆▆▆▆▆▆▆▆▆▆▆▆▆▆▆▆▆▆▆▆▆▆▆, and the second near the end of their training when they move down for ▆▆▆ months for FTC ▆▆▆▆▆▆▆▆▆▆▆▆▆▆▆▆▆▆▆. Goldstein was saying he thought the ex-military guys who taught in the ▆▆▆▆▆▆▆program were better than the ▆▆▆▆▆▆▆▆ instructors.

"You have Warren?" Goldstein asked.

"Oh yeah," I said.

"Talk about a teacher."

Warren was a craggy old Vietnam vet who'd joined the Agency after the war. Everyone joked that he had post-traumatic stress disorder, because his little black eyes darted constantly from side to side and he never spoke. He'd demonstrate something, and another instructor would narrate what he was doing. One day in the woods, he showed us how to move silently, picking his legs up and putting them down so slowly it took him a full minute to take a single step. In my class, at the end of the demonstration, one student called out, "You ever get anywhere going like that?" Another instructor said, "Takes a while, but you're alive."

Goldstein said that when he was in the course, Warren used to say, "Don't lose your map," over and over again, something he'd apparently given up on by the time I got there. Once, after a full-day escape-and-evasion exercise, Goldstein's squad had come out of the woods three hours late. When they finally reached the rendezvous point, their squad leader had to admit to Warren that he'd lost his map. Warren stared at the guy so hard Goldstein thought he was about to attack him. The squad leader, flustered and hot, unzipped his jacket, and the map tumbled down to the ground. Everyone stared down at it, but after everyone else had looked back up, Warren still had his eyes fixed on the map. According to Goldstein, he must have stared at it for three or four minutes, during which nobody said a word. Finally, Warren just shook his head and walked away.

We traded Farm stories for most of that afternoon. I told Goldstein about two guys in my group who, during a timed two-mile run, had sprinted out ahead at the beginning, at a pace that probably would have set a world record if they'd been able to keep it up. When I passed them two thirds of the way through the run, they were bending over and trying to throw up to the side while still running, the vomit dribbling down their chins onto their BDUs (battle dress uniforms—simple cammies, in this case). Goldstein laughed and said the same thing had happened in his class. It wasn't that surprising. At the Agency, you wouldn't stop running in that situation.

Goldstein told me about a guy in his class who'd been a major in Delta Force. SOTC wasn't that easy or that hard—it was often referred to as "Outward Bound with guns" and wasn't designed to produce actual paramilitary officers, but rather to give trainees basic military and weapons familiarization—so for a guy who'd been in Delta, it was obviously nothing. In order to make it at least a little bit of a challenge, this guy used to stay up every night until three or four in the morning drinking at the officers' club, then get up at five thirty with everybody else for the morning march. He wasn't showing off. He was a decent guy, and everybody liked him. But for him, the paramilitary training would have been like going back to third grade for someone with a Ph.D.

One morning, Goldstein happened to wake up at around four o'clock. He was lying in his bunk, listening to the various snores and whistles filling the barracks, when he heard the front door open. He knew it must be the Delta guy, Sam. Sam made his way quietly down the aisle between the bunks, then climbed up onto his top bunk, which was next to Goldstein's. Something plastic made a little clattering sound on the floor. Goldstein thought Sam had probably dropped his ID. And then Sam, who obviously would have thought everyone was asleep, said out loud, "I'll get that."

Goldstein snickered. Sam climbed down from his bed, picked up whatever he'd dropped, and whispered, "You awake?"

"Yeah," Goldstein said.

"Well, gotta be up in an hour and a half anyway. Let's go for a run."

"A run?" Goldstein said.

"Sure. Let's get the day started."

There was no saying no. Goldstein got out of bed and jogged three miles in the dark with him. Sam, who was usually quiet, talked the whole time, telling stories about Delta, making jokes, and doing imitations of their instructors. Goldstein felt fantastic. Later, when he had to do the morning march with a thirty-pound pack, he felt even better. After that, he'd stay up once a week with Sam at the officers' club and then go for a jog with him before everyone else got up. This quickly became easy for him, and he started to think that he probably had physical potential far beyond what he'd ever explored before.

After SOTC, trainees went back to Headquarters for a series of short-term assignments in various parts of the Agency. If you were ultimately headed for the Directorate of Operations, you were strongly encouraged to try at least one assignment in a different Directorate. I spent two months in ▮▮▮▮▮▮▮▮ in the DI, writing a paper on ▮▮ ▮▮▮▮▮▮▮▮▮▮▮▮▮▮▮▮▮▮▮▮▮▮▮▮▮▮▮▮▮▮▮▮▮▮. Goldstein asked for, and received, an assignment in the Directorate of Administration, where he processed field requests for ▮▮▮▮▮▮▮▮▮▮▮▮ ▮▮▮▮▮▮▮▮▮▮▮▮▮▮▮▮▮▮▮▮▮▮▮▮▮▮▮▮▮▮▮▮▮▮ ▮▮▮▮▮▮▮▮▮▮▮▮▮▮▮▮▮▮▮▮▮▮▮▮. Everybody made fun of him for doing an assignment in the DA, which was considered beneath a case officer, but he liked it. He said you got a whole new view on things by seeing what people were sending back and forth to the field.

Goldstein went back down to the Farm for FTC in the summer of 1996—I was there five years later. At FTC, you learned everything you needed to know to work in the field, from surveillance detection to communications methods. The instructors were almost all extremely likable, though most were midcareer, stuck at GS-13 or -14, and at the Farm in lieu of some better assignment.

Somewhere around halfway through the course, you started having mock ▮▮▮▮ meetings. Some of these were in a car, and the instructors made quite a point of the fact that you needed to have

food and drink ██████████, which they referred to as "amenities."
It was usually a thermos of coffee or tea, and some chips or cookies.
This was considered a very important means of making the agent feel
comfortable and taken care of, and anytime you went off to a meeting one of your homeroom instructors would say, "Don't forget the
amenities." Goldstein had heard a story from an instructor about one
easily flustered woman in his class who, as soon as an ████ instructor had gotten into her car, had actually said, "Would you like some
amenities?"

As you started running mock cases, you spent less time at the
Farm and more in ██████████. The heart of ██████████ was
█████████████████, a sort of town/theme park/museum that had
been made up to look just like it had in the 1700s. The "residents" of
the town dressed in authentic period costumes and carried on authentic period tasks. As you ran SDRs through the streets and the semipri-
vate gardens behind the colonial homes, you'd go by cobblers banging
away at shoes, or women in bonnets churning butter. Blacksmiths
were always popping up in your rearview mirror.

Goldstein said that when he'd begun the FTC, an instructor had
said, during a lecture, that the locals kept the Farm's existence and
exact location secret, though of course they knew about it. He'd said
that reporters nosing around were always told that people had no
idea what they were talking about. But then, about halfway through
the course, there was a front-page story in the ██████████ paper
about the Farm, with numerous quotes from locals about the CIA
trainees who were always turning around in their parking lots or
stopping in their stores for ██████████████████████████████
██
██
███.
██
██
██████████████████████████. Goldstein had had a car meeting once where
he'd gotten lost on the outskirts of the city (██████████ was, of
course, surrounded by the same thicket of highways, strip malls, and

fast-food restaurants as every other small city in America). He couldn't tell if his instructor, posing as a relatively new developmental, could tell or not. She'd been telling him that she had a brother with a drug addiction and that she was having trouble coming up with the money to help pay for his medical treatment (this would be testing a C/O's ability to appear compassionate, and also recognize the potential financial motivation the target would have for becoming an agent). Goldstein had responded by saying that he had a sister with a heroin addiction. Of course, the instructor realized this wasn't true—Goldstein was using a technique called mirroring to try to win the agent's trust and sympathy—so the question was whether or not he could pull it off. He thought he was doing a good job, regurgitating everything he'd ever seen or heard about heroin addiction, applying it all to his sister, but soft-pedaling it enough that he didn't appear false or overly eager to achieve intimacy. The instructor kept asking him questions about his sister's addiction, and although a few times he had to look wistful or contemplative while he took a moment to think, he came up with good answers to everything. But the whole time, he also had no idea where he was. He'd taken a wrong turn somewhere and gotten completely lost. He'd just finished a lengthy speech about the effect on his parents of his sister's addiction when the instructor broke character and said, "You have no idea where you are, do you?" Goldstein opened his mouth to speak, and just then saw a sign ahead for one of the main arteries back into ███████.

"Sure I do," he said.

I told Goldstein of a near disaster of my own that had taken place during embassy week, the final week of training where you simulate being in a Station full-time. Late one afternoon, in the middle of the week, I was called up to the office of the Chief of FTC and informed that I'd been detained and brought in to see the Chief of Police in ██████, the country my Station was supposedly located in. There was a lot of bustle around, with other students going in and out of nearby offices and instructors everywhere. Jeff, an instructor from another homeroom, was playing the part of the Chief of Police. I sat down across from him at his desk and he handed me a photo of another instructor, a contractor named Bill who I'd had a meeting with the previous day where he'd played an agent named Robert Binston.

"Do you know this man?" he said.

I looked at the photo. If I admitted knowing him, he'd probably be arrested immediately and charged with being a CIA spy.

"No," I said, looking innocently across the desk.

"You were seen with him yesterday afternoon," the Chief of Police/Jeff said.

I'd blown it completely. I was supposed to say that I knew him and, if asked what we'd been doing together the day before, use the cover story you put together before every agent meeting. Now, by lying about it after we'd actually been seen together, I'd as good as admitted that I was CIA and he was an agent I was running.

"Can I see that again?" I asked, pointing at the picture.

Jeff slid it back across the desk. It was an incredibly old picture of the instructor, probably from when he'd first joined the agency ten or fifteen years earlier. He had a full beard and mustache in the photo, which he no longer had. I picked it up and stared at it, squinting and trying to look uncertain.

"Y'know," I said, "now that I look at it, I guess that could be Robert Binston. It doesn't really look like him. But I guess that could be him. Maybe when he was a lot younger."

Jeff looked skeptically at me.

"So you do know him?"

I said yes and spun out the cover story.

When I finished, Jeff broke character.

"Okay, you got a lucky break there," he said. "You survived. But just barely."

He led me into another office, where a large pad on an easel had the names of every student at the FTC. There were two columns next to the names, one marked "dead" and one "alive" (referring to the agents who we'd just blown or not blown). There were check marks next to every student who'd gone so far, in one column or the other. It was running about fifty-fifty dead to alive. "It's been quite a slaughter today," Jeff said. He checked the "alive" column next to my agent's name. "Barely," he said. "Just barely."

I asked Goldstein how he'd done on that exercise, and he said, "I figured it out in time. Barely." Somehow, I didn't believe him. I had the feeling he'd had no trouble with it at all.

Goldstein and I had each had classmates who'd mysteriously disappeared near the end of ▮▮▮▮▮ week. The instructors wouldn't talk about it, and even the students exchanged rumors carefully. The main rumor in my class was that the student hadn't conducted an SDR that he'd claimed he'd conducted, and he'd been observed. So he'd been kicked out for lying—an integrity issue. Others heard he'd quit or had broken under the pressure. In each of our classes, the students who had disappeared had a native capability in a foreign language, and there was another rumor that they'd been taken away to become NOCs, nonofficial cover officers, who would never have any connection ▮▮▮▮▮▮. ▮▮▮▮▮▮▮▮▮▮▮▮▮▮▮▮▮▮▮▮▮▮▮▮▮▮
▮▮▮▮▮▮▮▮▮▮▮▮▮▮▮▮▮▮▮▮▮▮▮▮▮▮▮▮▮▮▮▮▮
▮▮▮▮▮▮▮▮▮▮▮▮▮▮▮▮▮▮▮▮▮▮▮▮▮▮▮▮▮▮▮▮▮
▮▮▮▮▮▮▮▮▮▮. This made sense, in a way. But it was hard to come up with a reason why they had to be spirited away from the FTC before finishing. It made some sense as a belated attempt to do a better job protecting their identities, but not much. In any case, they'd either failed or done well. Nobody knew which.

At the end of ▮▮▮▮▮▮ week, there was a graduation ceremony and banquet. Diplomas were handed out, looked at, and then handed back to be stored in a safe. Then we filed into a big tent that had been set up on the parade ground. There was beer and wine, and the mess hall served prime rib on fancy china. We ate at round tables, but there was one long table at the front for the various dignitaries. The ADDO (Associate Deputy Director for Operations) had come down from Headquarters, along with the Chief of Human Resources. The head of FTC, the Director of the Farm, and several lead homeroom instructors sat there too, as well as five students from the class, apparently chosen both to represent those who had done the best, and to provide some diversity of gender and race. There were no official class rankings in the FTC, so this was the closest we got to seeing who the instructors considered standouts.

At his graduation, Goldstein had sat at this table, between the ADDO and one of the lead homeroom instructors. Sitting next to the ADDO probably meant that he was considered the best student in his class, though of course he didn't say this to me, and it would be hard to be certain without knowing who was on the other side of the ADDO. As for my graduation, I sat at one of the round tables. Those of us sitting there kept looking up at our friends at the head table, trying to catch their eyes and make them laugh. They were all terribly serious, stuck there next to the big shots. You could see the strain on their faces from having to impress them. Essentially C/Oing throughout dinner. Not that we didn't all wish we were there. But we had a more relaxing meal than they did.

After the dinner we milled around the tent, and I ended up in a discussion with the Chief of Human Resources. He told me that most of the instructors at the Farm had never recruited anybody. I was surprised, and looked it, but he assured me it was true. He wasn't from the DO, and I wasn't sure he knew what he was talking about. In fact, it now seems ridiculous to me—a lot of the instructors talked about their recruits, and some had been COSs, who never would have gotten that far without recruiting anybody. On the other hand, recruiting was hard, and maybe it didn't go on as often as we assumed.

15

Goldstein and I hadn't told our stories in order. We'd jumped around, talking about whatever came into our minds next, or whatever the last person's story had made us think of. Eventually, we started talking halfheartedly about teaching again, and whether or not we thought we'd keep doing it. Goldstein had been teaching for a number of years and liked it. I told him that I was doing it more to make a little money, and had no idea what a future career might be for me now that the CIA was over.

It was getting dark, and we made some pasta and ate dinner. We seemed to be talked out. After dinner, we watched the news. Half the program was about Iraq, where things had only just started to go to hell. I had friends there, and I wondered about them, and about their wives. I thought about trying to operate in that kind of environment. Goldstein undoubtedly had friends there, too, although he wouldn't have known which ones unless he'd stayed in closer touch with people from the Agency than was likely.

After the news, Goldstein said, "Hike?"

"In the dark?" I said.

He produced two flashlights from a cupboard, then we drove in his car down to the bottom of the hill, continued a few miles on quiet back roads, then drove partway up a much larger hill. Goldstein pulled off to the side of the road, then led me over to a break in the trees. We started walking along a narrow path, barely navigable by flashlight. We walked for a long time, going steadily upward, twigs and leaves crunching underfoot. I wondered fleetingly if he was going to murder me. I was pretty sure the idea was absurd, but at the same time, he was leading me to a dark, secluded spot in the woods. What if this was some sort of ops test after all, maybe one to establish if ex-officers could be trusted, and I was failing, and the Agency murdered ex-officers it didn't trust? Or maybe Bobby himself was on some sort of weird personal mission where he killed ex-Agency officers after sending them postcards. Dismissing all this, I still thought I'd been CO'd by him. He'd been hostile and suspicious toward me, then he'd turned and become friendly. It was a recognizable gambit, but one that was hard to resist anyway. But should I be resisting? I had no reason to suddenly trust him. Still, I couldn't help myself—a certain belief in him was seeping into me. But why? Because we'd told each other some stories?

Eventually, sweating and breathing hard, we came out of the woods onto a bald mountaintop. Goldstein pointed out a little gathering of light and, farther away, a dark hump on the horizon—"That's Winville, that's Mt. Renoir"—then he lay down on a patch of grassless earth. I lay down next to him. With no trees to block the view, the stars seemed to wrap around you. I had an uneasy sensation of the earth moving under me, almost like I was riding it through the stars.

After a while, Goldstein said, "There was this one guy, Philip. I've always wondered what happened to him. He was from ███. God knows how he got into the Agency. Really who they should be hiring, I guess. Anyway, he was the sweetest guy—huge, almost a giant, always smiling. But he didn't really speak English. I mean, he did, but he didn't. If you talked fast, he was just lost. But he was always there, doing the exercises, getting everything wrong because he couldn't understand the lectures, but sort of . . . you could tell he was smart. And think of all the things he'd be able to do, if he went back to ███. Things we'd never be able to do, no matter how much language training we had." Bobby stopped for a second, then picked up again. "You think of all the fuckups you can have just by misunderstanding one thing somebody says. On my first tour, I was running a ███████████ in ██████, which I sort of spoke, but I always thought I might be misunderstanding almost everything he said. No idea when he was joking, or unsure of something. From his tone, I mean. All of that lost. And most of the words, too. Of course . . . I don't know how much better it is in English. I picked up a case that same tour, and the guy was ████████, and he spoke some English, and of course I spoke no ██████. So we worked in English. It was the same problem, just flipped. Was he understanding my instructions? Did he know what to do? Or was he just nodding after a while, just like I did with ██████, because there are only so many times you can say 'what?' I mean, you repeat everything over and over, try to get them to say it back to you. But still . . . they don't really seem to get it half the time."

"Even if you both really speak English, it's pretty fucking hard," I said.

"You can get in a lot of trouble a lot of different ways."

There was something cold and distant in Goldstein's voice as he said this. I turned my head to look at him, and even in the dark I could see the grim set of his jaw as he lay motionless underneath the stars.

16

The next day, I slept late and ate breakfast in Beekridge, then drove up the hill in the early afternoon. Goldstein hadn't even asked if I was coming back, but I knew he'd be expecting me.

He was chopping wood in front of the house when I got there. We shook hands, and I said, "Come on. You're actually chopping wood?"

"It's fun," he said.

"But do you actually use the wood?"

"Sure. For fires."

"Summer's coming."

"Gets chilly here at night, even in the summer."

He told me to try it, and after a few bad swings, I chopped a block straight down the middle. There was something enormously satisfying about hearing the wood crack and watching the two halves fall off to different sides.

Back in the kitchen it was chilly, and Goldstein made hot tea this time. As we sat down at the table, I saw the energy and joy he'd had while chopping wood suddenly drain out of him. He stared vacantly at his cup as he dunked his tea bag up and down. I kept my mouth shut, knowing what was coming.

"William ever tell you about TDTRACER?" he asked.

"Yeah, a little bit," I said. "And I saw part of the file when I was doing this file review. I don't really know what happened, though." And figuring it was now or never, I said, "And the other one. LXMALIBU."

Goldstein stopped dunking his bag and stared at me. The whole atmosphere of the room changed, and I was sure I'd made a mistake.

"He told you about MALIBU?"

"He mentioned it."

"How much did he say?"

"Not much. Just that it was another big case of yours."

Goldstein looked away, his mouth tight and his brow furrowed. Finally, he said, "Still talking about it, huh?"

"He just mentioned it. I don't really know what happened."

He took a sip of tea, winced because it was too hot, then said, "Well, here's what happened."

PART THREE

Before I tell the story that Bobby told me that night, I should make a few things clear. First of all, Bobby seemed to have an excellent memory, and mine is very good, too. Nevertheless, between his reconstruction of conversations that were several years old, and my reconstruction of his reconstructions, the dialogues I present here should obviously be seen as close approximations of what was said, not literal transcripts. Second, about five percent of Bobby's discussions with TDTRACER took place in ████████, which Bobby had studied in college. As previously noted, that opens the door to any number of potential misunderstandings, and it is possible some of the content and/or feel of certain discussions between the two is off base. Finally, since Bobby and I both served in ███████, I think it's possible that on occasion some of my own impressions and ideas have crept into my account of what he thought. I've done my best to eliminate all such instances, but undoubtedly a few remain.

1

Bobby did his first tour in ████████. He recruited three agents while he was there, including the █████████████████████████. This was something of a coup for a first-tour officer. He received a performance award and a midtour promotion to GS-11. At the end of his tour, he got his first choice for a follow-on assignment, ████. (I'd put it first on my ARL [assignment request list] because I thought it was exotic and because officers going there didn't have to do any language training. He chose it because, even back in 1999, he thought it was going to emerge as one of the world's most important countries.)

Bobby spent a month at Headquarters before his PCS. He met with Chief/█ twice, who told him he was "the future of the Agency." He had lunch with the DDO (Deputy Director for Operations) and turned down an offer to be his special assistant for a year instead of going straight out to █████ (the DDO ended up telling him he was right to get back to the field as soon as possible). Even the secretaries in █seemed to be smiling at him all the time.

The only person who didn't seem happy with Bobby was his girlfriend, Sulie. She was an Agency analyst who he'd met on one of his interim assignments during training. They'd been dating for a little less than a year when he left for ███████. They'd spoken on the phone and e-mailed a fair amount while he was gone, and Sulie had visited him once. While there, she'd shopped for food every day, cooked him dinner every night, and given multiple indications that she could be a happy case officer's wife.

The night before he left for █████, Bobby took her out for dinner at an Afghan restaurant in the International Conflicts Mall, a dingy little strip mall in Roslyn, Virginia (known as the International Conflicts Mall because an Afghan, a Cambodian, and a Vietnamese restaurant were all located there). In the middle of dinner, Sulie started crying. She said that she'd wanted to go with him to ███████, and he hadn't asked, and now she wanted to go with him to █████, and he hadn't asked again. She didn't think that seeing each other twice a year for four years was a real relationship.

After she poured all of this out, she looked up at Bobby, who said, "I can't really argue with you." Then he apologized for being a shitty boyfriend, and said that he felt like he'd wasted three years of her life.

The next morning, he was on a plane to █████.

2

Bobby arrived in ████████ on a typically stifling day at the end of August. An admin officer met him at the airport and took him to his house in ███, a beautiful district a few miles away from the embassy (on the other side of the ███████ from the house I lived in later). Instead of unpacking, Bobby drove into ████████ excited to get his first taste of the ██████ street. Beggars and cripples seemed to take up every inch of space between █████ and ███████████. The ████ and ████████ wandering through the streets were amusing at first, but quickly turned aggravating.

By the end of the day, Bobby's clothes were coated in yellow dust, and he couldn't get the smell of excrement out of his nostrils. He drove home. As the guards were waving him through the gate with their flashlights, he saw a small figure sitting on the front steps of his house. He stopped the car, opened the window, and said, "Who's that?"

"He work here, sir," one of the guards said.

Bobby parked, then went up to the boy. He was probably ten or eleven years old. He had on brown slacks and a blue dress shirt that was too big for him.

"I work here," the boy said, looking Bobby in the eye.

"You do?"

"My name is ████████. But the Lawsons called me Tom. You can call me Tom."

"Hello, Tom."

"I clean the house, and tend the garden."

"I'm not sure yet what I'm going to do for help," Bobby said.

"Also, I cook."

"You cook?"

"I am not a very good cook. But I can prepare your breakfast. The Lawsons had a machine which makes waffles, and I can use this."

Bobby didn't say anything.

"Do you like waffles?" the boy asked.

"Not really."

"Also toast. And jam. And the coffee machine."

3

At the Station on Monday, Bobby met William, who had been COS ███ for about a year at that point. Bobby thought he was surprisingly mild, not the type of hard-charger who usually made it to the SIS (Senior Intelligence Service) level. He asked Bobby questions about his life before he'd joined the CIA, which no other boss of his at the Agency had ever done. He wanted to know why he wasn't married, and spent a long time talking about his own relationship with his wife. At the end of their meeting, he patted Bobby on the shoulder and said he hoped they'd accomplish something together.

The DCOS took Bobby around the Station and introduced him to most of the C/Os and support personnel. He went over maps of ████████ with him, then took him out to lunch. When Bobby finally sat down at his desk in the afternoon, he found a note there from the officer he was replacing, Kate Lawson. She welcomed him to ███ and said that she was sure he would enjoy his tour. She told him she had instructed her ████████ Tom to speak with him, and that Bobby should consider keeping him. Her family had grown very attached to him, he was a hard worker, and he used his salary to help support his parents and three sisters. She said they'd actually fallen so in love with him that they'd considered adopting an ██████ of their own, but unfortunately, ███████ law prohibited it. At the end of the letter, she warned Bobby to watch out for ████████, which the ██████ intel service sometimes used for surveillance.

4

W ithin a few weeks, Bobby had his first developmental going, a ████████ diplomat he'd met at a conference the ████████ government had set up on foreign investment. He was named ██████████ (although not his real name, the ████████ and ████████████ I've chosen are representative of ████████████ in the ████████████ province where he came from). At the conference, the ██████████████ minister had given a speech in which he'd made several comments to the effect that the American treasury secretary ought to spend less time golfing and more time using his extensive understanding of world affairs to teach his government how to get along with other countries. The comments were unusually hostile for an ███████ official speaking in public.

Bobby had seen ██████████ sitting alone during the speech, a thin, distracted-looking man in a bad suit. Later, he found him looking at some pamphlets on a table at the back of the room. Bobby sidled up next to him and said, "Well, I do realize we need to learn a thing or two about getting along with other countries, but I don't understand what the minister has against golf."

"Yes," ██████████ had responded.

From the look in ██████████'s eyes, Bobby wasn't sure if he'd understood his joke.

"I don't like golf anyway," Bobby said, speaking more slowly.

"No sport," ██████████ said.

"Right," Bobby agreed.

As they continued to chat, ██████████'s English proved to be fairly difficult, but by no means impossible, to understand. Bobby learned that he had been in ▮▮▮▮ for a little over a year, and that he had served previously in ▮▮▮▮ and ▮▮▮▮▮▮▮. He currently worked in the ▮▮▮▮▮▮▮▮▮▮▮▮▮Department of the ▮▮▮▮▮Embassy.

5

His first lunch with ▮▮▮▮▮▮▮, ostensibly to discuss their respective countries' interest in a trade pact with ▮▮▮▮, took place a week later. They discussed the implications of the potential trade pacts for a while, then Bobby turned the conversation in a more personal direction. He learned that ▮▮▮▮▮▮▮ had grown up in the ▮▮▮▮▮▮▮▮▮of ▮▮▮▮. His father had died when he was young, in some sort of industrial accident. ▮▮▮▮▮▮didn't give any details about the accident, but when he mentioned it, he winced in a way that made Bobby think it had probably been gruesome. The manager of the father's factory had been kind to ▮▮▮▮▮▮'s family afterward and, when ▮▮▮▮▮▮was old enough, pulled strings to have him admitted to the ▮▮▮▮▮▮▮▮▮▮▮▮▮▮. It was an impressive school for the son of a factory worker, and ▮▮▮▮▮▮ had been the top student in his class, resulting in an invitation to take the ▮▮▮▮▮▮exams and ultimately receive a position at the ▮▮▮▮▮▮ ▮▮▮▮▮▮▮▮ Ministry in ▮▮▮▮▮. Eventually, a mentor there had sponsored him for the diplomatic service exam.

After lunch, Bobby wrote ▮▮▮▮▮▮ up as a potential source on ▮▮▮▮ economic policy. There was also an outside chance that, by virtue of being in the embassy, he might come across intelligence, or might have or develop contacts with access to intelligence, on the separatist movement in ▮▮▮▮▮▮as well as other terrorist targets the ▮▮▮▮intel service was known to collect against.

Bobby also wrote that ▮▮▮▮▮▮, although in his late thirties, seemed naïve and overly earnest. But he appeared to be quite bright.

6

After his first few months in ████, Bobby fell into a straightforward routine. In the morning he'd come downstairs, where Tom
had toast and coffee waiting for him on the kitchen table. He'd eat
and read the newspaper, while Tom stood against the wall, occasionally coming over to refill the coffee. After breakfast, Bobby
would drive to the ████, check in at the Station, then work at his
████ job until lunch. Then he'd eat with a developmental or potential
developmental if he had one, and if not, he'd case neighborhoods and
restaurants for an hour or so. Back to his ████ job in the afternoon.
Then paperwork, cables, and meetings at the Station until six or
seven.

On nights when he was home early enough, he'd see Tom squatting
in the garden, pulling weeds and pruning even the tiniest plants and
flowers. He had a surprisingly complicated set of gardening tools,
which Bobby assumed the Lawsons had left for him.

7

Bobby had liked living in ████████, where he'd spent his first tour.
It was pretty, and orderly, and even if there were tensions in the
society, they were generally accepted. ████ was different. Bobby felt
like the whole country was teetering on an edge where falling either
way would result in complete catastrophe.

But at the same time, the filth and poverty, as depressing as they were, gave the streets a life and energy that excited Bobby. The desperation itself seemed to make everything in ████ feel important. As if anything you did here could only make things better.

8

By the end of October, Bobby had had two lunches and a dinner with ████████, who had been assigned the crypt TDTRACER. He also had two other developmentals going, a mid-ranking ████ police officer and ████████ a sixty-year-old businessman who owned two of the largest ████████████████████ in the country. The businessman was over six and a half feet tall and extremely thin. Despite being a respectable ████████ he came off as somewhat slimy, although Bobby wasn't sure if that impression was justified or just the result of a slight but permanent leer that seemed to be built into his facial structure.

His tour was off to a good start. He had more to discuss at the staff meetings than some of the C/Os who'd been there over a year. William seemed to listen intently when he talked about his cases, and the two of them would often stay in the conference room after everyone else had left and go over what had happened at the meeting. They'd also discuss world events and try to decide if the Station was failing to cover anything important.

Bobby was pleased to have his COS take such an interest in him. But the truth was, he wasn't surprised. Even though he worked for William, he could talk to him as an intellectual equal, which most of the other officers in the Station couldn't do. Bobby also knew that he inspired confidence in people. William didn't have to worry about him screwing up, which probably made it a lot easier for him to deal with Bobby than with some of the younger guys in the Station who practically oozed inexperience and questionable judgment.

9

At a lunch in the ▮▮▮▮▮▮▮ District, TDTRACER said that his friend ▮▮▮▮▮▮▮▮ had played a practical joke on him a few days earlier. When TRACER had arrived at his desk, there was a note for him to pick up a package in the mail room. The package was a large, almost weightless box. He brought it back to his desk, and when he opened it, there was a tiny piece of ▮▮▮▮▮▮▮▮▮▮▮▮▮, a ▮▮▮▮▮▮ delicacy, at the bottom. The entire office had gathered around, and everyone had a good laugh.

TDTRACER had an expectant grin on his face when he finished the story. Bobby didn't understand the joke—it seemed to hinge on some sort of cultural reference that was lost on him—but he laughed appreciatively. It felt like a time to give TRACER exactly what he was looking for, not ask him to explain ▮▮▮▮▮▮ culture. Back at the Station, he looked up TRACER's friend who had played the joke. He was a mid-ranking officer in the embassy's political section. Bobby had hoped he would turn out to be an officer in the ▮▮▮, but that was asking a lot. In any case, having a direct connection to a source of information in the political section did raise the potential value of TDTRACER as a source.

10

One morning, while refilling Bobby's coffee, Tom said, "The Lawsons ordered many items from America. With a waffle machine, I will make you delicious waffles." Bobby said that he didn't like waffles, but Tom suggested that since he had never had the waffles Tom made in the waffle machine, perhaps he did like waffles and he didn't know it.

A few mornings later, Tom said, "It is a shame to eat only toast for breakfast."

Bobby looked up at him, and Tom continued, "My sister will eat only toast, and my mother says that her hair will fall out."

Bobby said that actually he'd like to have eggs or cereal some mornings, and that in fact he'd asked Tom to put out cereal for him. Tom frowned. He said that ██████ eggs were not clean, and that cereal was very expensive. Waffles, on the other hand, were economical and healthy.

11

Every time Bobby reached out to TDTRACER, he responded positively. Eventually, he began calling Bobby and suggesting plans. He was obviously open to a friendship.

But whenever Bobby brought up anything in the least bit political, TRACER became detached. He didn't like to talk about his work at all, and he seemed uncomfortable when Bobby talked about his. The

██████ security apparatus was one of the most formidable in the world, so this made sense. It even demonstrated good security awareness, as Bobby pointed out in his cables to Headquarters. But Bobby also realized that nothing was coming out of him anytime soon. It would be a long, slow recruitment, if it happened at all. There was nothing wrong with this, per se. In fact, slow recruitments were the norm. But Bobby had initially thought it would go quickly, and he was starting to get annoyed. The sooner he made his first recruit of the tour, the more likely he was to top the three recruits he'd made on his previous tour.

One night, Bobby and TRACER were drinking wine in an underground bar near the ██████████. TRACER, who was normally fairly cheerful, had a faraway look in his eyes. Bobby thought he looked homesick. They sat drinking quietly for some time before Bobby finally broke the silence.

"So what do you do in your free time, ██████████?" he asked.

"Read so many books. Cook."

"Just for yourself you cook?"

"Yes. Sometimes my friend ██████ too, but very quiet."

"I like to read," said Bobby.

"Yes?"

"Books about history. Sometimes . . . well, when I was younger, poetry."

"Poetry, yes. In heart. You read ██████?"

"No, I missed him," said Bobby.

"He write, '██ ██████████████████████████████.'"

"That's beautiful," said Bobby.

"About man's heart."

"Yes."

"You are alone?" asked TRACER.

"Alone? Yes. You mean not married? Alone, in ██████? Yes, I am."

"Do you feel bad?"

"Sometimes."

"I have girlfriend. Before. When I go from ████, she cannot. So many years. She marry."

"Women," said Bobby.

"Women," said TRACER.

12

Bobby eventually concluded that Tom himself wanted a waffle, and wanted one quite desperately. He went ahead and ordered the waffle maker. The morning after it arrived, Bobby came downstairs to find his usual toast and coffee waiting, as well as a waffle with bananas and ██fruit on top.

"We do not have syrup," Tom said gravely.

He had moved from his usual position against the wall to hover closer to the table.

Bobby took a bite of the waffle, then said, "Make one for yourself."

Tom shook his head no.

The next morning, another waffle was waiting for Bobby. This time, halfway through eating it, Bobby said, "I think I'll have another one."

Tom had already washed the dishes, but he pulled a bowl off the drying rack and made batter. He poured it onto the waffle maker, and a few minutes later he put the waffle down on the table. Bobby finished his first waffle, then said, "You know what, I'm not actually hungry anymore." He looked down at the second waffle. "A shame to waste it."

With that, he picked up his briefcase and headed out the door.

That night, he tried to figure out if Tom had eaten the waffle. But since Tom never left any garbage, it was impossible to tell.

13

After a three-month development, Bobby recruited the ███████████ businessman ██ ██ ███████████████████████████NRLIGHTHOUSE. Things had gone by the book. LIGHTHOUSE was completely unsurprised when Bobby pitched him. He was forthright about the fact that he was motivated primarily by a desire to secure an American visa and American business contacts. He was hardly poor, and he didn't blink when Bobby offered him ████████████████████a month.

LIGHTHOUSE wasn't going to have them bursting out in song back at Headquarters, but he was a solid recruit. Although his access to intelligence on █████████████████████████would obviously depend to some degree on circumstance, he had the potential to access all kinds of ██████████information from his many contacts in the ███████████. Even if he didn't, he was smart and smooth enough to serve as a cutout for recruiting ████████████████████████████ ██████████████████████████.

The only thing that bothered Bobby was the crypt. At first, he thought it was a reference to LIGHTHOUSE's height, and he didn't like it. But before complaining about it, he'd gone over the cable again and recognized the pseudonym of the officer who'd originated it. He wasn't the joking type. Bobby thought about asking for a new crypt anyway, but the chances of a cable being intercepted and decoded were close to zero. And if that did happen, there would be a lot of things more revealing than the crypt.

In any case, the first recruit was out of the way. Now Bobby had to focus on getting someone truly significant. It probably wouldn't be a local like LIGHTHOUSE. Very few ████████were going to rock the intelligence establishment. Maybe it would be TRACER. He certainly came from a significant target country, and could be run in place if he were posted back there someday. As for what he came across in the ██████████████, the potential there was pretty good, too. He wasn't obviously on the level of the ██████████████████ ███████ Bobby had recruited in ████████. But once he started producing, he might get there.

14

After several weeks of wondering if Tom was eating the extra waffles he left for him, one morning Bobby said, "Tomorrow, go ahead and make me two waffles for when I come down. Maybe I can eat them both if they're both ready when I start breakfast."

Two waffles were waiting the next morning. When he sat down, Bobby said, "Tom, I don't think I can eat both of these after all. Why don't you sit down and have one with me?"

"No, sir."

"But I want you to have a waffle with me," Bobby said.

Tom shook his head.

Bobby had Tom continue to make him two waffles every morning. He tried several more times to get him to sit with him and eat the extra one, but he never would.

15

His first post-recruitment meeting with NRLIGHTHOUSE was a car pickup. The SDR was his first full one since getting to ███. It was as bad as the first one he ever did. The conditions in ██████ were nerve-racking, with █████████████████████████████ ██ ██ ██████, the streets were wider and less crowded, and at least you could ██ ██████. In ██████, there was no █████████████████████████████ ██████. Bobby was sweating through his suit so badly he was afraid that, if he was pulled over, he'd be detained just for looking so nervous.

He tried to calm down, telling himself to concentrate on the █████ markers and stop thinking about anything else. But somehow his brain wasn't cooperating fully. It wasn't sealing off the areas it usually sealed off when he worked. He started to wonder if it was possible that he'd just never been challenged by a truly difficult operational environment before.

He saw NRLIGHTHOUSE in the distance as soon as he turned onto ████████████. Bobby felt a slight tremor in his arms, and loosened his grip on the steering wheel. He was afraid he'd missed surveillance, which you were always afraid of, but he was more afraid than usual. He wanted to stop and compose himself, but he was way too close now. He pulled up at the curb, and LIGHTHOUSE got in.

As soon as they pulled away, Bobby said, "You remember we discussed how it's important to have some sort of story, or excuse, for why we're together, in case somebody questions it? If anyone pulls us over, or asks you later, let's say that we were ████████████████████

██████████████████████████████████████
███████████."

LIGHTHOUSE nodded. The top of his head was actually touching the roof of the car, and Bobby thought about the tradecraft problems he was going to present because of his height. It would be easy to pick LIGHTHOUSE out of a crowd, which meant public meetings and countersurveillance were both going to be tricky.

They turned onto ██████████ and Bobby looked down the dark stretch of the esplanade, with the flashing yellow lights on all the corners. The double pricks of headlights and the barely discernible shapes of cars were coming into his rearview mirror now.

"Sorry, would you mind repeating it back to me, just for practice?" he said. "Why are we together tonight?"

"Well, I will say we are ███████████████████████████████ ███████████████. Yes?"

"Good," said Bobby. "Perfect. Here, would you like some tea, and some cheese?"

He handed LIGHTHOUSE a thermos and a bag with cheese and crackers inside. As soon as LIGHTHOUSE started rooting around in the bag, Bobby felt that cheese and crackers was the wrong choice. It was too fussy. And the crackers would make noise, and leave a mess in the car.

He had a route planned that would take them through ██████████████████ and ██████████████████, down ██████, and through the ████████████████████████. He turned onto █████████, a narrow conduit between ████ and ████████. Suddenly they were the only car on the road.

"How are you?" Bobby asked.

"Very good, very good," LIGHTHOUSE said. He'd cut a piece of cheese off with the knife Bobby had put in the bag, and stuffed it in his mouth with a cracker, not bothering to put the cheese on top of the cracker first. Now he unscrewed the top of the thermos and poured the steaming tea into the cup, then took a gulp.

"Jesus," Bobby said. "Isn't that hot?"

"No, not for me."

Headlights appeared in the rearview five or six blocks back. Bobby kept the gas steady.

"So, did you speak with your friend this week, about the consortium on ████████████████████?"

"Mm, yes," said LIGHTHOUSE. He dug back into the bag.

"He say anything interesting?"

"He tells me the chairman of ████████████is absolutely decided to open the ████████████within a year."

"Really?"

"Yes."

LIGHTHOUSE took another gulp of tea.

"I believe this man is reliable," he said. "He is very smart, especially for an ████████. One year, then. Obviously too soon. Any fool would know."

"Why?" asked Bobby.

He went around a curve and ██████turned onto a brightly lit avenue crowded with cars. The car behind him on ███████was gone, but if surveillance had seen him turn onto ████they could just pick him up here.

"You must understand the rules of development in ██████. If he has not yet paid off the ████████████████, which I know that he has not, he will wait two years at the minimum for the fees to make their way down to the ground."

"How do you know he hasn't bought off the ████████████████ yet?"

"████████████told me."

"How does he know?"

"He worked at ████████████████████████████ for many years. He knows everything that goes on there."

Bobby exited at ████████████. This plunged them back into darkness. Four other cars turned off with him; two went left at ████, two stayed behind. At a red light, one of them pulled up next to Bobby. LIGHTHOUSE started to crane his neck to look past Bobby into the car, but Bobby put his arm out and said, "Don't!" LIGHTHOUSE sat back and poured more tea.

"Well, that's interesting," Bobby said. "That's good to know."

"Yes," LIGHTHOUSE said. He was peering into the bag now and pulled out what appeared to be the last of the cheese. Bobby found himself slightly offended that LIGHTHOUSE hadn't offered him any.

Bobby went at least ten blocks on ███████████. The car that was on their side at the light was gone, the one behind was still there. He turned north onto █████. He spent about ten minutes giving LIGHT-HOUSE a preliminary lesson on contact procedures. He also gave him an emergency meeting site. Then he decided to cut his loop back to the drop-off point short and take ██████ to █████. He'd planned to debrief LIGHTHOUSE on ████████████████████████████ ████████████████████████████ also, but he thought the meeting had been clean, and he sensed he should let it go.

Later, at home in bed, Bobby still felt jittery. He wondered if he should talk to William about it. After all, William would probably tell him it was perfectly normal, and even tell a few stories about similar things happening to him. But Bobby decided not to. You just didn't tell your COS that kind of thing.

16

One morning, Bobby came down to breakfast and saw Tom standing against the wall waiting for him as usual. Bobby sat down and took a sip of coffee. Then he got up, picked up the plate with the extra waffle on it, walked over to Tom, and thrust it at him.

He sat back down and stared hard at his newspaper. After a few minutes, out of the corner of his eye, he saw Tom eating the waffle with his hands.

17

"Pull up a chair," William said as Bobby came into his office. "I've been wanting to talk to you. How are things? I feel like I haven't kept up with what's going on in your life."

"Good. Great."

"Fine, fine. Glad to hear it. You comfortable in the house?"

"Very nice. Living like a king."

"Making any friends?"

Bobby was stuck for a second. He wasn't sure he'd been asked this since grade school.

"I don't know. Some. You can't really socialize too much with the Station people, so that's hard. You mean friends like . . . not developmental friends, right?"

"No, no, friends. A man needs friends. And a wife!"

William smiled, communicating that he knew he'd already told Bobby this.

"You get along so well with everyone here," William went on. "Even the ██████ folks say good things about you."

"They just like me because I work fast."

William laughed. "Well, you need to do some work on your personal life," he said. "What about the job? LIGHTHOUSE has been interesting, I think."

"I think he's promising."

"How about the SDRs, et cetera? Tough in ██████, isn't it?"

Bobby shrugged. William looked closely at him.

"It's okay if it's hard," he said. "It is hard."

"I'm having trouble with the ████████████████████" Bobby said.

"Try taking a ███████████. Other than that, there's not much you can do. You sweating?"

"A little."

"It's hot here."

18

After a concert in the ████████, TDTRACER invited Bobby to come to his apartment the following week, where he wanted to cook him a "traditional ██████ banquet." Bobby was immediately alarmed, because ████████████ tended to live together in the same buildings, and TRACER would surely be noticed coming in and out with an American ██████.

"I'd love that," Bobby told him. "I can't think of anything nicer. But you know, I have an idea. Maybe we should do it at my house. I have a really nice, big kitchen. It's fun to cook in. And it could be a little bit more private."

Bobby was primarily concerned with avoiding TRACER's apartment, but at the last moment it had occurred to him to bring up privacy. Raising the privacy question was a conversational move you could make to determine where a developmental was at. If they balked at the mention of privacy, or didn't seem to understand why you were bringing it up, it was more likely they saw your relationship as purely friendly. If they quietly acquiesced, it probably meant they had some sense of what was going on. And if they seemed surprised but were still potentially open to recruitment, it could start the process of opening their eyes to what they were in the middle of.

"Okay," TRACER said. "I cook in large kitchen. Very good."

He seemed so cheerful about it that Bobby couldn't deduce anything from his response other than the fact that he was happy to cook in his kitchen. Bobby started talking about the excellent appliances he had, then TRACER looked timidly at him and said, "Yes . . . now you call me Ralph, okay?"

With TRACER's accent, Bobby didn't immediately understand what he'd said. But after a few moments, he sorted out the sounds.

"Ralph?" he said.

"My name in English class. In █████."

"Wasn't I doing good with ███████?" Bobby asked.

TRACER insisted at first that Bobby had done well with it for a foreigner. But Bobby finally got him to admit that the way he pronounced it, it sounded less like his name and more like the ████████ word for ████.

19

The day of the dinner, Bobby felt tense and irritable. At the Station, he almost argued with the DCOS over a few minor corrections on an NRLIGHTHOUSE intel report. And when a first-tour officer named Theresa asked him a harmless question about an SDR route, he said, "Don't you think you should know the answer to that yourself by now?" This behavior was so out of character for him—or really for any C/O—that three separate people asked him what was wrong. Each time Bobby just shrugged and said he was fine.

The truth was, he had no idea what he was so edgy about. Although he didn't love having developmentals at his house, figuring that ██████████████████████████████████████ ██████████████████████████████████████ ██████████████████████████████████████ ██████████████████████████████████████ ███████████████████. The DCOS had also turned down his request to do a ██████████ sweep, saying it was more likely to attract attention than actually find anything. But maybe he was just drinking too much coffee, or, more likely in ██████, not enough water.

When Bobby got home, Tom was on his hands and knees in the garden. He'd seemed very busy planting things the last week or two. Bobby sent him home, then went inside and closed the curtains on the windows with an open exposure. He did a useless manual inspection of the phones and power-drawing appliances. Then he sat in the den and waited.

Ralph came at seven o'clock, carrying a bulging cloth sack. In the kitchen, he unloaded ██████ herbs, vegetables, wrapped parcels of meat (which it occurred to Bobby must have been very expensive for him), and a few strange-looking cooking utensils. Bobby poured wine, then went into the living room to turn on a CD. By the time he came back, two ███ were already sizzling and smoking on the stove.

As Ralph cooked, he told Bobby about the ingredients he was using, giving him something close to a botanical and political history of each one. He was just starting to describe the role of the ███ onion in the ███-century court of █████████████████ when Tom walked into the kitchen.

Before Bobby could react, Ralph said, "Hello!"

"I did not change the paper in the bathroom," Tom said, looking down at the floor.

"It's okay," said Bobby. "You can do it tomorrow."

But Tom was already heading to the bathroom. He came back a minute later and stood at his regular place against the wall. He stared at the incredible variety of ingredients laid out across the counter. When Ralph saw him looking, he motioned him over with his hand, but Tom stood still.

"It's okay," said Bobby.

Ralph started to run through the ingredients again, describing them to Tom. But then he noticed that Tom seemed to be more interested in his unusual cooking utensils, and he started to tell him about those instead. He picked up each one, said its ██████ name, then waved it through the air in a pantomime of its intended use. Then he said the ██████ name again and told Tom to repeat it, which he dutifully attempted. When he'd gone through all of them, Ralph handed

Tom an enormous cleaver, positioned it over a gnarled ginger root, and guided his hand as he chopped it.

Once Tom had the hang of it, Ralph took a small, hooked knife, put it in Bobby's hand, and showed him the ████ way of cutting ████. He took some of Tom's ginger and the first few pieces of Bobby's ████, and sprinkled them into the boiling oil in the ██.

As Tom and Bobby built up mounds of onion, carrot, celery, ginger, ████, Ralph went to work on the beef and chicken. He used the tip of the cleaver to dig into the meat, then tore pieces away from the bone. When a strand of tendon was exposed, he'd carve out the rest of it and toss it into the oil with the vegetables.

Ralph talked almost nonstop as he cooked, telling odd little folktales about vegetables, describing meals he'd had in ████, and chuckling at jokes that Bobby never seemed to catch. Pillars of steam were rising from the ████, a frying pan, and two pots of sauce. The kitchen smelled like a greenhouse. Bobby tuned out Ralph's monologue and tried to figure out how big of a problem Tom was. His first thought was that there was a possibility Tom was spying on him. He was just a boy, but there was no reason to think he couldn't be reporting to the ████. He'd worked for the Lawsons before, and if they'd been blown, which was always a possibility, the ████ may well have realized another Agency officer was likely to move into their house. ████ ████. He couldn't completely dismiss these thoughts, although on balance, he thought it was unlikely. The ████ wasn't thought to be so active against the Americans that they'd go to any lengths ████. And he'd never heard of a ████ being used in this way. More than anything, though, Bobby just didn't feel suspicious of Tom. He'd probably shown up that night out of curiosity, or loneliness, or God knew what else. Maybe he really had forgotten to put toilet paper in the bathroom.

Ralph suddenly started moving very quickly. He scooped ████ out of the ████, pots and pans in a sort of giant curved spatula, then let them down onto the platters and into the bowls with a gentle flourish. He sprinkled parsley and ▮▮▮▮▮ on top of the dishes. Then he and Bobby brought everything to the table. As they stood looking down at the food, Ralph said, "Authentic ▮▮▮▮▮cooking from ▮▮▮▮▮▮▮▮."

Bobby and Ralph sat down, and Tom, who had been bringing water glasses to the table, went back and stood against the wall.

"Tom, sit," Bobby said.

Tom didn't move. After a few moments, Ralph said quietly, "He no eat?"

"Not at the table," Bobby said.

Ralph made a plate of food and brought it over to Tom. When Tom took it, Ralph put his hand on his head and mussed his hair.

As soon as they started eating, Bobby wanted to steer the conversation toward the most innocuous subjects possible. Not because Tom was a spy, but simply because there shouldn't be a third person at a developmental meeting at this stage, and if there was, he should learn as little as possible. For several disconcerting moments, though, Bobby couldn't think of any topics at all. The phrase "the weather" kept popping into his head. Finally, he raised his wineglass and said, "Well, it's nice to have everyone here. A toast to the world."

Bobby forced a smile, but he couldn't believe what had just come out of his mouth. If that was the best he could do, he should probably just resign. Ralph raised his glass and took a sip of wine, then Bobby launched into a monologue about ▮▮▮▮▮ restaurants in America, and how his father had enjoyed going to them, and what all of his favorite dishes were. Ralph responded by talking more about the history of ▮▮▮▮▮ cuisine. Then, to Bobby's surprise, Tom said, in a quiet voice, "You are from ▮▮▮▮?"

"Yes," said Ralph.

"I know ▮▮▮▮," said Tom.

"Yes. You know how make ▮▮▮▮▮▮▮▮▮▮▮▮▮? Put ▮▮▮▮ in shoe."

Ralph and Tom burst out laughing. Then Tom said, "How are boys in ▮▮▮▮?"

"Fine," said Ralph.

"Like boys from ████?"

"Yes. You come ████ and see."

"What do they do?"

"Oh, school. Work. Many boy live farm."

"Do you live on a farm?"

"I live here."

"But in ████."

"No, I live city. When boy. But I go farm."

Then Ralph told Tom the following story. (I'll render this as closely as I can to what Bobby told me, but I don't think I'll be able to capture it perfectly—you have to picture Bobby sitting across the kitchen table from me, doing a fairly poor imitation of a heavy ████ accent.)

"We go my grandfather in ████████ one time every year. He farmer, owner one steer. You know steer very very expensive ████. When boy in city, I do not know steer. But grandfather say, '████, go with steer to village. Into water. For buy wood.' My mother, I know, will go say, 'No, no, he cannot,' but nothing. I go water, walking behind steer, yes?, but he know. Stop, stop. When I push, go over here, walk me into tree. Yes? Big steer. He think funny. In water, we walk bridge, he push me down into water. For his fun. I think . . . how you say? . . . top steer . . . sharp . . ."

"The horns," Bobby said.

"Horns go in me. If? This what I think. Maybe dead. We go village, buy wood, go home, steer push here, there, into tree, more tree, hill. Then arrive grandfather, nice steer, now. Parents see. We walk, me and steer. Everyone smile, 'Oh ████, you good steer.' I am very happy. I say, 'I good steer.' I say, steer turn, push me side of steer, I fall down, he make all wood fall on me."

Tom, who was still standing against the wall, said, "Did your brother laugh?"

"No brother," said Ralph.

"Oh."

"You have brother?" Ralph asked.

"No, I have three sisters."

"Ah, three girl, one boy. In ███ we say ██████████████."

"My parents love to have a big family," Tom said.

"What work father do?" said Ralph.

"He repairs shoes. And my mother stays at home and tends the house and children."

"Hard, life for father, yes?"

"Yes, sir. He works very hard. I work to help him also. I work here every day for Mr. Goldstein, and also some nights I work at the General's."

"The who?" Bobby asked.

"The General, sir."

"Which General?"

Tom seemed unsure if Bobby was being serious or not.

"Sir, General ████?"

General ████ was the Deputy ██████████ of the █████ Army (he held the same position, but with one extra ██████████, when I met him several years later). Bobby knew that he lived just a few miles away in the ████████████Alarm bells started going off in his head. If Tom worked for General ████, maybe he did need to worry about him spying on him.

"You work for General ██████?" he asked. "When? You're always here."

"Only sometimes, sir. When he is having a large party and requires extra help. Or when his servant ████is unable to come. Then I work at his house in the evening. But only if everything is done here, and you do not need me. I will always be here first."

Bobby wondered why Tom had never told him about this. But the truth was, he'd never really asked him anything about his life outside the house. And Tom seemed perfectly calm discussing it. Once again, Bobby tried to dismiss his concerns. If Tom was spying on him, he never would have mentioned that he worked for the General in the first place. For that matter, no remotely competent handler would have sent him barreling into the middle of an evening like this.

"Sir, on the farm," Tom said to Ralph, "do the chickens wake you up in the morning?"

Ralph smiled, lifted his thumbs to his underarms, and imitated a chicken flapping its wings and squawking.

"Tom, have you been to a farm?" Bobby asked.

"I don't know," said Tom.

Bobby talked about the farms his parents had taken him to visit when he was a child. Then Ralph started asking questions about growing up in America. He was curious about the ways in which children were and weren't obedient to their parents there. He also wanted to know how old Bobby was when he got his first computer, and he asked him several questions about operating systems that Bobby could only shrug at.

The weedy smell in the kitchen had turned sour. Bobby was sucking the insides of his cheeks, trying to get rid of the taste of the food. The vegetables had been stringy and a bit slimy, the meat tough and almost flavorless despite all the things Ralph had put into the dishes. Bobby wondered if Ralph was a bad cook, or if food from ███ Province just didn't agree with the American palate.

Tom, on the other hand, had obviously enjoyed the food. He'd actually had a look of almost burning pleasure in his eyes while he'd been eating. Now, he was doing the dishes. He'd wash a few, then turn around to look at Ralph, then turn back to the sink.

20

It was three A.M. Moonlight was coming in through the bedroom window, and the ███ were chirping, a softer noise than crickets make. Bobby lay in bed alternately thinking about Ralph and Tom. The night with Ralph had undoubtedly been a success. Bobby could tell that he was both comfortable and happy, maybe considerably happier than usual. Coming from ███, he probably felt an air of freedom just spending a night in a Westerner's house.

Tom had seemed happy, too. He had been curious and talkative, and his extreme deference had relaxed a bit. Or at least it had around Ralph.

Bobby could feel in his bones that this kid was not a spy, for the ▮▮▮▮ or anyone else. But still, you weren't supposed to rely on your bones. And Bobby couldn't quite get over the fact that Tom worked at the General's. He still thought Tom hadn't had to tell him he worked there, and obviously wouldn't have mentioned it if he were spying on him. But on the other hand, he was eleven years old, and could have made a slip in a fit of forgetfulness or exuberance.

He started thinking back to the day he'd met Tom, sitting on the steps of his house. He tried to recall different conversations he'd had with him. He pictured him working in the garden, and he thought of the elaborate set of gardening tools he'd originally assumed the Lawsons had left for him. It looked like a set that would have cost a lot of money, and it seemed too elaborate and fussy for an Agency officer, even if she'd been an avid gardener.

Bobby tried to picture the tools more precisely, but he couldn't.

He turned and tried to go to sleep, but he wasn't even drowsy. He tried to think about Ralph more, but once he'd remembered Tom's tools, that was all he could think about.

He put on a pair of jeans and a T-shirt and went downstairs without turning the lights on. At his front window, he looked out at the gate. He saw one clear shape standing still in the moonlight, and a few feet away, to the side of the guardhouse, the burning nib of a cigarette. He went to the kitchen, got a flashlight, then went out the back door.

Moving slowly and quietly, he walked across the lawn to the toolshed. He opened the latch and pulled the door, keeping forward pressure on it to keep it from creaking.

Inside, he moved a box onto a metal shelf to block the window. Light could still get out around the edges, but he didn't want to take the time to seal it properly. He closed the door and turned on the flashlight, keeping it pressed into his palm.

He opened Tom's gardening box and took out the tools onc by one. There were two hoes, two spades, a miniature rake, three sizes of shears, and a few pieces he didn't know the names or uses of. Pulling the flashlight away from his palm enough to get a bigger sliver of light, he inspected each piece closely. He looked for cracks on the handles, and he held each tool up and shook it next to his ear. The larger of the two spades was the only one that seemed a little off. It wasn't as solid as the others, and the handle had a two-inch section in the middle that was shinier than the rest of the wood grain.

He put the flashlight down with the beam shining onto his leg. He tried twisting and turning the spade in every possible way. He pressed up and down the handle, tapping it against the floor of the shed as he went. He repeated every action with the spade facing up, down, and to both sides. It was a warm night, and he was sweating now. He stood up with the flashlight and looked around, letting more light out of his palm. There was some sort of club in the corner. He wrapped it in a piece of dirty cloth, then balanced the spade on a turned-over wooden tub with the handle sticking out.

He hit one hard crack in the middle of the handle. The noise was dull and wouldn't carry to the gatehouse. He hit it again, and then again. On the fifth hit, he felt the wood crack, and two blows later, the handle separated in the middle and split down the center seam.

There was nothing inside. No listening device. No recording equipment. No notebook or invisible ink.

Bobby carefully scooped up all the wood splinters from the ground and wrapped them in the cloth with the pieces of the spade. He brought the bundle back into the house, went upstairs, and put it in his briefcase. He'd dump it somewhere on the way to work.

21

The next morning, as Bobby sat down at the breakfast table, he said, "That was nice last night."

"Yes, sir," said Tom.

"Glad you came."

"Oh, thank you, sir," Tom said.

Bobby motioned for him to sit down at the table to eat his waffle. Tom, looking down the whole time, came over and slid into a chair. Bobby poured him a glass of orange juice. After he did this, Tom got up and refilled Bobby's coffee.

If he weren't embarrassed for himself, Bobby would have laughed at what he'd done the night before. He'd known all along that Tom was no spy. He looked at the boy for a moment, then stared down at his newspaper.

He wondered what Tom saw and heard at the General's. Of course, it was possible the General was very security conscious and never said anything in front of him. Then again, that was more of an American mind-set, or at least it wasn't an ███ mind-set. If Tom was serving tea and cleaning up, all kinds of things were probably said around him. Even if that wasn't the case, he would know who was at the house, who the General was close to, and, if he was perceptive, who the General did and didn't like.

But he was a kid. So that was that.

Though Bobby wondered if kids were actually on the cannot-recruit list. It was possible that it was so obviously wrong that they didn't even bother to officially prohibit it. On the other hand, what about the children's armies in Africa and the teenagers in terrorist groups? Weren't there any sources there?

And couldn't you get an exception to any rule anyway?

He could ask William about it. But maybe it was too crazy to even mention.

22

Bobby and NRLIGHTHOUSE met inside a park near the ███ ███. It was dusk, and the wet heat of the day was fading, leaving behind a sticky mist.

Bobby had given LIGHTHOUSE a cover story at the end of their last meeting, and he was pleased when he repeated it now unprompted.

"So, we are ███████████████████████████████████████
███████████████████████████████."

Bobby nodded. Then he asked after LIGHTHOUSE's wife and made a few other pieces of small talk. When he sensed the time was right, he started talking about walking countersurveillance.

Over the next forty-five minutes, they moved through the park, ██
██
████████████████████████████████Half the people who walked by looked up at LIGHTHOUSE, often registering what looked like dismay at his height. Bobby tried to impress on him that ███████
██
█████████████████████████████the rest. When Bobby was satisfied he'd gotten it, he turned the conversation back to ███████. After a few minutes, LIGHTHOUSE started debriefing himself.

"The ████████████████████████████████will be going to a summit in ███████. He plans to object to the ████████████████████
██
████████████████████████████████. Several of his advisers are furious, and the ███████████████████████is considering resigning."

"Yes," said Bobby, "I read about this in the paper."

"Yes, but what you did not read is that the ██████████████████ is standing behind the ███████████████████████, but he is ready to shove him aside if the opportunity comes to strike."

Bobby had read that too, or something very close to it. "How do you know about this?"

"My colleague ███████is a cousin of the ██████████████████. His wife hears everything from his wife."

"The wives discuss the Upper ██████████████████████████?"

"Very political, women these days."

LIGHTHOUSE was talking too loudly. There were people sitting on the grass to their right and others walking close to them who were going around the lagoon in the opposite direction.

"████████, remember, this is confidential."

"Of course."

"No, I mean, we have to be a little quieter."

"Ah. Yes. I am too loud?"

"Maybe we're a little loud for this environment."

"Okay."

"What about the ███████████████ project?"

"Still delayed, as I forecast. Have you heard anything about ███████████████?" (This was the American subcontractor working on the ███████████████)

"Just that they're pissed," said Bobby.

"I would like to meet this man, ███████████████. He is in ███████ from time to time, yes?"

"I think he comes, yes," said Bobby. "But I can't arrange a meeting. It would look suspicious."

"What kind of man is he?"

"A good man, I think. Very corporate. A very big American businessman."

"Open to all kinds?"

"What do you mean?"

"Does he welcome ███████ input into his business decisions?"

"Well, when he's working in ███████, I would hope so."

"I have some things to tell him. Perhaps, if not a meeting, you would give him a memorandum I will write. This could be vital to his future."

"I could show it to the appropriate people, see if they thought they could get the content to him, if it's important."

"Very important," said LIGHTHOUSE. "I could help his business very much."

Bobby and LIGHTHOUSE parted at the entrance to the park. Bobby thought about going back to the Station to write up the meeting, but it could obviously wait until the next day. The intel was just recycled garbage from the newspaper. It wasn't uncommon for an agent to pass on this type of information when they didn't have anything better. The C/O just had to be careful not to pass it on to Headquarters as if it were something valuable.

He was almost flattered that LIGHTHOUSE thought he could hook him up with ▓▓▓▓▓▓▓▓▓▓▓. On the other hand, if LIGHT-HOUSE were a hugely important agent, maybe he could. In any case, Bobby knew it would come up again, and it would have to be finessed in order to keep LIGHTHOUSE happy.

23

A week after the dinner with Ralph, Bobby came home after work one evening and saw Tom sitting in the garden. It was strange to see him sitting down outside—Tom was usually in motion, picking things up and moving things and digging things. Bobby walked over to him. As soon as Tom saw him coming, he stood up.

"Shouldn't you be going home soon?" Bobby asked.

"Yes, sir. I will go."

"I'm not trying to get rid of you. It's just that it's getting late. Why work harder than you have to?"

"Yes, sir."

Bobby saw that Tom's gardening tools were laid out in front of him in two neat rows.

"Those are nice tools," Bobby said.

"Yes, sir," Tom said. Tom looked down at the tools, and Bobby realized that he was on the verge of crying.

"Is something wrong?" he asked.

"No, sir."

"Are you sure?" Bobby asked.

"I am sure."

"Why are all your tools out?"

Tom stared down at his feet.

"I am a careless boy, sir. I have lost one of my spades."

"It's only a spade," Bobby said.

"It was an important gift from the Lawson family. Mrs. Lawson, Mr. Lawson, and their two children, Henry and Susan Lawson."

Shit, thought Bobby.

24

A few days later, Bobby came home early from work and looked all over the house until he found Tom in the laundry room. He handed him a package.

"What shall I do with this, sir?" Tom asked.

"Open it."

Tom put the package down on the washing machine and carefully untaped it. When he saw the spade inside, he looked puzzled.

"That's to replace the one you lost," Bobby said. "It's not exactly the same. But it's a good one."

"Sir, I can work very well in the garden with the tools that remain. There is still one spade."

"No, no, it's a present," said Bobby. "It's for you. To replace the other one. Just like the Lawsons gave you a present."

"Thank you for your kindness, sir," Tom said.

They stood without saying anything for a moment, then Bobby went upstairs. He watched from the bedroom window as Tom went out the back door and into the shed with the spade. He felt like less of an asshole now. He also knew it would bind Tom to him, so if he wanted him, he was a step closer.

25

At a quiet restaurant in ▇▇▇▇▇▇, Ralph gave up his first, tiny little tidbit of information about the economic section at the ▇▇▇▇▇ Embassy. In response to something Bobby made up about the American Ambassador arguing with Washington over a bilateral trade agreement with ▇▇▇▇▇, Ralph mentioned that the ▇▇▇▇▇ Ambassador opposed a new treaty between ▇▇▇ and ▇▇▇▇▇.

Bobby tried not to look overly interested. "I never know if these ambassadors are the ones everybody should be listening to, or if they don't know a damn thing," he said.

"In ▇▇▇▇, no freedom for this," Ralph said. "Ambassador is with ▇▇▇▇▇▇▇ and ▇▇▇▇▇. He oppose every treaty with ▇▇▇▇▇."

Bobby wrote up Ralph's willingness to share this information as a minor development, and in truth he wasn't sure it wasn't just a momentary slip. But he hoped it was a crack in the ice, and that soon it would spread.

26

Ralph told Bobby that he was going to ▇▇▇▇▇ for a conference on international ▇▇▇▇▇▇▇▇▇▇▇▇▇▇▇, and Bobby responded that he was going as well. He quickly made arrangements to attend the conference, and a week later, he was at a crowded, spartan resort in the ▇▇▇▇▇ Mountains.

The first night he couldn't find Ralph, but the next morning he saw him sitting at a table in the dining hall with a ███████ delegate. This meant there probably weren't any other ██████ delegates, which was good. Bobby stayed away at breakfast and at lunch, then approached Ralph between afternoon sessions. They agreed to take a hike together after the final roundtable of the day.

Bobby studied the resort map to guess which hiking trail would be the least popular. He spent an hour at a lecture on ███████████ ████████████████. Then he met Ralph outside the main hall and brought him to a secluded path that wound for miles through a ██████ forest. The tangle of █████ branches turned long stretches of the path into a near-dark enclosure. It wasn't exactly cool in the mountains, but it wasn't hot, and with ████████ singing and the sweet smell of ███████████ Bobby wished he could just walk instead of conducting business.

They did walk quietly for a while, but finally Bobby launched into a story about an alleged fight he was having with the Chief Secretary of the ████████ Section. He claimed that the Secretary (who in fact he rather liked) was a buffoon, and that he was constantly pressuring Bobby to exaggerate the potential for investment in ██████████ █████████████. Bobby said that he refused to do it, but had received several direct threats from the Secretary in response.

"Will Secretary hurt you?" Ralph asked.

"Well . . . yes and no. I have friends who look out for me. But if he complains to Washington, I could suffer repercussions."

"How repercussions?"

"Might not get promoted. Trouble influencing where my next post is. Anyway, what can you do. All our information . . . all of it, including some very confidential, says the next two years in ████████████████ are going to be a disaster. We really know this."

Ralph, who was looking down at the ground as he walked, locked his hands behind his back. After a minute, he said, "My ████████████ bad man too. People in Embassy make him to 'do this, say this,' and he do this, say this."

"What if he didn't?" Bobby said.

Ralph laughed. "No good. No more future, too."

"You have a lot of those guys? Who make people do the wrong thing?"

"Yes, very many. I cannot fight. All we say about ███████████ lies. They go to money. But █████████ do not know."

Bobby nodded.

"Little things like this—they help me understand ██████ so much better," he said. "How things work. How they are. I want to understand ███████. Really, we must understand each other's countries to keep from destroying each other . . . and the world. Don't you think?"

Ralph nodded.

27

Bobby stopped by Ralph's room on the last day of the conference. He stood by the television, away from the window, while Ralph sat on the bed.

"Interesting conference," Bobby said.

"Yes, I think."

"Got to the heart of the ██████████████████████████ ███████████████████████████."

"Yes. Also ██████████████████████████████████ ████████████."

"That's true," said Bobby.

They were quiet for a minute.

"You looking forward to getting back?" Bobby asked.

"We three day gone."

"That's true."

Ralph was looking down at the floor.

"It's good to see you here," Bobby said. "Don't have to worry about anybody seeing us. Being suspicious. The way people are of diplomats. And friends. Always better to keep a low profile when you can."

Ralph looked at Bobby while he was talking, then he turned his head and stared at the blank TV screen.

28

At breakfast one morning, before beginning his waffle, Tom said, "I will not come to work next week, or the next week after that."

"Why not?" Bobby asked.

"I must go with my family to ▉▉ for a festival. It is important for us to go every year."

"What kind of festival?"

"A very important festival."

"What do you celebrate?"

"It is not to celebrate."

"What do you do? Commemorate something?"

"We honor many Gods."

"What about the General?" Bobby said. "He lets you leave whenever you want?"

"Of course," Tom said.

Tom started eating his waffle. He looked slightly nervous, as if he were afraid Bobby would give him a hard time about the festival. To put him at ease, Bobby smiled and said, "Who will make the waffles when you're gone?"

Tom looked up, panic in his eyes, until he saw Bobby smiling. Still, he said, "I am sorry I will not be here to cook breakfast for you, sir."

"It's okay, it's okay," Bobby said, regretting his joke. "I'll be fine. I got along very well by myself for a long time without you."

This came out wrong, too. Bobby didn't know why he was having trouble saying the right things around this kid. How hard should it be to keep your ███████ houseboy happy?

Tom was eating more slowly now, his eyes locked on his waffle. Bobby thought that if he did ever recruit him, the money he could put away for him would be about the best thing that could ever happen to the kid.

29

Bobby had Ralph meet him for dinner at an out-of-the-way ████████████████████ several miles off the ████████████████. Ralph was, as usual, on time, and obviously hadn't had trouble finding it. These were good early signs that he had at least the basic capacity to learn tradecraft.

While they were eating, Bobby said, "I always prefer going to more out-of-the-way places. It's just quieter. Don't have to worry about anything, or anyone."

Ralph simply nodded. But later, as they walked back to their cars, Bobby saw him turn his head several times to look around the dark parking lot. He was becoming careful.

30

After morning staff, Bobby logged on to to his nonsecure computer and searched for "Festivals ████ June." He found a list at the ██████ Department of Culture and ████████. There were about fifteen the weekend Tom was going away. One was for ████████████, two for ███████████████, and there were four separate festivals for different kinds of ███████████████. None of these made any sense. Two festivals for ████████████ struck Bobby as vague possibilities, but unless Tom's parents were extremely old, those weren't right either. Then, at the bottom of the page, he saw "Festival To ██████ Orphans."

Something churned inside of him. He went quickly back over the entire list to make sure there were no better possibilities, but the other festivals seemed even more ridiculous now. If this was right, he couldn't believe that he hadn't even suspected it. But why would he? He hadn't been looking for holes in Tom's story.

It all made a terrible sort of sense. The few things Tom had said to Bobby about his family had all the dreaminess and insubstantiality that lies often had. And the boy had a heaviness about him that seemed now to be the indisputable effect of aloneness.

For a moment, Bobby felt something almost like grief. It was harder to think of anything sadder than this poor kid having to survive all by himself in this shithole country. But then he found himself tumbling down the path of wondering if it was perfect. If Tom was an orphan, the possibilities for using him were stronger, weren't they? Not exactly that there was less at stake for him, or that no one would be looking out for him—though these were true in a sense—but that there was just a certain logic, or symmetry, to the idea. There was no one to take care of the kid. He could do it, in a way, if he were his case officer.

Then again, it was obviously wrong and cruel and ridiculous.

But it was bold.

And what about the product? The General was the Deputy ████████████████ of the ██████ Army. He was connected to practically everyone important in every branch of the armed forces. And as a result of four years as the Chief Military Officer at the ████ and having the trust and the ear of the ██████████████, he knew as much about ████████ nuclear program as anyone in the country. The potential for intelligence on nuclear issues alone was almost breathtaking. Couldn't this, grandiosity aside, actually save the world someday?

31

On the way to his fifth meeting after recruitment with NRLIGHT-HOUSE, Bobby ran a four-stage SDR, less because he was worried than because he had to ███████████████████████████████████ ████████████████████████. Everything felt good. It was a pleasantly warm night, and he was driving with the window open. No █████████ ███████████████████████████████ and he hadn't seen anything unusual. He'd been slowed down by a traffic accident on ██████, but easily made up the time on ████████████.

Four minutes before the pickup, a █████████████████████turned onto the street a block behind him. It looked identical to one he'd seen on ███████. He could just make out the shape of the driver—he seemed to be the same height as the one on ████████, and to occupy the same amount of space behind the windshield. But he had a different ████████. That could be a ████████████████████████. He had to decide in about thirty seconds if he should abort. It was or wasn't a █████████████ ███████████. The car and driver ███████████████████. On the other hand, how many █████████████ were there in ████████? Just in █████ at this hour? It was too easy to get spooked and miss meetings. Ultimately, this was one of those moments where you gritted your teeth, held your breath, and just went.

LIGHTHOUSE was waiting at ████████████████████████████. Even here, his looming figure managed to be the most noticeable thing on the street. Bobby picked him up and drove onto the ████████████. The █████████████████ was gone two blocks later and nothing popped up in its place. Bobby went two miles on ████████████, then merged onto the █████████████. The highway was crowded, and the glaring headlights and dimmed street lamps made it seem even darker inside the car now. Bobby felt close to invisible. He'd felt like this at times during ops in ██████████, but never before in ██████.

He debriefed LIGHTHOUSE on ████████████████████████ ████████████████████ and ████████████████████████ ████████████████, then offered him coffee and cookies. They rode silently for a while, LIGHTHOUSE crunching the cookies loudly and sipping the coffee. Then LIGHTHOUSE said, "Tell me about fucking the American women."

"Same as anybody else," Bobby said.

"Yes, but, how do they do it? With . . . much of the . . . ooomph?"

It was the only time Bobby ever heard an ██████ say "ooomph."

"They're really just like other women," he said.

"No, please," said LIGHTHOUSE.

"Really."

When LIGHTHOUSE got out of the car on a quiet street a few blocks from the ████████████████, Bobby imagined running him over. The drop-off spot had been well selected, and no one would have seen.

32

Tom poured Bobby his coffee, then sat down across from him. When Bobby started eating his waffle, Tom started eating his.

"How was the festival?" Bobby asked.

"Very good, thank you, sir," Tom said.

Bobby stared at him, but Tom looked straight down as he ate.

"Tom, do you . . . where do you live, exactly?"

"In the ██████████."

"Have you ever gone to school?"

"I cannot, sir. I must help to support my family."

"But you . . . you read, don't you? I know you can read."

"Yes, sir."

"And write? Can you write?"

"I can read, sir."

"No writing?"

Tom looked back down. "I attended the ██████████████ ████████████ for only one year, sir."

33

In early summer, Bobby was sent to ██████████ to service a dead drop. He'd been in ██████ almost a year and hadn't left one single time. He hadn't gone back to the States to see his parents, he hadn't taken a weekend in ██████. He'd barely gone to the outskirts of ██████, and even that was only for operational purposes.

So he was glad for the assignment. And he liked traveling in alias. Despite the increased risk, he felt good in strange hotel rooms under fake names. It was as if he hardly existed. Which was certainly the right way to run an operation, and in truth felt infinitely more secure than ██ ██████████████████████████ he felt almost liberated from his ██████████ immunity.

The actual unloading of the drop was incredibly routine, but when Bobby got back to his hotel an old ██████████ woman started shouting at him in the lobby. He had no idea what she was saying and he was sure the police were about to break in and arrest him. He tried to smile at the woman and indicate with his hands that he meant her no harm.

Finally, a hotel clerk came over and sent the woman away. He explained to Bobby that she was upset because her son, who lived in America, had been turned down for a loan. Bobby couldn't decide if this made any sense or not, and he was awake all night, changing his mind back and forth about whether or not to destroy the ████ from the drop.

When he got back to ██████, he found out that NRLIGHTHOUSE had called for an emergency meeting while he was gone. A first-tour officer named Craig had gone to meet him. According to Craig, "The Lighthouse," as he called him, had found out that the CFO of ████████████████was pressuring two members of the ████ to help his company win a government contract for ████████████. He was expecting one of the members to offer the minister of ██████████ a licensing deal on ███████████████████████ on behalf of the CFO within a day or two.

Headquarters graded the intel report from the meeting "Excellent," which Bobby thought was a bit much. He knew he was probably pissed because someone else had debriefed his agent and gotten some of the credit for the intel. But still, he thought a "Good" or "Very Good" grade would be a little closer to the truth.

34

Bobby ran an ops test in which he ████████████████████ ███████████████████████████████████████ ████████████████████████████████. ██████████ ██████████████. Bobby wasn't terribly worried about him being deceptive after that.

(This was the only piece of tradecraft Bobby told me about where I doubted his judgment—I'd heard a story about a similar ops test where the whole thing had been misleading because the agent, assuming it was some sort of incriminating evidence, thought the officer secretly wanted him to hide it and never mention it again. You could understand that kind of misunderstanding.)

35

There was a flurry of progress with Ralph in July and August. While drinking at a ██████ in the ██ District, he told Bobby about a communiqué his embassy had received from ████ detailing a new government policy toward █████████. Bobby had responded by saying, "That's really interesting. You should know, I'm very careful who I repeat these things to about your country, but I think they're very useful to the people in my government who actually work to understand ████ and how we can set the best policy with regard to her."

The intel was very solid and would be eaten up by ██ analysts, State, and Commerce. Getting a report like this from a potential agent boded extremely well for the intel to come if they were recruited. When Bobby wrote it up, William didn't even say anything, he just nodded and gave him a smile that indicated he was very pleased. Headquarters responded a day later with a high grade and a special mention in their cable of how interesting TRACER's intel was becoming.

A few weeks later, Ralph and Bobby were eating dinner at an outdoor café near ██████ Park. Ralph, who normally ate lightly, had ordered two courses of ████████ and finished both. Near the end of the meal, while drinking tea, Ralph said, "This make understand my country more. Section Chief yesterday say we work support ████████████████████████████ ████████████████████████████ ████████████. This mistake. Maybe trade war. But if████████ ████████████████████████████ ████████████████████."

Not only was this first-rate intel again, it was so precise and cleanly offered that it almost certainly meant Ralph was starting to feed Bobby information on purpose. The development was picking up speed, just as it should have been, and Bobby felt a rush that made him realize just how flat and dull his tour had been up to this point. It was going to really kick into gear with TRACER's recruitment, and become more like his first tour, when his own abilities and the Agency's tools seemed to fit so perfectly together.

The following weekend, Bobby and Ralph went to the ██████████████ Nature Preserve near ████. The drive up was easy, and they got there before the heat of the day had fully set in. They strolled through the grounds for almost an hour, hardly talking at all. Deep inside the park, they came upon a ███████ temple in a clearing. They approached, and followed the directions on a placard for saying a quiet prayer and lighting a candle. Afterward, they sat on a bench across from the entrance.

"How are things at the Embassy?" Bobby asked.

"Criminals. Not below, but high. Ambassador send new rule for us. Cannot visit ██████████████████. He think we going prostitute. So stupid. One man in ██████ going prostitute, make trouble. With police. Drunk. So go back █████ now. Easy. But father and Vice-Minister ████████████████, now he stay. Ambassador want fight. No, only lose, but this answer. Hah."

"Is the vice-minister in the group with ██████████████? Or do the leaders of ███████████████████████████████ ████████████████████?"

"No, fight everyone. Safe with ████████████████watch for him."

Bobby shook his head to indicate that he shared Ralph's frustration. Then he said, "You know, ████████, I would like to make sure my country can continue to know what's really going on in ██████. The things you tell me like this are so useful. Would you be willing to keep helping me, and my government, to understand these types of things you explain to me?"

Ralph nodded. Bobby waited a few seconds, looking right at him. Then Ralph said, "Yes."

"Good. I think that will be very good for both of us. And I think I should do some things for you, in appreciation of your help. I'm sure it's not very easy, trying to plan for the future, with uncertainties about how crazy the ██████ economy can be and everything. You certainly know about this."

"I know," said Ralph.

"Perhaps I can help with this a bit."

"How help this?"

Ralph looked confused, and Bobby had a momentary panic that he'd misread him.

"Well, I can provide some help with financial matters," he said.

Ralph nodded slowly.

"What I can do is have some money for you. Not a fortune. A ████ ████████████████████████. Which could be helpful to you, like you're being helpful to me, and my government. And I could put it somewhere safe, and private, for you. It's not really a good idea for me to give you money straight. Not here. Too easy for people to notice, if you spend any of it. Because why do you suddenly have this extra money to spend? But probably you'd want to save it anyway. For a rainy day, as we say. For the future. So it's better, I think, in this special place I can set up for you. Better to have your money in America anyway. Then one day, if you retire, in ██████, maybe things will have eased up there by then. Easier to have money and everything. If not, we still have ways we can get it to you. Or you might come visit the States, too. You could use it there. Or pass it on to your children, if you have children someday. A fair amount could get saved up."

"Okay," Ralph said.

They sat quietly for a minute.

"Ralph, we'll have to make some changes now. No one should see us together after today. That'll be hard, it'll be harder to have dinner and do the things we enjoy in our friendship. But it's for the best. We don't want anyone to be suspicious. So I'll explain how we can meet, how we can contact each other, without anyone knowing about it, or getting suspicious. I'm a professional with this, and I can keep you safe and . . . things unknown. Still, it has to be said . . . you understand there are risks, yes? But I'll do everything I can to keep this safe and secure, and we'll make sure no one finds out about it."

Ralph nodded.

"I'll get into everything in more detail next time we see each other. But even then I want us to start to use some of the techniques to keep everything quiet and between us. So I'll pick you up in my car next week, at a specific place. And I'll show you some of the things I'm talking about. Are you free on Thursday night?"

"Okay."

"Go to the corner of ▮▮▮ and ▮▮▮▮▮▮▮ at eight o'clock at night. Don't get there early. Walk around if you have to. And at eight o'clock, I'll pull up. You know my car. Get in, and we'll go for a ride. Do you understand?"

"Yes, I understand."

Bobby looked hard into Ralph's eyes. Ralph looked back at him then turned toward the temple. Bobby followed his gaze. Two thin lines of smoke were still rising up from the candles they'd lit earlier by the door.

It had taken one year, just as he'd predicted.

36

▮▮▮▮▮▮▮▮▮ was dark, short, and likely to be empty, but when Bobby turned onto it there was a vagrant sitting in a semicircle of garbage against a wall on the west side of the street and an old man walking down, probably from ▮▮▮▮, on the east side. It was far too clumsy a setup for surveillants, and Bobby quickly focused on Ralph, who was standing at the pickup point wearing an old baseball cap. The hat made him stand out much more than it disguised him.

Bobby glided to a stop in front of him and Ralph hurried into the car. After Bobby pulled away from the curb he squeezed Ralph's shoulder, then gave him a cover story and had him repeat it back. For the next hour, as they drove through ▮▮▮▮▮ and ▮▮▮▮▮▮ ▮▮▮▮▮▮▮▮▮▮▮, he gave him his first lesson in tradecraft. He ▮ ▮▮▮▮▮▮▮▮▮▮▮▮▮▮▮▮▮▮▮▮▮▮▮▮▮▮▮▮▮▮▮▮▮ ▮▮▮▮▮▮▮▮▮▮▮▮▮▮▮▮▮▮▮▮▮▮▮▮▮▮▮▮▮▮▮▮

Ralph took it off and put it in his lap.

██████. His affect was essentially flat, though he had a sharper mind for this than Bobby had expected, an almost mathematical ability to absorb and repeat back the details as well as the reasons for everything.

Nearing ████, Bobby brought out the contract. (I never understood why the Agency insisted on these—maybe they added a certain clarity to the enterprise, but I thought they showed a lack of trust. They also had to be successfully transported back to the Station concealed in ████████████████████████████████████. To me, it seemed reckless to have them out on the street at all.) Bobby went over the main points, then handed the contract to Ralph. He signed it without comment.

As he turned onto ████████████████, Bobby told Ralph they would review everything they had discussed at their next meeting and then move on to the next level with ████████████ ████████████████. They went over the cover story in advance, then Bobby dropped him near the ████████████████ ████████████████.

37

Tom was sitting at the kitchen table when Bobby got home from work late on a Monday afternoon. He had two pencils and a dirty composition book in front of him.

Bobby took off his jacket, got the books from the Embassy library out of his briefcase, and sat down.

"It's almost like drawing," he said. "Can you draw?"

Tom opened up the composition book and drew a chicken.

"Not bad," Bobby said. "Now try this." He took the pencil from Tom and drew an "A."

38

At his second post-recruitment meeting with Ralph, Bobby picked him up on a side street off the main ████████████████ ████████████████, so as part of their cover story they could say that they'd
██
████████████████████████████████. After going over the cover, Bobby asked him a number of questions about himself to fill in a few holes on his 201 form. Then he told him in detail about the kinds of information he was hoping to get from him. As an example to show that he understood, Ralph ████████████████████████████
████████ he'd heard about from a colleague in the political section, and also talked about the tenuous ties between the ambassador and a small clique of ████████████████████████████████
████████████████████████████.

Bobby had brought sandwiches and hot tea, and he took them out. Normally, he wouldn't have eaten anything himself, but Ralph's seriousness was almost too intense, and he wanted to add a casual element— or at least a routine element—which meant having a sandwich with him and appearing relaxed. So with one hand on the wheel, he started eating the ████████ with the other. But between driving, keeping up the conversation with Ralph, staying mentally a step ahead on his route, and keeping his eyes open for surveillance, eating at the same time was one piece too many. He had the odd feeling of his brain hitting its limit.

After Ralph finished his sandwich, Bobby went back to ████████████████████████. He asked Ralph if he understood what they'd discussed last time, then he had him repeat ████████████████████
██

back to him. Then he went into ████████████████████████████

Back at home, Bobby had a glass of wine and thought about where he might want to go on his next tour. He could probably get a slot outside of the Division, even a soft post in Western Europe somewhere, where he could relax and maybe find a French or Swedish girlfriend to fall in love with. But he knew he'd never request that. Even if it was tougher in ███████████ for fifty different reasons, it mattered more, and that was why he was in this business in the first place.

39

The first word Bobby taught Tom to write was "cat." He had him go through his workbook until he found all three letters, then he told him to write a "C," an "A," and a "T" right next to each other (I thought why not just teach him "S-P-Y"). When Tom finished, his word looked more like "oar" than "cat." Bobby said, "You could be a doctor," then immediately regretted it when Tom said, "I do not think so, sir." For the rest of the lesson, they worked only on "C."

40

It was probably unprecedented, but Bobby decided to have a meeting with TDTRACER at the ███████. Not only would it get them out of the car, but they certainly wouldn't look conspicuous there, between the ██.

They met at the entrance on a Saturday afternoon. It was too crowded to debrief in the main pavilion, so they talked about the art and Bobby kept his eyes on the other visitors. After about an hour, they went out to the gardens behind the ████████ where they had more privacy. Bobby asked Ralph for the latest on the ambassador and the ongoing negotiations with ██████████████████████ ██████. He also asked if Ralph knew anything about ██████████ ████████████████████████. He told him to keep his ears open for information on it, but he made it plain that he didn't want him to take any risks. He gave several examples of how over-eagerness to obtain information could create problems, trying to strike a balance between alarming Ralph enough to keep him careful but not so much that he'd never do anything again.

When they were done debriefing, Bobby gave Ralph a lesson in walking countersurveillance. Some of the features of the ████████ grounds, with their natural blinds, traps, and turns, were so perfectly suited to the task, and at the same time created so many unique problems, that Bobby found himself unusually interested in what he was talking about. At least one of the major tenets of █████████████ ████████ seemed to break down when you put ████████████████at right angles to each other. Bobby had to think fast so he wouldn't look like an amateur, but he came up with something of a work-around, which was to █████████████████████████████████████ ████████████████.

Bobby ended up so involved in the lesson that he didn't notice Ralph wasn't following everything with his usual attentiveness. When they turned off of a long, sheltered pathway running along the ███ and onto a brick path heading back toward the main ███, Ralph said, "Bobby, we are friends for this?"

Bobby tried to look shocked and a little bit hurt. "No, of course not," he said. "No. This was . . . all of it . . . a real surprise. When we met, I just thought you were this interesting guy. That we had some things in common. It was fun to talk to you, spend time with you, learn about you and . . . yes, your country, because I'm interested in these things. That's why I like to live, and serve, abroad. But frankly, I never thought you'd have access to the type of information we look for. It just didn't seem like it. With your job. And then, it turns out, you did. I wasn't sure what to do. So then, this happened. But no, it wasn't what I thought at first. It's not why we're friends."

Ralph was looking in front of them at a small band of children who were lining up around the ███████████.

"I promise," Bobby said.

He remembered a meeting he'd had at the Farm where an instructor named Kim had been playing the role of a ███████████ minister who he'd recently recruited. He'd pulled over to drop her off in front of a municipal lot where she was parked. Instead of getting out of her car, she'd said, "You lied to me about everything. You never cared about me, or even liked me. You just wanted me for this." Bobby had said almost word-for-word the same things he'd just said to Ralph. Later, Kim had told him he'd handled it beautifully.

He knew it had worked on Ralph, too. His hurt expression had disappeared, and he looked almost cheerful as they walked toward the exit. But Bobby suddenly felt sorry for him. Somewhere in his imagination he pictured him as a sad kid walking alone through a playground.

41

Tom worked as hard as ever during the day—the house continued to be spotless, and the garden was newly ringed with a waist-high canopy of broad-leaved ████████. But now, every night that Tom wasn't working at the General's, he stayed late at the house to practice his writing. Bobby would come home and find him in the kitchen bent over his composition book. If it wasn't a lesson night, Tom would pack up as soon as Bobby came in, say, "Good night, sir," and with his eyes down walk out the back door. Bobby had the sense he was waiting to make sure he got home from work safely, and he was both a little bit touched and somewhat annoyed.

After their lesson one night, Tom said, "I have written something for my mother."

"Okay," Bobby said.

Tom handed him several sheets of paper. The first one read:

> Mother,
>   I can write now. I will write a beautiful story about you and about our family. Also, my big hope is to get a cat. I love you.
>
>   ████████

What followed was a story about a young boy, obviously Tom, who finds five million ██████ and brings them home. The boy's father tells him to return the money to where he found it, which he dutifully does. At the end of the story, the boy, his siblings, and his parents are sitting around a hearth, and the mother says that love is better than money.

The handwriting remained blockish and uneven, but there wasn't a spelling error in the entire story.

"It's very good," said Bobby. He almost added "She'll love it."

42

Bobby came home early one Friday afternoon, looking forward to a quiet night with no meetings and no parties. After he went into the house and made himself a cup of tea, he realized he hadn't seen Tom. Tea in hand, he went out to the garden to look for him.

He wasn't in the garden or in the yard behind the house. Bobby assumed he'd left early for some reason, but he went over to the tool shed anyway to look there. When he opened the door and stepped in, he heard what sounded like a cat panting. The shed was crowded with all sorts of junk and it took a moment before Bobby made out a human shape lying on the floor against the wall. It was Tom. Bobby could sense as much as see that he was running a high fever.

"Tom, what's wrong?" he asked.

"Very sorry, very sorry," Tom muttered.

"You're sick," Bobby said.

"No, sir," Tom said.

"What happened? Did you just . . . did anything happen? When did you get this way?"

"I am fine, sir. Please. I will go home very soon."

Bobby bent over and tried to pick Tom up, but he writhed out of his arms.

"Please, sir."

"Tom, I'm taking you inside."

"No, sir. Please. I will go. I promise to go. I am sorry."

Bobby grabbed him more forcefully and practically ripped him up off the floor. As he carried him to the house, Tom stopped struggling, though it was clearly out of weakness rather than resignation.

Bobby took him upstairs and lay him down on the bed in the guest

room. He fluffed the pillow under his head and went for a thermom-
eter. Tom's temperature was 104.

"I have to take you to the hospital," Bobby said.

"No, please. Do not take me there. I will go home."

Bobby realized Tom was right, the hospitals in ███ were a disaster, especially for a boy from the ███████. He looked at his
watch. It was just after four o'clock.

"Wait here," he said.

He ran down to the kitchen and poured a glass of cold water,
grabbed aspirin from the bathroom, and went back to the bedroom.
He practically forced the pills and water down Tom's throat.

"I won't forget you. I'll be back very soon," he said.

He ran out to his car and drove back to the ██████.

He got there at four thirty. He sprinted up the stairs and made it to
the infirmary just as the doctor was walking out.

"I need to see you," said Bobby, using his hand to hold the infirmary door open.

"You look all right to me," the doctor said. "It's Friday afternoon.
Come see me Monday."

"It's not me, it's my . . . well, it's my houseboy. He's got a hundred
and four temperature."

"I only treat American ████."

"I know, I know," said Bobby. "But I can't take this kid to the hospital. He'll wait all night. He could be dead by the time they get to him."

"I don't think he'll die from a hundred and four," said the doctor.
"Look, I need to get home. Come see me Monday."

Bobby used his body to press the doctor back inside the infirmary,
then he shut the door.

"Doctor, I'm sorry," he said. "I really am. But I need your help."

"And I can't help you. Even if I wanted to, the rules I operate under
are clear. American ████████ only. Now get out of my way."

Bobby barely resisted the impulse to hit him. It was good that he
did, because in addition to being unlikely to produce the desired result, the doctor had been in the navy, and Bobby had heard he was a
theater-wide boxing champion.

"Doc," he said, "there are a lot of favors I could do for you. Things that you might really want someday."

"No go," said the doctor.

They were standing by the desk in the waiting room, and Bobby picked up the phone and called the Station. He asked for William, and got him immediately.

"I need some help in the infirmary," Bobby said. "Sorry to bother you."

"Be right there," William said.

Bobby couldn't believe he was calling the COS of a major CIA Station down to the ███████ infirmary to help with a problem that he should have been able to handle on his own. But William had treated him from day one like a real friend, and Bobby didn't think it was an act. Now he'd find out.

William walked in half a minute later. The doctor's eyebrows went up just enough for Bobby to see that he knew who William was. Bobby said, "My houseboy, Tom, is sick as a dog. Hundred and four fever. If I take him to the hospital, who knows what'll happen. I need a good doctor for him."

"Friday night," the doctor said. "And I have clear rules about who I'm supposed to treat. And this houseboy is not one of those people. They'll take care of him at the hospital, ███████ hospitals aren't as bad as they say."

"Hundred and four," William said to the doctor. "That sounds high. Can't a fever that high be dangerous?"

"It can be, of course," the doctor said. "But usually it'll go down with a few aspirin. Did you give him aspirin?"

"Yes," said Bobby.

"Don't you want to help this boy, no matter what the rules are?" William said. "I often find doctors feel that way."

"He can go to a hospital," the doctor said, recovered now from the surprise of seeing William. "It isn't like I'm abandoning him to die."

William stared hard at the doctor for a few seconds, letting him know that he was appraising him. Then he walked up to him and put a hand on his shoulder.

"I've got an idea," William said. "You go home with Bobby. You bring your doctor's bag. You treat this boy and make sure he gets better."

"Why should I?" said the doctor.

"Because then I won't call Admiral Rickens and tell him it's a disgrace that you ever wore a naval uniform."

The doctor's face froze. A moment later, he went into his office, came back with his doctor's bag, and led the way out the door.

Bobby had him back at his house in twenty minutes. Tom was unconscious when they got there but breathing more calmly than he had been before. The doctor woke him up and performed what seemed like a very thorough examination. Then he gave him an injection in his arm.

"He'll be fine," he said to Bobby. "It's ████████, fairly common here. I'll give you a short course of antibiotics for him. He'll be better in four or five days. Keep him in bed until then."

Tom didn't seem any better the next day, though by late afternoon he'd gotten out of bed, dressed himself in his dirty clothes, and staggered downstairs before Bobby caught him and carried him back up. The day after that, his fever was down to a hundred and two. He begged Bobby to let him go home, insisting over and over again that it was wrong for him to be sleeping in the house. Bobby just told him to be quiet. He brought him tea and crackers every few hours and sat in the room with him when he looked delirious.

On the third day, Bobby had to go to work. Tom's fever was down to a hundred and one, and he could sit up now. But Bobby didn't want to leave him alone. He thought about letting one of the guards into the house to watch him, but he didn't trust them. Finally, he put a phone by the bed, gave Tom his office number, and left.

At work, Bobby sat silently during morning staff. Afterward, William came up to him and said, "How's the boy?"

"Fine, fine," Bobby said. "He's doing better."

"He'll be fine," William said.

"Yeah, I know," Bobby said.

"Maybe you should take the day off. Stay home with him. Or if you want to stay here, maybe a little work would be good for you."

Bobby was momentarily puzzled. He didn't see why William would suggest he take the day off. He decided to stay, but he couldn't focus well and he didn't get anything done.

When he got home, Tom looked almost normal. The next morning, when Bobby checked his room, he was gone. Bobby started to run downstairs, but as soon as he smelled waffles he slowed down, then walked casually into the kitchen.

"Feeling better?" Bobby said.

"Thank you, sir," Tom said.

On his drive to work, Bobby opened all the windows and took a deep breath. There was a fine dust in the breeze, and the rancid smell of ██ manure swept into the car. Everything snapped back into place. Bobby started thinking about TDTRACER and whether or not he could task him more specifically at this point. He thought TRACER was up to it, but it probably made more sense to wait a little longer.

43

A few nights later, Bobby came home late after a developmental meeting with an ████████████ and was surprised to find Tom there waiting for him. It was almost eleven o'clock, and it wasn't a night when they were supposed to have a lesson.

"I would like to show you something," Tom said.

He handed Bobby a piece of notebook paper. On it was written:

Dear General ████,

I write to thank you for my job with you and the help you give to me. I want very much to serve you for many years.

I write also to tell you about the man I serve on ██ Street. His name is Bobby Goldstein. He works at the American ████████. He asks me to eat with him. He teaches me to write

so I will be educated. He is an American man who can be an
example of a very good man. Maybe you will be his friend.

Bobby read the note and, before he could stop himself, grimaced.
Tom saw the expression and was crestfallen.

"No, no, it's okay," Bobby said. "It's a very nice note."

"The General is a very important man. He should know that a
man who lives near to him is an important man, too."

"I know. Thank you, Tom. Really."

Tom looked like he was about to run away.

"Tom," Bobby said, "listen . . . I don't know how to explain this
exactly. I think maybe it's a grown-up thing. But I don't want you to
give the General that note."

"I will not," said Tom.

"Good. Can you just . . . can you just trust me, Tom, that it's better this way?"

"Yes."

"No, I mean, really. Really understand that I'll look out for your
best interests, and that if I say something's better for you, you should
have faith in me?"

Tom's sour expression seemed to lift a little. "Yes, okay," he said.

44

The signal from TRACER came in at seven o'clock, just a few minutes after Bobby got home from work. ███████████████████
████████████████████████████████. It wasn't nearly enough
time. Bobby had made it clear you had to give more notice, and if you
didn't, there might not be anybody there to meet you.

He called the Station but everyone was gone, so he had to dial
back to the ██████ and tell the Watch Officer to contact the DCOS
and give him the code for an ████████████████. Then he sat down

in the den for ten minutes and went over his preplanned ████████
SDR. With so little time before the meeting, he adjusted the last leg
and put himself on ███ so he could cut off at any time and go to
████████, where their ████████████████████████, half a block
from ██████ in front of a ████████.

He left the house with exactly an hour and forty-five minutes to go.

The sidewalks in ████████████████ were fairly crowded with
pedestrians, but the streets were almost empty. It was a good trade-off
for the first leg of an SDR if you ████████████████████████████
████████████████████████████████. Bobby looked at everyone he
passed, but he knew it was a waste of time. Even if there were a surveillant, they'd be a ████████████████, and never show up again later in
the route. He ███
██
██
████████████████████ with an hour and fifteen minutes to go. The
██████bridge was crowded, but he could make that up at the ████████.
He started getting nervous in ████████████. He must have passed six
or seven men who looked directly at him, which was perfectly normal for a Westerner in ████████ at night, but on the way to an
emergency meeting, it was unnerving. ████████████████████████
██
████████████████████████. Forty-two minutes. He went a little faster
than he should have over to ██████ in case he got slowed down on
████████. But it was clear. A small, junky sedan followed him for
three blocks on ████, turned with him onto ████, and six blocks later
turned with him again onto ████████. It was too obvious to worry
about, especially since the car was right behind him most of the
way, but Bobby memorized the dark shape of the head and shoulders in the rearview mirror anyway. The car sped up and turned off
on ████████. Almost certainly someone going to ████████████████
██████████████████████████████████.

He was onto the third leg before he really had time to wonder
what the hell was going on. If it had been NRLIGHTHOUSE, he
wouldn't have worried too much about it. But Ralph wouldn't call an

emergency meeting without a real reason. At least Bobby didn't think he would.

At ten minutes, he was three miles and ███████ from the pickup point. Bobby hoped to hell Ralph would follow instructions and not arrive early and then stand there like an idiot waiting for him. But if he was nervous about something, who knew what he'd do? █████ was empty and he slowed way down to kill the time. Very alerting if anyone was watching, but there didn't seem to be a soul around. If they were on him at this point, they'd get the pickup anyway. But it looked, and felt, clear.

Coasting toward the spot, Bobby saw Ralph standing on the edge of the sidewalk with his hands in the pockets of a boxy ██████ rain-coat. Then he saw a small sedan turn onto ████ two blocks behind him. His heart raced, and he almost slammed onto the gas pedal and sped past Ralph. He braked lightly instead, and as the car came up on him, he saw it was the same shape as the one on ██████ but newer and a different color. It went by, and Bobby pulled up in front of Ralph.

"You okay?" he asked as soon as they turned the first corner.

Ralph didn't answer. Bobby turned to look at him and saw him staring glassily at the windshield.

"Ralph, what's wrong?"

"Sister . . . mother . . . I . . ." His voice was shaking.

"Your sister? Your mother? What?"

"They take sister."

Bobby turned onto ████████. They could cruise down it for several miles without having to worry and he could focus on Ralph before turning onto ██████.

"What do you mean?"

"Take sister. Mother . . . call. Today. In apartment. Say men . . . men come take sister."

"Somebody took your sister?"

He had to focus on the road for a curve around ████, but in his peripheral vision he saw Ralph nodding.

"Do you . . . do you know who?"

"She say men. Two men. Like . . . look like police."

Bobby turned onto ███████████. If he doubled back on ████ and got onto ███████████, he could take him to the safehouse in ███████████.

"Ralph, I'm going to take you somewhere. Where we can talk."

"Where?" said Ralph, turning to look at him now.

"It's a special place we have. To have a conversation or something, when you don't want to be driving around like this. We should sit down."

Ralph turned toward Bobby. His lips started to move but then stopped. He turned back and faced the windshield. Bobby wondered momentarily if Ralph was afraid of him, if he thought he might be taking him somewhere to kill him.

They drove in silence for a few minutes, but when Bobby turned onto ███████, Ralph said, "Where go?"

"We have a safe place to have meetings. I'll take you there, we can talk more easily."

"Why . . . why we . . ."

Ralph couldn't finish his sentence.

In the hills of ███████, Bobby checked every driveway they went past and looked into the windows of every house, light and dark. There weren't any guards here, and it felt like half the neighborhood was already asleep. He'd never been to the safehouse and when he didn't see a small park he was expecting on a corner, he thought he'd screwed up the directions. But he went over everything again in his head, and he remembered it clearly. The park appeared a few blocks later. Bobby turned onto an almost totally dark street two blocks past it. A minute later he killed his headlights and pulled into a garage next to a small bungalow.

Inside the house, half the curtains were already drawn, and he closed the rest. In the darkness, he searched for the lights, which he'd forgotten to locate before closing the curtains. He finally got the lights on and Ralph seated at a little Formica table in the living room. Bobby went to the kitchen and came back with a bottle of whiskey and two glasses. He didn't want to drink, but he poured for both of them, and Ralph immediately started taking a series of small sips.

"What's going on?" Bobby asked.

"Mother . . . in ███████ . . . call every week. Two week. She call three day before, now call tonight. Say two men come, go inside house, take sister. They take sister."

Bobby tried to remember if he knew that Ralph had a sister. He must have put it on the 201, but somehow he couldn't remember.

"How old's your sister?" he asked.

"She twenty . . . nine."

"She lives with your mother?"

"Yes."

"What does she do?"

"She . . . account. Work in account. At factory in ██████████."

"Does she have any . . . is there anybody who would want to take her? Any . . . people who don't like her?"

"Nice girl. Very good. Very, very good."

"You said your mother thought it was the police?"

"Look like police. ██████████, police look like . . . police. Always same. Suit, shoes. Police."

"Are you sure?"

"Mother say."

"Is there anybody . . . any boyfriend?"

"No. No boyfriend. ███████ very nice. Nice girl. Home, with mother."

"No boyfriend?"

"No."

"Somebody . . . mad at her about anything?"

"No! Nobody mad! Nobody!"

"Is there anybody . . . at the factory . . . anybody who might have problems with money? Something with her work? The accounting? Something with the money at the factory? Somebody stealing? That she might have known about? Anything like that?"

"No. I don't think."

Bobby tried to think of more questions. He could hear Ralph's breathing across the table, almost a pant, with the smell of whiskey on it now.

"Because me?" Ralph asked quietly. "What we do? Because me?"

"Oh, Ralph, I don't think so. No. It's almost impossible. We've been very careful. We've run what we call a very secure operation. Completely secure. I don't think anyone could know."

"Why police? For sister? Why?"

"There could be a lot of reasons. I don't know. But I can put a lot of resources into play, and see if anyone knows anything. Maybe we can find something out. And maybe your mother will know something more. They didn't say . . . did they say anything to her?"

"Take sister, go. Say nothing."

"Well, maybe she'll know more soon."

"No, nothing. Police do . . . police do."

"I know. But listen, Ralph, let's try to calm down. Not panic. We don't have any idea what's going on. We don't even know absolutely that it's the police. I know it's hard, but let's try to figure this out. Is there . . . tell me more about your sister."

"She work ██████████ textiles factory. Good girl. School in ██████ ████████ Account School. Very good girl. Very good. Love mother. Love me. Only small, like nothing, when father die. Very alone. Small. Never do bad. Never. For police, no. No."

"Never married?"

"No."

"Who was her last boyfriend?"

"No! No boyfriend! With mother!"

"Okay, okay. Let's keep thinking. I think we're going to have to . . . we need to get more information."

For the next hour, Bobby went back and forth between pacing up and down the living room and sitting across from Ralph, asking questions. But nothing led to anything. ██████ was twenty-nine. She was an accountant. She was single. She'd never had any trouble at work. Never had any trouble with men. Didn't participate in any political activities, underground or otherwise. She was an accountant. She worked at a textile factory.

Ralph stayed virtually motionless in his chair, but his breathing never slowed down, and he was sweating so much Bobby was afraid he might collapse. He couldn't calm him down, but he did force him to drink several glasses of water. Finally, when he couldn't think of any more questions, Bobby set up a meeting for the next night. He went over the pickup spot and the cover story multiple times to make sure Ralph was getting it. Then he drove him back out of the hills, saying over and over, "We'll figure it out. Hopefully it'll be okay. We'll figure it out."

45

After he dropped Ralph off at the ███████, Bobby improvised an SDR to get back to the Station. At first he was in a zone, executing the turns and seeing the ████████ with total confidence and precision. But then he hit a multiple █████████████ and knew he was clean. Suddenly, he couldn't believe what was happening. He knew he didn't have enough information to figure it out, but whatever it was, there was a possibility it was his fault. That he'd screwed something up, made some tradecraft error or error in judgment that had led to this.

It could easily be the end of his career, or at least the end of his golden-boy status.

And Ralph's sister . . . Bobby hadn't even remembered that he had a sister. Now she was God knew where, for God knew what reason. He found himself wondering what she looked like. Then he imagined her being beaten by █████ policemen.

He caught himself. The important thing now was to stay calm. He knew he could do it—this was his strong suit, what he'd always been best at, staying cool and making good decisions under pressure. Maybe he'd had some minor trouble with nerves since getting to █████, but now, with the chips down, he was fine. He focused back on the mirror, and his awareness sharpened and took in all 360 degrees as everything else drifted away.

When he was within a half mile of the Station he did a ████████ ████████████. He hated going there this late ████████████

██

████. When he walked in, he told the Watch Officer to contact William and the DCOS and let them know he was back from the meeting. Then he went ████████ and unlocked the vault. He got Ralph's file out, and started writing.

Half an hour later William came in, and before Bobby could even start talking to him the DCOS arrived. They stood next to Bobby at his desk while he explained what had happened.

"Okay, let's take it easy," said William after he'd finished. "We don't know what this is. It could be anything."

The DCOS turned to William and said, "We need to put this together very tightly. Steven's going to go berserk if this is ops related."

"Okay. Bobby, let's see what you've got."

He scanned the cable over Bobby's shoulder.

"Fine. Add a timeline of everything, I mean everything that's happened with TDTRACER. And put it in ████████████████. I'm getting on Milton's radar about this now. Stu, why don't you check in with Alan, let him know Bobby's cable is coming." He looked at his watch. "Okay, they'll still be there. Let's go."

Twenty minutes later, Bobby's cable was out and he was in William's office with the DCOS.

"What did you set up?" William asked.

"Tomorrow night, eight o'clock, pickup at the ████████████."

"That's too soon."

"I think it's fine," said the DCOS.

"I don't want to alert anybody by getting sloppy," William said.

"We can't keep him floating out there like this," said the DCOS.

"He's not going to do anything risky with his sister missing and us working on it. Bobby, move the meeting back to Saturday night."

"It's too late," said the DCOS. "Better to move than wait. He could be gone by Saturday. He could be gone already."

"All right, all right. Keep your meeting. We'll see where we're at tomorrow."

46

The next morning, Bobby was driving by ███████████ when he saw ███████████████████████████ ██ ███████████. He squinted at it, actually wondering for a moment if there was any other way it could have gotten there. But there was no mistaking it. Ralph was signaling that he'd loaded a dead drop. (An agent usually loads a dead drop at a prearranged time, then leaves a signal to confirm that it can be retrieved. It's less common to use them in an emergency, because if the C/O isn't looking for the signal, it's easy to miss it.)

Bobby turned off ███████ and onto ████. He needed time to think. What the hell was Ralph doing leaving a dead drop? Did he even know how to do it? Bobby had explained the basics, that was true. And he'd gotten the signal right (assuming he was, actually, leaving a dead drop). But the training had been pretty rudimentary. Bobby certainly hadn't expected him to use it yet. He'd planned to go over everything two or three more times, and do a dry run together. He'd told Ralph this was something for the future (though he hadn't said that it might not be used at all unless he was back in ██████, and that then it would be with another officer).

Under normal circumstances, Bobby wouldn't have unloaded the drop until that night at the earliest. It was best to let a site settle so that ██████████████████████████████████ also were supposed to have a meeting with Station management before unloading any static ███████████. But this was an emergency situation. He could go to the Station, go over everything with William and the DCOS, and waste the entire morning while Ralph was out somewhere waiting for his help. Or he could unload the drop. They were always telling you to take initiative, to make decisions yourself if you could. It was early, but he was going to do it. (The truth was, they pushed initiative and absolute adherence to the rules at the same time—when the two came into conflict, it was hard to know what to do, and how things worked out tended to determine whether or not you had made the right decision.)

He stopped at a ███████ and picked up ████████████████████ ██████████ while trying to plan the most extensive SDR of his life in his head. He ██████████████████████████████████████. It was eight thirty when he left with two ████████████████ and a satchel of ██████████ under his arm.

██
██
██
██████████████████████.
██
██
███.
██
██
███████████████████████████████████.

He coasted up to the ████████████. It was right where it was supposed to be. He'd hardly gone into any detail at all with Ralph about how to ████████████████████ and he had it ███████████████████████████ ██. Bobby almost laughed when he pulled it out of the ██████. It was completely ridiculous, all wrong, and yet he couldn't help thinking it was perfect. No one would ever ██. It reminded him of one a student had made at the Farm during their first dead drop exercise. It had been a ██████████████████████████ ██. The instructors had chewed her out in front of the whole class, but by the time they were done they were shaking their heads and laughing. One of them finally said, "Or it's possible you're a genius."

Bobby drove out and turned onto ████████████. The site had been clear—there was no way anyone could have seen him unless they were literally right behind him, which no one was. ███████ looked clear, too. He was as sure as you could be that he was clean.

Two more hours of SDR, then Bobby went to the Station. He kept his head down as he walked through the hall, hoping to avoid having to talk to anybody. He was normally hyped up after any kind of op, but now he felt exhausted. He ██████████████████, went to his desk, and opened Ralph's package. A slip of paper inside read:

Maybe go home. Section Chief say.
Why? Help.

"Fuck," Bobby muttered. If there was any way for this to get worse, it just did. He took the message into the DCOS's office and handed it across the desk.

"What's this?" the DCOS said before reading it.

"TRACER signaled for a drop this morning. I thought I'd better get it right away, with everything that's going on."

"You what?"

"I unloaded the drop."

"When did he signal?"

"Early this morning."

"You unloaded a drop right after he left it?" His voice was getting louder.

"I thought under the circumstances . . ." Bobby said.

The DCOS read the note.

"In case he was in trouble, needed immediate help . . . ," Bobby said.

"You do not unload a dead drop like that without talking to me first!" he yelled.

William walked in. "You got a drop?" he said.

"Yeah," said Bobby.

William held out his hand and the DCOS handed him the note. He read it and sighed.

"Do you know how much you could have jeopardized?" the DCOS said.

"Oh, take it easy," said William. "Were you clean?"

"Yeah," said Bobby.

"You sure?" said the DCOS.

"Sure as you can be."

"All right," said William. "What does this mean?"

"Well, it's not good," said the DCOS.

"Obviously," said William.

"Why would they call him home?" said Bobby.

"It's looking more likely that they're onto something," said William.

"Could be a coincidence," said the DCOS. "Still could be something else."

"He hasn't told you about any trouble with anybody?" William asked.

"No."

"What's his expertise again? In economics?"

"████████████."

"Could be calling him back for something on that."

"He's not at that level," said the DCOS.

"Fuck," said Bobby, rubbing his forehead. He knew he shouldn't be showing outward signs of being upset—the "fuck" was okay, the forehead rubbing was not—and he lowered his hand slowly.

"Why's this guy using a drop anyway?" William asked. "When did you recruit him, three or four months ago?"

"I know," said Bobby. "It's crazy. I haven't even finished training him on it yet. And why not a ████████ signal? I don't know. He's called back home, he doesn't want to see me because . . . he's scared. Figures it's riskier to see me than do the drop? He thought I taught him this so he could use it, so now he's using it?"

"That's complicated, what's simpler?" said the DCOS.

"What's simpler? I don't know. You think he's a double? And he's . . . what . . . setting me up? To get arrested? A ████████ guy in ████? That doesn't make sense. What else? If he's a double, what?"

"No, no, I don't see that," said William. "Let's look at the possibilities. They might be bringing him home. Fast or slow. They might be interrogating him in the embassy. He might have scrammed, sensing the hammer about to drop. They might not be onto anything at all. If he shows up at tonight's meeting—"

"Cancel it," said the DCOS. "If he's out there, how much sneaking around do you want this guy to do in one day?"

"If he's leaving, we have to get him first," said William. "You'll be okay. Just keep your eyes open, be careful."

47

Bobby turned the corner, squinted into the darkness, and saw an empty door frame.

48

Let's try again," said William.

"One more time," said the DCOS.

"Okay," said Bobby. "I guess if he's gone, he's gone."

"If they're moving that fast, it's trouble," William said. "Let's hope he shows up this time."

"If they've got him and they're getting stuff out of him, they could be looking for Bobby at these meetings," said the DCOS. "Let's set up some CS [countersurveillance]."

"I'd go armed, too," William said.

"Well, if it's the ████, that's not gonna help," said the DCOS.

"I'm just thinking there's an outside chance the ████ or █████ could be involved in this. Better safe than sorry."

"Send the signal, Bobby," the DCOS said.

██
██
███████████████████████████████████
██
███
██
██
███████████████████████████████████████

He couldn't stop feeling the gun against his hip. He didn't know what the hell he was going to do with it anyway. If the ████ was there, obviously he wouldn't pull it. The odds of some kind of terrorist assault seemed remote. Even if that did happen, either countersurveillance would catch it or he'd be ambushed, in which case he'd be gone before he got a chance to pull his gun anyway.

He felt watched in the same way he had while running SDRs at the Farm. Instructors watched you in the same way CS watched you—they were on your side, but if you did anything wrong, it went in their report. They were spaced at █████████████████████████████████
██
██
██████████████████████████████████.

About a mile from the pickup he felt his legs starting to shake, first in his calves, then moving up to the backs of his thighs. He gripped the steering wheel and forced himself to focus. He worried that if he shook any worse he might lose control of the car. Then he thought about Ralph. He hadn't really been thinking about him during the SDR, or he had been but only in some remote way. He still didn't know what was going on, or if it was related to what he was doing with Ralph. But if it was, Ralph could spend ten, twenty years—the rest of his life—in prison. He could be executed. Still, Bobby couldn't figure out what any of this could have to do with his sister. They easily could have just called Ralph back home. Unless they thought he'd flee, and the sister was insurance. But it didn't quite add up, which was a slight comfort.

He turned onto ███. A man of Ralph's height and build was walking south toward ███, and Bobby's heart jumped. But almost as soon as he saw him he realized it wasn't Ralph. Bobby drove past the pickup spot.

He had twenty extra minutes to drive around and wait. If Ralph came, CS would ████████████, and Bobby would make a second pass. He drove up ████, around a ██████████████, and down ████. At every corner, he imagined getting ████████████████████████ and turning back toward ██████.

████████████████████ Bobby checked his watch. At ten minutes, he knew it was over. At twenty minutes, he kept straight on ████ and headed toward home.

49

The next night, he went to the pickup spot for the alternate ████████████████████████. He was so sure Ralph wouldn't be there that he was hardly even nervous. A few blocks away, he felt a stab of something like longing to see Ralph, a desperate wish to have him standing there when he turned the corner onto ██████.

When the spot was empty, he banged both fists down onto the steering wheel. The need to keep the gas pedal steady while so much frustration was coursing through him was almost unbearable.

50

et's get a ▮▮▮▮▮▮ team down from Headquarters and do a hot watch on the ▮▮▮▮ Embassy," William said.

"He'd probably be out of there already if they had him," the DCOS said.

"You're probably right," William said, "but let's try it. Forty-eight hours, I think."

The ▮▮▮▮▮▮ team came out on an ▮▮▮▮▮▮▮ and arrived the next evening. The watch started at 2200. The DCOS ran it, and he spent most of his time at the site or at home trying to get sleep. Bobby only saw him twice over the next two days. Both times, he just shook his head.

At the end of the watch, they hadn't seen a thing.

51

et's give it one last shot," William said.

The DCOS rolled his eyes.

"Countersurveillance?" Bobby asked.

William shook his head, and the DCOS said, "If anybody was on you who wanted you, they would have moved already. Just keep your eyes open. It's Hail Mary time."

Bobby signaled for an emergency meeting for the following night. For the next twenty-four hours it seemed like hardly a minute went by when he didn't think, Last chance, last chance. When it was finally time to go, he ███████████████ and did a regular SDR. The whole way, he kept imagining seeing Ralph as he pulled up to the pickup spot. He could almost feel the rush of relief that would go through him. But he knew perfectly well it wouldn't happen, and it didn't.

52

The next day, they sent out cables tasking the ████████████ ███ ███ ███ ███ ██. Bobby asked if there was anyone who could ████████████ ██████████████████████████████, but the DCOS shot it down right away ██ █████████████. Bobby knew he was right.

A week passed during which Bobby slogged through his ████ job, slipping ███ to the Station every chance he got to read the traffic. After the flurry of cables back and forth detailing all the attempted meetings and speculating on what could be going on, now there was nothing.

The other C/Os kept looking at him sympathetically. He couldn't even walk down the hall without someone patting his shoulder. William came by his desk three or four times a day, never to talk about the case but to try to get Bobby's mind off it. They talked about the weather and their Thrift Savings Plans. They had a few conversations about football, even though it was clear neither of them was a fan. But Bobby couldn't manage to get rid of the haggard look that he knew was on his face. At one point, William squeezed his arm and told him not to assume anything. He said he'd been through tougher situations than this that had turned out fine. When Bobby asked if any of them had turned out badly, he just frowned.

53

Tom and Bobby had breakfast together every morning, but Bobby hardly registered his presence. He didn't talk to him, and he forgot to pay him for two weeks. When it was time for one of their lessons in the evening, Tom would sit at the kitchen table with his workbook out and wait. But after Bobby walked right by him on his way upstairs three or four times, Tom started going straight home after work.

54

The cable came up on Bobby's screen the following Monday.

TDTRACER ARRIVED CONUS 10/10/2000.
REQUEST ANDREW L. SEEGRAM TDY HQS ASAP.

Bobby stared at the cable. At first, he couldn't even make sense of it. Ralph was in the United States? How could that be? Then he realized that if it was true, it meant he was alive. An instant of relief came, and disappeared just as quickly. What on earth was he doing in the U.S.? What had happened to his sister? The cable stopped making sense again.

He walked into the DCOS's office carrying a copy of the cable. The DCOS just shrugged.

"Got me," he said.

They went to see William, but he didn't know any more than they did. "At least he's alive," he said.

"Can we call them on the ▇▇ line?" Bobby asked.

"They would have called if they wanted to talk," said William. "They'll probably have a cable here by tomorrow explaining everything. But you have to go ASAP."

Bobby went to Admin and made arrangements to fly out the next morning.

When he got home that night, he put his briefcase down and went to make tea. Standing in front of the stove, he was overcome by the feeling that Ralph was nearby—somewhere in the kitchen where he couldn't see him, or just outside the window. He stood completely still, listening. He immediately understood it couldn't be Ralph, but something was out of place.

And then he realized what it was. Tom wasn't sitting at the table.

He'd hardly thought of him since the TDTRACER catastrophe had begun. This was perfectly understandable—after all, a man's life was on the line. But now Bobby wished Tom were there so he could at least tell him he was going out of town.

He sat down at the table and scribbled a quick note. He wrote that he had to go back to America for a family matter, and he wasn't sure exactly how long he'd be gone. But Tom should continue working, and Bobby would see him when he returned. He left a few weeks' pay on the table with the note.

Then he drank his tea and tried to come up with even one scenario that could explain why Ralph was in the United States.

55

From the plane, Washington looked orderly and bleach white. Driving down 267 from Dulles felt like a different world, haphazard and unrelated to the city he'd just flown over. But everything seemed neat and in place again as soon as he arrived at Headquarters—cars evenly lined up in the enormous parking lots, the marble Old Building next to the double-paned, green glass New Building.

Bobby collected his badge from security, strung it around his neck, and headed up to ██ Division. The secretary was expecting him and sent him right in to see DC/ ██.

The Deputy Chief was new, and Bobby hadn't met him before. He was in his late forties, and had the same boxy build as a lot of the ex-military C/Os at the Agency. They shook hands, and Bobby sat down.

"Well," the Deputy Chief said, "he got here Friday night. Ended up getting half the Division in here to deal with it. He was on an Air ██████████, no ticket, no passport. Just had a note with him in ██ ████████████████████████ stationery. He just handed it to the customs agent. Took two hours to find a guy who could read it. It said . . ." The Deputy Chief rummaged around his desk, then found the translation. " 'You want him, now you have him.' Customs didn't know what the hell that meant. But they figured the stationery was something, so they called us. You know Teddy Senko? He went out to the airport, but he didn't know who he was. He'd never heard of the case. But TRACER figures out who he is, pretty much says, 'I work for you.' We finally figured out it was him, got him to a hotel, gave him something to eat. Yesterday we moved him into a temporary apartment. And there he sits."

"So . . . what happened?" Bobby asked.

"He was blown. We don't know how. They called him home . . . Bobby, this is the rough part . . . they killed his sister. Right in front of him. Then they put him on a plane, with that note."

For a moment, everything was perfectly still. Bobby understood the facts that the Deputy Chief had just told him, but for an almost blissful few seconds he couldn't understand what any of it had to do with him. Then something deep inside told him to sit up straight, to remember that his reaction was being watched and judged. He snapped back into place.

"They . . . but . . . why would they kill his sister?" he asked.

"Who knows? These people are barbarians. I'm always saying that, but nobody believes me. They want you to think it's some wonderful culture. Maybe it is. Somewhere. But these people, the ███, they're barbarians."

"But . . . do they do things like this? Kill sisters? A family member? I've heard of the ████████ doing that, but the ███?"

"Sure. They're just as bad as the ███████. Figure blowing a guy away isn't enough. When they can really make him suffer. And they can send us a message, too. 'Here, he's yours. You want him, you got him.'" The Deputy Chief looked back down at the note. "'You want him, now you have him.'"

"So, he's where now? In an apartment? How is he?"

"He's a fucking wreck. Yeah, we got him in an apartment in Arlington. For a few weeks, until the relocation guys find him something permanent. But yeah, obviously he's not in good shape. We got a ██████-speaking shrink over, but he wouldn't talk to him."

"Jesus fucking Christ," said Bobby.

"It's a goat fuck."

"So . . ."

"Yeah, you'll go over there. Talk to him. We want you to stick around a few weeks, help him get settled. Best if you explain all the arrangements to him."

"What are the arrangements? I haven't done . . . I don't really know anything about resettlement."

"Well, he's only been working, what, four or five months, so there isn't much in his ██████ account. Regrettable. But we'll cover housing for a year, extendable to another year if he needs it, and language training if he needs it. Vocational training, or retraining, as the case may be. We'll get him resettled."

"What's he got in the ███████? ███████████████dollars?"

"I think about that."

"But . . . that's nothing. Now he's here. Because of . . . us. Can't we . . . you know . . . get more for him?"

"I'll talk to Milton about it. We can probably get a special allocation ████████████████████████."

"That's not gonna do that much."

"It's not nothing. It'll help him get on his feet. There's not much more we can do. Things worked out badly. You told him there were risks?"

"Sure."

"Well, he's an adult man. He chose to take them. Now he's here. It's not the worst place to be. I'd rather be here."

"But his sister . . ."

"I know, Bobby. It's a bad break. But our work, these are the risks. If you want to serve your country, you have to take them. His sister—that's a tragedy. No way to make that up to him."

"I can't . . . I can't believe this is happening."

"It's tough," said the Deputy Chief.

56

It was a fairly new development, a light gray, two-story building designed to look like a row of attached town houses (half the developments in Northern Virginia near the Beltway fit this same description). Bobby sat in his car looking at it for a long time before he finally went up to the second floor.

When Ralph opened the door, he stared blankly at Bobby's chest, then looked down at the ground. His cheeks were yellow and flabby and his forehead was heavily lined, as if he'd aged twenty years in the two weeks since Bobby had last seen him.

They stood there until Bobby said, "Let's go in." Ralph turned and moved back inside. The apartment was furnished with a sofa, lounger, and chairs, all upholstered in a blue-and-green floral print. Ralph sat down just outside the kitchen at a table with a waxy tablecloth on it that matched the upholstery. Bobby sat down next to him. He'd prepared a few things to say, but now that he was actually in a room with Ralph, the order he'd intended to say them in slipped away.

"Ralph, I . . . I can't tell you how sorry I am. I have no idea how this happened. No idea. It shouldn't happen. But . . . I'm just so sorry."

Ralph looked at Bobby, then lowered his head into his hands and started to sob. Bobby waited, then put a hand on his shoulder.

"I know," he said. "It's horrible."

"They kill ███████," Ralph said, forcing himself to stop crying. "Shoot. Bang. Sister. ████████████████████████████████. What she do? Work. Go with mother. Shoot."

"I know," said Bobby. "They're . . . beasts. Evil, evil . . . barbarians. People like this shouldn't . . . this is why we . . ."

Ralph put a hand on the table as if to steady himself. They sat silently for a while, then Bobby said, "I don't know what to say."

A bit later, he went out and bought groceries, then brought them back and loaded up the refrigerator and the shelves. He had Ralph come into the kitchen so he could show him how to use the microwave. Then he made them bologna sandwiches. But Ralph wouldn't touch his, so Bobby didn't eat his either.

When he left, Bobby said he'd come back the next day and they could discuss where to go from here.

57

know it's hard to be practical at a horrible time like this," Bobby said the next day, "but we should discuss the future. How we're going to help you. Get you set up and adjusted to life here. I think eventually . . . way down the line, when things are at least a little bit better, you'll . . . you'll find opportunities here unlike those you've had before. And . . . well, things will be a little better way down the line."

"My mother come," Ralph said. "Never. They no let. For me. For hurt me, no mother. She alone now, no ███████████████. Me here. Mother █████."

"I wish we had some way to get her. But you're right, I suspect they won't let her go."

"For what?" said Ralph.

"For . . . what for what?" said Bobby.

"This."

"Right. I . . . you know, the world is such a fucked-up place, Ralph. We can see that here. It's the reason to do things, the reason we do these things, to try and make it better. To try and stop this. This kind of thing. That's what you were doing, fighting for something better for your country, for a country that doesn't do this kind of thing. For your family to live happily and freely in that kind of a country. It just . . . it's a long, painful fight."

Ralph turned toward Bobby. He squinted, as if he didn't quite recognize him. They sat silently until Bobby went on.

"Anyway, I know it's hard, and the timing isn't quite right, but I should explain some things to you. About how we'll help, and what we'll do, now that you're here. There's about ███████████████████ that you earned, which is what we discussed, before, in █████████, about the money we'd give you. That I'd put away for you. Now, we're hoping we can get some more, what we call a special allocation, because of the circumstances, so we could up that, and there'd be more. Which would be good. But it's not just the money. We'll pay your rent for a year. Hopefully, after a year, you'll have a job, but if you don't, it can be renewed, so we can pay for another year. And during that time, we can send you for vocational training . . . that's job training, to help you prepare for a new job . . . there's lots of things you can do, a smart, talented guy like you, we can discuss this, and you can discuss it with a vocational specialist, too . . . and English training, not that your English isn't good, but if you want it, I think it'd be a good idea, to get it even better, so that if you're going to work here and live here, it should be really top-notch, obviously. I think you could quickly advance to your English skills being really excellent."

Ralph got up and went into the bedroom.

Bobby stayed on the couch for a while. At first, he was hoping to hear some sound from the bedroom, something to indicate that Ralph was awake and would be coming back out. But the apartment stayed quiet, and after a while, Bobby's mind started to drift. He pictured Tom standing over the sink in the kitchen in ████. He wondered if he called the house if Tom would answer. Of course, he never answered the phone, so that wouldn't work. He didn't know what he had to say to him anyway.

Or maybe he did. Because now it seemed like Tom would be his only chance to resuscitate his career after this. They'd certainly been getting closer, the English lessons had a real feeling to them and were turning into something important. Bobby could start getting the intel from him without any kind of formal recruitment, then recruit him later after everyone saw how valuable the intel was. Meetings would be easy, they could just do them in the garden every week. Run a quick ████████ and start talking. This was all assuming the intel would be good, but Bobby could feel it, he knew there was something there. This was also assuming he was even going back to ████, which seemed iffy at this point.

Eventually, he got up from Ralph's couch and went out to his car.

Before getting in, he kicked the panel over the front wheel hard. He heard it dent. He'd never done anything like that before, never once thrown something in anger or punched a wall. He looked around, because in these suburban neighborhoods anything could get the police after you.

As he drove away through the ███████████ streets, he saw that there was no way to case officer this. Ralph was wrecked. That was that.

58

The next afternoon, Bobby sat at the same table with Ralph and the relocation officer. The officer was young, dull, and officiously competent. He had everything on paper: Ralph's ███████████ balance, the amounts and timing of living and educational expenses, the legal requirements for citizenship. He spoke about Ralph's "obligations" and the Agency's "assistance protocols." Finally, he gave a pep talk in which he discussed the differences between successful and unsuccessful relocations. He said that if you did it right—had the right attitude, took the proper steps—"the sky's the limit here in America."

After the relocation officer left, Bobby took Ralph out to dinner at a ██████ restaurant. He ordered the favorite dish of his father's that he'd told Ralph about the night they had dinner at his house in ████. He didn't know what he was trying to spark with that move. Maybe nothing.

They both picked at their food but didn't really eat anything. Bobby couldn't decide if he should be trying to get Ralph's mind off of what was happening, or more clearly onto it. He made small talk, but Ralph didn't respond. Finally, Bobby asked him outright if he wanted to talk about what was going on.

"What is going on?" Ralph said.

"Yes, what . . . what's happening," Bobby said.

"What happening?" Ralph said.

"Yes I . . . I . . . I'm sorry, Ralph," Bobby said.

He'd never had a training exercise for this, for a situation where there was nothing left to say.

59

He saw him three more times that week. The first time, he took him to the Tyson's Corner Mall and bought him a suit. With his thin frame and bony arms, he didn't look good in it. A few nights later, Bobby brought over takeout and they watched country music videos, which he told Ralph would be good for his English. And over the weekend, on a hot, airless night, he drove him to the Vienna Town Center, where they walked down the half-real, half-mock Main Street, and Bobby tried to explain everything he could about living in America. Among other things, he spoke glowingly about the vibrant ███████ community in Virginia and the District, and how Ralph could make friends that spoke his native language and understood his original culture.

60

Bobby went to Headquarters for a few hours every day. They gave him an empty desk in ██, and he'd sit there and read the traffic. Occasionally, he wrote a cable if the desk was busy. Everyone was perfectly nice to him, and the ones who knew what was going on made an effort to buck him up. But it was a far cry from when the secretaries used to smile at him and everyone knew he was turning down job offers from the DDO.

The more he sat at his desk, the more he wondered if he could make some sort of career at Headquarters. The idea almost made him laugh at first because he'd been so sure he wanted a career in the field, to be a great operative. That was actually what all the C/Os said they wanted, but he'd really meant it. He didn't even want to become a COS because it would take him off the street. But now, for the first time since joining the Agency, he was wondering what else he could do if his career in the field was over. He'd dropped out of a Ph.D. program in ███████ Studies to join the Agency. He remembered all the reasons he'd hated it—how it had been stressful but boring at the same time, how he'd felt like he was literally wasting the minutes in his life. He would rather sit behind a desk at Headquarters than go back to that.

61

One afternoon, after he'd been in the States for about three weeks, Bobby was at his desk when a cable came in from William.

STATION REQUESTS ANDREW L. SEEGRAM RETURN BY NOVEMBER 15. PLS ADVISE IF C/O SEEGRAM IS AVAILABLE FOR SECURE TELECON ON NOVEMBER 1 1600 HRS.

The following afternoon, Bobby was at his desk by 1500, waiting for the secure line to ring. He pictured William in the ███████ ███████████████████ where he'd have to go to make the call. It got hot in there, and William would probably be uncomfortable.

At 1603 HRS, Bobby picked up the phone on the first ring.

"Time to come back," William said.

"TRACER's not really settled in yet."

"He won't be for a long time. You've got to move on with your work."

"I feel radioactive."

"You might be a little hot. We don't know, honestly. That's part of the business."

"But how can I do anything?"

"We'll have you spot and assess, probably take it easy on the recruiting. What have you got, seven more months? It'll go fast."

"But if I'm blown—"

"We don't know that. In fact, I doubt it. I think it's probably something else. That's my instinct. And you can't leave early anyway, that raises more flags than anything else. Any foreign service would wonder about that, wherever your next tour is. 'Why'd he leave ██████ early?' "

Bobby didn't respond, and William said, "Have you thought about that at all, by the way? Where you want to go next?"

"Well, I was thinking ████████. But that seems like a bad idea now. Might be better to go to another Division. Temporarily."

"Not a bad idea."

"William, you sure you want me back?"

"Are you kidding? Of course we do. You're still one of the finest young officers at the Agency. This doesn't change that at all, Bobby."

"It's such a disaster."

"Don't be so hard on yourself. You know this happens all the time, right? And it particularly happens to good officers, because they're the ones taking the big risks. That's how it works."

"Really?"

"Of course. And when something goes south, a case officer has to be able to deal with it and move on. I ever tell you about when I was in ████████████ in seventy-four?"

"No."

"The ████████ ran a double on me. I know it's not exactly the same thing, but believe me, it was bad. I gave him every goddamn piece of tradecraft in the book. My COS said it might have blown half the cases in the Station. I've never been so devastated in my life. I almost quit. Well, we found out about five years later he'd been

turned because an ███████████████████████████████. How about
that? And three years later, I brought a ██████████████ on board
who gave us █████████████████████████████. Imagine that,
Bobby. How much good that did us."

"Good stuff during the cold war. Great stuff."

"Yes, it was. You have to give yourself that chance. Look, I never
served in ████████ or ████████████ again, never went after any ███ officers. So what? Bobby, you're young, and it's early. Early in your career. I know this is painful. But you have to get back on the horse and
not get derailed by this."

"Mixing your metaphors there."

"I certainly am."

62

A case officer named Omar, who Bobby had trained with, was back
at Headquarters for the next two years. He'd been one of the best
students in their class, and even though Bobby wasn't close to him, he
respected him. Bobby asked DC/██ if Omar could take over Ralph's
case. DC/██ worked it out, even though Omar was in a different Division.

The last time Bobby saw Ralph, he brought Omar over to his
apartment. He explained that he had to go back to ██████, and that
Omar would take care of him. Omar didn't say much, which was
just right, and Bobby was glad he'd arranged to transfer the case to
him.

The next night, he was on a plane back to ███████. At some point
late in the flight, he woke up suddenly and remembered an afternoon
in language training, not long before he'd left on his first tour. He was
talking to Nick Tynan, a senior officer at the Agency who was in
Bobby's █████████████ class because he was going out as COS ████████.
Nick was telling him about an agent he'd run in ███████████who'd

been executed after a meeting they'd had was ███████████████ ███████. Tynan had said, "When you lose one, it's like losing a member of your own family." (James McDunne, one of my instructors at the Farm, had told me the same thing, word for word.)

Sitting there in the sky, somewhere between America and ███████, Bobby asked himself if Ralph was like a member of his family. And he wasn't. Maybe he should have been, but he wasn't.

So what was he, then? His agent? His blown agent?

That didn't seem to cover it.

Bobby looked out the window, where he could barely make out the shape of the plane's wing against the dark sky. He realized what it was. After all the dinners and lunches, all the talking and getting to know each other, even going through the recruitment together—for God's sake, all of the times he'd said it to him, and still not really noticed it—Ralph was his friend.

He'd done this to his friend.

63

Bobby's plane landed late in the afternoon, and he got home just as a gray dusk was settling over the city. He'd already opened his front door when he stopped and stood still. He wasn't sure why he wasn't going forward. Then he turned and walked around to the little garden at the side of the house.

He stopped at the low hedge of ██████ bushes Tom had put in a few months earlier. One dirty, green-yellow gourd was growing in a corner of the garden. Next to it, a string of little cucumbers were hanging from vines almost flush to the ground. Bobby couldn't tell if they were baby cucumbers or just some small variety. Between the cucumbers and the ██████ bushes, a patch of tiny green buds were sprouting, but he couldn't tell what they were going to be.

64

The next morning, Bobby came downstairs to an empty kitchen. He spent a few minutes looking around the house for a note from Tom. Then he made his own coffee and sat at the table quietly.

When he got to the Station, he went to the DCOS first and filled him in on everything that had happened with Ralph in the States. Then they went together to William's office, where Bobby repeated it all. When he was done, William looked at the DCOS and said, "So we'll have Bobby lay low. Not go after any more recruits this tour. Just spot and assess. Maybe develop a little if it feels right."

"I think that's appropriate," said the DCOS.

"And NRLIGHTHOUSE," said William. "Why don't you turn him over? We'll move the whole thing ████████. Just playing it safe, I know you hate to lose him. But I don't want to risk it in case you are blown."

"I understand," said Bobby.

"Craig?" William said to the DCOS.

This was the officer who'd met LIGHTHOUSE when Bobby was in ███████. He was a first-tour, and Bobby didn't think highly of him, but William liked him.

"Sure," the DCOS said. "But it's a little risky to have Bobby there, isn't it? Why not just do it cold?"

"He can handle it," William said, nodding at Bobby. "Get a little denied area practice."

The DCOS shrugged.

"Set it up," William said.

Bobby nodded.

"We'll keep you busy," William said. "There's plenty to do. You could spend a whole tour targeting and developing and it could be very worthwhile. More than most tours, I think sometimes."

Bobby left the office with the DCOS. When they were back in the hall, Bobby said, "I thought for sure I'd have to leave the Division. At the least."

"Good lord, no," said the DCOS. "We wouldn't have anyone left."

65

When Tom didn't show up the next day, Bobby casually asked the guards if they'd seen the kid who worked there. They hadn't. The day after that Bobby searched the house again for a note or any kind of clue. He didn't find anything. On the fourth day, he realized Tom was never coming back.

He knew he'd ignored him while he was dealing with the TDTRACER mess, but he was surprised Tom would give up his job over that, especially in ███. He had obviously formed even more of an attachment to Bobby than he'd wanted him to.

He wished he could just call him and apologize. But it wasn't like the kid had a phone.

66

The ███ C/Os who were doing the countersurveillance gave Bobby a completed map. He'd be covered with ███ long nets at ██-mile intervals. It wasn't what you'd put up for the most important meeting in the world, but it was good enough.

He left his house at nine o'clock and drove through ████████.
He ██
██.
Thirty minutes through ████████, with hardly any traffic for some
reason and nothing interesting behind him. He went through the first
catch zone in ███ minutes, sitting back and letting CS do their job.
He got the clear signal ███ minutes out. The second zone was
████████████████ away and he coasted through it calmly again. He
was actually enjoying this SDR. He did the final leg in ████████
██
████████████████████████.

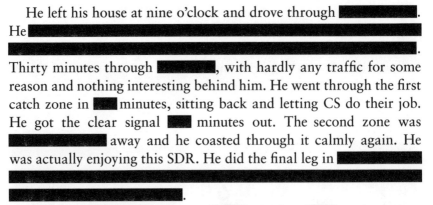

He got out and walked the last ████. The air in ███ was less grimy
than ████ or ████████ and filled with a soapy smell. He saw the go
signal on a ████ a block ahead. He did the final turn and ████ and
then he was there. He went in through the front and heard LIGHT-
HOUSE and Craig talking before he saw them. He turned in to the
next room, where they were sitting at a card table.

"Here he is," Craig said.

LIGHTHOUSE got up, and Bobby shook his hand.

"You met my colleague once before, am I correct?" Bobby said.

"Yes, when you were away," said LIGHTHOUSE.

Bobby sat down at the table and gestured LIGHTHOUSE back
into his seat.

"I understand you got along well," Bobby said.

LIGHTHOUSE shrugged.

"Well, in any case, I think you two would like each other," Bobby
said. "And I haven't had a chance to tell you this before, but I'm leaving in several months. And to prepare for my leaving, I'd like to have
you start talking to someone who can continue to talk to you after
I'm gone."

LIGHTHOUSE stared at him, and Bobby sensed everything was
about to go to hell.

"So I wanted you to meet again," he went on, "because I think you
would be very good friends. I think you would get along very well.
And frankly, of all the people I know, of all the colleagues I have, he's
the very best. By a mile. The very, very best."

"I fail to see the purpose," said LIGHTHOUSE. "You are here for several more months, why can we not continue to speak with each other? Perhaps then we could consider some other arrangement. But I prefer to speak with you."

"I'm sorry," Bobby said, "this is the procedure. Of course I argued for it to be different. I agree with you, it's not necessarily . . . necessary. But there's nothing I can do about it. You understand this, I'm sure. How organizations work."

He thought that would do it. Not that LIGHTHOUSE would be happy, but that he'd give in. If what he wanted was American contacts, why did he care who got them for him? But LIGHTHOUSE surprised him by saying, "This is unforgivable."

"Can't do anything about it, I'm afraid," said Bobby. "I'm sorry."

Craig said, "I think if you give me a chance—"

"This does not concern you," said LIGHTHOUSE.

"Please watch how you talk to him," Bobby said.

It came out in the wrong tone. Far too hostile. But if this guy couldn't be pacified, maybe he had to be intimidated.

"How dare you," LIGHTHOUSE said, standing up from the table. In his anger, he stretched up to his full height, and even at his advanced age there was something frightening about it.

"How dare I?" Bobby said, bolting up and staring hard at LIGHTHOUSE.

"Guys," Craig said.

"I will report you," said LIGHTHOUSE.

"We should terminate this asshole," Bobby said to Craig.

LIGHTHOUSE turned red. "You will terminate me?" he said. "This is unacceptable. You made me promises. We are working together. No? How could you . . . how could you . . ."

"No," said Bobby.

"Why do you do this to me? Why do you do this to me? I have done nothing to you."

"He didn't mean 'terminate' like that," said Craig calmly. "It's a special term for us. It just means 'fire.' 'Stop working with.' "

"Oh," said LIGHTHOUSE.

"I'm out of here," Bobby said.

He turned and left the room. He did a quick visual check of the ████████████████ and then went out the front door and back toward his car. He had the strange feeling that he'd just done something terribly wrong, but that he was going to get away with it. The whole thing could be played off as a strategy. He was out, Craig and LIGHTHOUSE were in, and Craig had just delivered the greatest relief of LIGHTHOUSE's life—that his life was going to go on. It was a total accident. But the turnover was done.

CS covered the first leg on his way home, then he was alone. It wasn't that late, but ████████████ was quiet and empty. He listened to the hum of his engine and to the uneven roll of his wheels across the pitted streets. He wondered if he would ever see NRLIGHTHOUSE again. Probably not. And he was glad about it. The man was an idiot. And his intel was low-grade, too. It had never deserved an "Excellent" rating or anything close to it. Bobby thought it must have been some junior analyst who was right on topic, and whose boss let him do the evaluation.

He wondered why he'd ever recruited him. The truth was, on his previous tour, he wouldn't have even looked at him.

And then, as Bobby rounded a corner off a small side street in ███, the question he'd been avoiding hit him smack in the face, hit him so straight-on and hard that he knew it had been hovering there for a long time. Was TRACER's intel worth it?

He started scanning his memory for every TRACER intel report he'd filed. There wasn't that much—insider information on the ████████Embassy and policy toward ██████. Nothing anyone was going to go crazy over. Of course, there was the potential. That's what this recruit was really about. Getting information down the line. But even there, how far was this guy going to go, without family connections in a country that was run by them more than most places, even if they pretended otherwise?

TRACER was better than LIGHTHOUSE. There was no doubt about that. But he was no superagent. Bobby saw it clearly now for the first time. There was nothing there worth risking his life, or his sister's life, for. If there had been a real cause—a real benefit at the end of it for the United States, or for the world—that would be justifiable. But Bobby had asked him to risk it all for nothing.

67

The next morning, Bobby was writing up the turnover when William's secretary called and asked him to come to the office. Bobby assumed Craig had already told William everything and that he was about to get chewed out. He even wondered if he might get fired.

William ushered him into a chair and made small talk for a few minutes. He didn't bring up anything about NRLIGHTHOUSE. Then he told Bobby that General ████ was having a party to celebrate ████ ███ ████████████████. He wanted Bobby to go. He said that he needed to get back on his feet and take the opportunities he'd have to spot and assess targets on the rest of his tour seriously, even if his cover status at this point was too weak to recruit. In particular, he wanted him to look for an ███████████████████, where the Station had a gaping hole.

Bobby thought that Tom might be working at the party. And then it all started to play out in his mind. Maybe there was still a way to redeem himself.

68

Two nights later, as the guards waved him through the high stone wall surrounding the General's estate, Bobby thought simply, Be there, Tom. He followed the driveway as it twisted through a stand of ██████ trees then ended in front of an enormous lawn. He gave his car to an attendant, then walked up the steps to the castle-like house.

In the foyer, he took a drink from a waiter and went into the main ballroom. He moved through the crowd, smiling at strangers and striking up conversations. The wife of a ██████████ flirted with him for some time. Military targets were everywhere, their epaulets and ribbons giving half the information you needed in order to know if they might be worthwhile. Bobby met two different colonels and actually turned down a lunch date with the second one. He was only supposed to spot and assess.

He'd been there for about half an hour when he saw Tom. He was all the way on the other side of the ballroom, carrying a tray. Bobby moved through the crowd toward him, but as he got closer, it became clear that Tom had seen him and was trying to stay away from him. They played a strange little game of cat and mouse for a few minutes until Bobby finally managed to corner him.

"Hello, Tom," he said.

"Hello, sir."

"You're angry with me."

"No, sir."

In case anyone was watching, Bobby took an hors d'oeuvre from Tom's tray.

"Yes, you are. I ditched you, didn't I? When I went back to the States."

"Please, I must work, sir." Tom started to move away.

"Tom, I have to talk to you. Come to the house."

Tom shook his head no.

"Where do you live, then?" Bobby asked.

"I cannot say, sir."

"Damn it," Bobby said, "I—"

Before he could say more, Tom had blended into the crowd. Bobby thought about going after him, but that would look too suspicious. And then he heard, "You are acquainted with young ██████████, yes?"

He turned around to see the General smiling at him.

"Yes, I am."

"He works for you, isn't that correct?" The General didn't seem to know that Tom had quit.

"Indeed, he's my ███████," Bobby said, wondering where the hell "indeed" had come from. (Like me a few years later, he was somehow compelled to overmirror this plump little military man.)

"I hope you will not have him planting devices in my house."

"Oh . . . well . . . I hadn't planned on it," said Bobby, trying to keep the tone light.

"Permit me to introduce myself. I am General ██████, from the ████████████████████████████████████."

"Of course. Thank you for your hospitality this evening. I'm Bobby Goldstein, ███████████████████████."

"Yes, ████████ has told me something about you."

"Well, nothing bad I hope. I try to be a good employer."

"As do I. It's quite difficult for these ████████. You can only do so much for them."

"Yes, it's terrible. But . . . well, we have our own problems. In America."

"Of course."

"You have a lovely home."

"My grandfather built it with money he stole from the ████████."

Bobby laughed. "I wish my grandfather had stolen more money."

"Yes. Well, perhaps you will do it for your grandchildren. Now if you will excuse me, I must attend to the many guests."

Bobby went to the bathroom and stood in front of the sink. He assumed the General had been joking about him bugging the house. But maybe he knew he was Agency and he was making a joke and being slightly serious at the same time. Bobby wished he knew for sure if he was blown. In any case, bugging the General's house wasn't such a bad idea. He'd have to think about that.

He took a towel and dabbed some cool water on his forehead. Some part of his brain wondered if he should have asked him to lunch. The instinct actually made him smile. He was awfully far away from that possibility. There would be no way to develop him anyway—too rich, too happy. But in other circumstances, maybe Bobby would have tested the waters a little bit, just stuck a toe in to see if there was something there not visible to the naked eye. After all, it would be a recruit you could make your whole career on.

He wanted to go home, but he didn't want to risk the General seeing him leave so soon after his remark about bugging the house, which could create the impression that it had affected him. He stayed another forty-five minutes, twice ensuring that he was in the General's line of sight. He saw Tom once more, this time handing out ███████.

69

It was a tricky stakeout, and Bobby had to recon the area three times to figure out how to do it. The main problem was that the General had security, and the secondary problem was that there were only two roads, one on each side, that accessed the General's street. Bobby would have to leave his car hidden off the road on one side, do the surveillance on foot, and hope his car was on the right side when the time came.

He stood in the woods about a hundred yards east of the General's main entrance starting at eight P.M. on a Monday. The first night, he gave up and went home at midnight. The second night, most of the lights in the house went off at eleven, and Bobby waited ten more minutes, then went home. The third night, Tom came out the front gate at around ten o'clock. Bobby watched him turn and start walking west. The fourth night, nothing. And then the fifth night, Tom came out just after nine o'clock. Bobby was parked on the right side this time, and he got to his car quickly and swung in fifty yards behind him.

Tom went down the hill and out of ████, then waited at a bus stop on ████. Bobby idled a block back. After twenty minutes, a crowded bus lumbered up, and Tom got on. Bobby followed it through ███, ███, and ████████. Finally, after about forty-five minutes, Tom got off in ████████.

Bobby parked—even in the dark, his car stuck out like a sore American thumb between the broken-down ████ and the few ████ ██████████████████████—and he followed Tom on foot past the

rubble-strewn lots and decrepit buildings. Each block was more forlorn than the one before it. He could just make out a low expanse of
shanties on the face of a hill a mile or so in the distance, the boxy
shapes jutting out at all kinds of angles from each other. They accomplished the almost impossible task of making the area Bobby was
walking through seem better than something.

He hustled to get closer to Tom. He couldn't have asked for a better area to follow somebody in, with the ███████████████████████
██ counted his paces
and checked his watch. They'd gone a mile and a quarter when Tom
finally stopped and went inside a dirty brick building that was leaning
at an almost cartoonlike angle over the street. A group of men were
milling around outside the entrance, but they parted for Bobby when
he followed Tom in.

He couldn't get his bearings at first. Wherever he was, it was almost completely dark, and the air tasted stale and wet. He heard footsteps, and then his eyes adjusted enough for him to walk forward to a
staircase. He moved quickly up the steps. At a landing, he stopped
to listen. The footsteps were still ascending. At the next landing he
didn't hear anything, and he went through a curtain into a narrow
hallway.

Two or three small fires were burning on the floor, and the smell of
████ cooking blended with the stench of the smoke. Bobby started
walking down the hall. He tried to ignore the stares of the thin men
lingering next to the fires, although they looked more perplexed to
see him than hostile.

He didn't see or hear anything, and he turned around and came
back to the stairway. He went up to the third floor and through another curtain. This hallway was empty. He walked to the end, where
he saw a pair of brown shoes outside a door. He thought he recognized them. He took a deep breath, then said, "Tom."

A moment later, the door opened.

"Oh," was all Tom said.

Bobby nodded.

"You are here?" Tom said.

"Tom, listen . . . can I come in?"

Tom looked at him, bewildered. Without waiting for an answer, Bobby stepped past him into the room.

Inside, a candle illuminated a tiny space, with a rug on the floor and a row of religious medallions hanging on the wall. There was a pot in one corner, Tom's workbook and a few other books in another. The ceiling was so low that Bobby's head almost touched it.

"Please, sir," Tom said, "you should not be here."

"I need to talk to you about something."

"But it is not right, sir."

"Tom . . . your parents . . . where are they?"

"They are not home right now."

"Yes, I know, I mean . . . I think maybe they're not . . . home at all, Tom."

Tom's eyes instantly filled with tears. "You are angry I did not come to work?" he said.

"No, no."

"You would like me to pay back some of my salary, yes?"

"No, no, I don't want your salary. I just want to know the truth."

"Why, sir?"

"Why? Isn't the truth just . . . isn't it enough of a reason to want to know the truth?"

"I don't know, sir."

"Tom, do you have parents now?"

Tom looked away. One of the tears that had been glistening in his eyes rolled down his cheek, but his expression was stoic.

"They have left," he said.

"Left like . . . went somewhere? Or left like died?"

"They have died."

"How long ago?"

"Five years ago, my mother died, and one year before, my father died. Sir."

"Sisters?"

"No."

"Did you live somewhere else before?"

"Yes, a little. In the ███████."

"Is that much better?" Bobby said, looking around.

"I do not know."

"Why did you lie to me?"

"Sir, I am afraid I will lose my job if you know that I have no parents."

"Why would you lose your job for that?"

"To employ a boy with no parents is not good."

Bobby wondered for a moment if that was true, but said, "Why not?"

"Sir, I . . . I am only sorry."

"Tom—"

"You will not recommend me to the next family, I know."

"I will, Tom. If you want that, I will."

"Please, sir."

"Okay, but . . ." Bobby stopped. He thought about Ralph, and his sister, and the million and one reasons this was a bad idea. But he reminded himself it was Tom's only real chance for a better life, and then he pushed all the other doubts out of his head. "Tom," he said, "do you trust me?"

"Yes, sir."

"Well, you did. But not now. Now you don't. But Tom, I need you to trust me again."

"All right."

"No, really. I need you to really trust me. Can you do that?"

"I only wanted to learn how to write, sir. I am sorry if I was not good. I know I was very slow."

"No, Tom . . . that's not it."

Bobby looked Tom right in the eye. Then he said, "I need you to tell me something about the General. Something only you would know."

"Sir?" Tom said.

"Something you've learned while working at the General's that somebody who didn't work there would never know. Like what the General believes about ▇▇▇▇▇▇▇. Or if he does anything that surprises you, something a little strange or different."

It was a long time before Tom spoke.

"Sir, there is a man who sometimes comes to see the General . . ."

For the next ten minutes, Tom poured out pure gold.

70

That night, Bobby stayed up until four in the morning. The next day was the point of no return, and he wanted to make sure he wasn't missing something. He sketched the plan out in two stages, with eleven discreet steps. When he finished, he only had to look at the diagram for a few seconds to see that it might work.

Once he'd gone over it enough times to have it memorized, he burned the paper and flushed the ashes down the toilet. After TRACER, he had no right to even chance this. But at the same time, he couldn't leave things the way they were. This time, he'd just have to make it work.

71

He kept the first intel report short and sweet. General ▮▮▮ met once a month with a ▮▮▮▮▮ man, who was always brought to the back door of his house by one of the General's bodyguards. The General met the man there and ushered him into the den. During their meetings, a briefcase filled with American dollars was sometimes open on the table, though it was unclear who the money belonged to.

William showed up at Bobby's desk five minutes after he sent him the report. He stared at him for a second, then motioned him to his office.

When they got there, William said, "This is fantastic. Did you squeeze this out of somebody at the General's party?"

"Well, in a way," said Bobby.

"Who was it?"

"That's the thing. The source is a problem."

"What kind of a problem?"

"Well . . . I can't even believe I'm saying this. But my ███████, Tom, also works at the General's. On weekends, and when he has a party or something. The General likes him, and apparently talks freely when he's around. Not to him directly, of course, but with other people when he's in there, serving tea or cleaning up or what- ever. He—"

"Your ██████ is the source?"

"I'm afraid so."

"How old is he?"

"Eleven."

"Jesus Christ."

"I know. I didn't seek this out. Obviously. I didn't even know Tom worked for the General. He never told me. What happened was, I was at the party last night, and there he is. Serving. So this morning, I say, I didn't know you worked for the General. 'Oh, yes,' he says. I say, 'He's an interesting guy' . . . I really wasn't trying to do anything, I was just responding, just saying . . . nothing words. Well, Tom starts talking. 'The General's this, and this . . . he's such an important fig- ure in █████' . . . Tom's seen the ████████████████████ at his house. Heard them all talking. I guess I looked interested. I didn't mean to, I just must have looked interested. Because now he starts saying, 'Well, just the other day this ███████████████ ██████ comes over and ██████████████████████████ ███████████████████████████████when I was serving the tea. I heard the ████████████████████████████ ███████████████████████████.' I can't shut him up. I mean, I didn't try, the stuff is gold. But right, it's from a kid."

"We can't use a kid as a source."

"I know. Believe me, I know. But what could I do? There's the in- tel, it's huge, it's falling right into my lap."

"I think you're supposed to run out the door."

"I know. Right. So . . . I figure, what do I do now? I mean, I didn't ask for it. And at this point, can I keep it from the U.S. Government? Isn't that kind of a violation? Of my duties, and responsibilities? I don't know. So I figured I'd write it up, see what you say."

"State would kill for this. DOD would kill for this."

"Our own analysts would be jumping out of their cubicles."

"Of all the fucking problems."

"I know."

"Maybe there's some back-channel way to do it. Let me talk to Headquarters."

"They'll have the lawyers shoving paper up our asses."

"That's right. We'll probably just have to let it go."

"Well, maybe we have to. Maybe that's just the rules."

"For Christ's sake, do not go after this kid for anything else."

"No. I didn't go after him for this. It just . . . happened."

72

The next day, the DCOS came up to Bobby's desk and said, "You run cables by me first."

"You weren't in the office when I finished it, so I just had William sign off."

"I was here all morning except for the ten minutes in which you just happened to finish it?"

"I'm sorry. I was just . . . the whole thing is so crazy, I just wanted to get it dealt with right away."

"That's what I'm here for, Bobby. To help deal with stuff. People who go far in this organization don't pull bullshit like this."

"What did you think of the intel?"

"It's obviously very good. But the source issue is impossible. You can't use an eleven-year-old kid."

"I know. I don't want to. But I can't sit on that intel either."

"William's talking to Milton today. We'll see what he says, after he finishes hitting the roof."

73

Two days later, Headquarters sent a four-page cable, three pages of which were warnings and restrictions. Bobby went in to William as soon as he'd read it. William was talking before he even sat down.

"Milton called this morning. The cable's just the half of it. One-time-only, ███████████, ██████, which is a code word I think they made up for this. ████████████, and highly limited internally. From what he said, though, I think they might brief the president on this."

"Jesus," said Bobby.

"Your source description won't fly, either. Creative, but no good. They want 'an unwitting source with no ████████████████████ ███████████████████████████████████████.' And get him a crypt. I don't care if he's one-time-only, if we end up in front of Congress over this I don't want this kid's true name within a million miles of anybody."

"Okay."

"And don't forget to add General Counsel on the distribution."

Twenty minutes later, the crypt request was out. A few hours after that, the DCOS came by Bobby's desk and dropped a cable in front of him. It was from Headquarters, assigning Tom the crypt LXMALIBU.

"Why isn't he an NR?" Bobby asked.

Tom was ██████ and should have had the same prefix as LIGHT-HOUSE and half the other cases run by the Station.

"Cases that require a DDO waiver get their own prefix," said the DCOS. "It's like putting a special warning on the file. It means that you'd better not screw up."

74

Bobby wanted everything to look as normal as possible. Tom came to work every morning. He made Bobby's breakfast and later cleaned the house and worked in the garden. And since it was already part of their routine, twice a week, in the evenings, they had a writing lesson.

During the lessons, Bobby would have Tom copy passages from novels he had in the house—*David Copperfield*, *Wuthering Heights*. Tom would sit and write row after row of carefully formed letters. He took three or four seconds with each one, looking back and forth between the samples in his writing manual and his composition book. He had the same look he had when he was working in the garden, intently focused but calm.

When he was done, they would discuss the passage. Then Bobby would have him write a few sentences about his own life. Tom's early sentences were all about things he did at work—"I plant tomatoes in the garden," or "I clean the dishes very fast." But then he started to write about his family—his mother standing over the stove cooking dinner, his father bringing home pomegranates or pencils for him. At first, Bobby wondered how Tom could still be making these things up after the truth had already come out. But then he realized these were real scenes from Tom's life before his parents had died.

75

Tom's next piece of intel was just as good as the first, maybe better. A few months earlier, he'd served tea at a meeting the General was having in his parlor with five or six other uniformed officers. He remembered hearing the General say that the U.S. ought to ███████████████████████████ in order to get them to give up their ██████████████.

The reaction to this report was worse than the first one. William, visibly upset, told Bobby that he'd been perfectly clear about the fact that this was one-time-only. It was the first time he'd ever spoken to Bobby sternly, and Bobby could hardly stand it. The DCOS was so angry that he kicked a garbage can from one end of the conference room to the other.

Bobby said that he'd in no way encouraged it. Tom liked talking about what he saw and heard at the General's. What could he do? "And look at the product," he said helplessly. If the General was saying that ████████████████████████████████, didn't the U.S. really have to know in order to ████████████████████? Bobby even got genuinely defensive at one point, saying, "Isn't this the whole point of intelligence?"

William finally authorized the cable, but when it went out, he said to Bobby, "I don't feel like you've given me any choice here."

Headquarters responded with a stinging cable that suggested, among other things, that ██████ Station reread line one of their previous cable, granting a nonrenewable exemption to ████████████ ██████████.

76

He waited three weeks before the next one. This time, Tom told him that the General had been reading a file one day in his office that had been titled ███████████████████████. This was a little thin. Bobby had known that Tom would run out of good information sooner or later, but he'd hoped it wouldn't be this soon. Still, it only took an hour's worth of research to figure out how he could expand it. Bobby added ████████████████████████ ████████████████████████████████████ ████████████████████████████████████ ████████████████████████████████████ ██████████████████████████. Bobby thought it was a masterstroke, though he was a little worried that there might be actual policy implications. Still, if the U.S. did ██████████████████ ████████████████████████████████████.

The DCOS told Bobby he wanted to send him home. But William was turning. He told Bobby they might both get fired over this, but that it was probably the best intel he'd seen in his entire career.

"How often do you get a chance to get something really good on the nuclear target?" he said. "Not often, that's how often."

A lawyer came out from Headquarters and read all three of them the riot act. He told Bobby to fire Tom from his job as his houseboy, but Bobby flat-out refused, saying it would look suspicious. He said he was half or maybe all blown anyway, and he had to step extra carefully to avoid doing anything alerting. The lawyer "strongly recommended" he stop getting intel from Tom until the operation was officially approved or disapproved, and Bobby asked him if he had any idea how to stop someone from talking who is in your house and really wants to talk. The lawyer said, "You're a goddamned case officer, you should be able to get someone to stop talking."

"My job is to get them talking, not to shut them up," Bobby said.

It wasn't OGC's (Office of General Counsel's) call in the end, and mixed signals were coming from Headquarters. The president had been briefed twice. The distribution list for the intel had expanded. And Chief/█ had told William on the phone that it was a fine cap to his career, as long as it didn't blow up.

77

Now that Headquarters was buying in, it was time for the next step. Bobby wished he could have done this first, but he didn't want to get the kid's hopes up when the whole thing might fizzle before it got off the ground.

As Tom was preparing breakfast one morning, Bobby said, "I don't think I'll have a waffle, Tom."

Tom stopped mixing the batter and started to put everything away.

"But Tom, I want you to make yourself one."

Tom stared at Bobby. Bobby looked back seriously, and kept looking until Tom turned around and started mixing again. When the waffle was ready, Tom came and sat at the table with Bobby. After he'd had a few bites, Bobby said, "I'm going to be leaving soon. Hopefully I can get you hired by the next family, and I'll try to do that. But there's some chance . . . I'm not saying this is possible, I'm just saying this might be possible . . . if there was some small chance I could make it happen, would you want to come with me? To America?"

"To America, sir?"

"Yes."

"To be your ██████ in America?"

"No. Just to come to America . . . to do the rest of your growing up in America."

"I know no one in America, sir."

"You know me. You would live with me."

"To be your ██████?"

"No, no, you don't have to be my ████████. Just to live with me. For growing up."

Tom didn't speak for quite some time.

Finally, he whispered, "Yes, sir."

78

After two more intel reports, Headquarters stopped kicking at all. The DCOS, thoroughly on record as opposed to the whole thing, realized he'd lost and decided to stop glaring at Bobby every time he saw him. William repeatedly reminded Bobby never to elicit or in any way affirmatively pursue information from Tom, but to just keep his ears open. And LXMALIBU settled into place as, Bobby suspected, the best source in ██████.

Now that the pressure was off, he could stop using Tom's information at all, which was good because there wasn't really anything left. But there were suitable items in the paper almost every day. Tensions on the ████████████████ were rising, and after playing with different angles, Bobby finally came up with the idea that ███████████ ██ ███████████████████████████████████████ ███████████████████████████████████████ ██.

It wasn't exactly impossible to disprove, but it would take a stroke of incredible luck, or an agent in place he didn't know about. Even then, he could argue it was a mistake if ██████████████████████ ████████████████.

He wrote the cable:

79

L XMALIBU was regularly producing, or at least everyone thought
he was producing, very high-quality intel. Headquarters was on
board. And Bobby's tour would be over in two months. It was time to
begin the second stage.

He had security duty at the Station on a Thursday night. After the
DCOS left, he waited half an hour, then went to Admin and unlocked
the ███████████████ He pulled out the ███████████ protocol and memorized the combination for the ███████████. He
locked the protocol back up and went ███████████████ where
he opened the ███████████. He chose an ALD-1 battery ████
transmitter from the back. (This was a beautiful little bug, ████
███████████ We were on to the ALD-2 by the time I was in
training, and the instructors used to always complain that we should
go back to the ALD-1 because it was so much clearer and more reliable.)

He secured the vault, then he drove down to ████ and had a
████. From there, he went to ███████████. Finally, he drove
down to the ███ Canal. It was late enough that there weren't many
people around. He did a potentially alerting ████ and saw nothing. He picked up a few stones from the ground and tossed them into
the water, trying to look meditative. After the second stone and before the third one, he slipped the ALD-1 from his left hand into his
right and let it fly. As it sailed through the darkness over the river,
Bobby surprised himself by asking God to make sure things turned
out all right.

80

The next day, Bobby went into William's office and stood in front of the desk.

"Something seems like it might be going on with the General," he said.

"What do you mean?"

"Tom said he's acting a little weird. He got quiet when Tom came in to serve tea last night. He was with the ████████████████ and he stopped talking, which he never does."

"They could have been talking about something sensitive."

"Right. It's just that that doesn't usually stop him. Tom thought he looked at him funny, too. He thinks the General's mad at him."

"For what?"

"He doesn't know."

"Probably just being a sensitive kid."

"Yeah, probably."

"You can't jump at every little thing like this, Bobby."

81

The following Tuesday, the DCOS opened up staff by saying, "Has anybody seen an ALD-1?"

Everyone around the table shook their heads.

"There's one missing from the ████████████████. Nobody has any idea where it might have gone? Speak up now, if you do. I don't care.

You had a ███████████ on one of your ██████. Realized it at the last minute, Alison wasn't around, you got it out of ██████████████████. Fine. It's no big deal. But if we have to do a full audit, that's a big deal. Just come to me and tell me if you needed it for anything."

82

At the staff meeting on Friday, Bobby sat quietly while everyone went around the table giving updates on their cases. He was going to take the final step that night—or at least the final step before it was more or less out of his hands—and he felt like if anyone looked closely at him, they would realize what he was doing. He wondered if this was what a double agent felt like right before they took a stash of documents out of a secure location. Or what a regular agent felt like before meeting a case officer, for that matter. It was a kind of fear, very deep and physical, but surrounded by a steadiness that was more like calm.

Craig started blabbing about something clever he'd done during an SDR, and Bobby was jolted back into the heart of the meeting. William was looking at Craig. The DCOS was taking notes. Bobby knew that he had to be perfect that night, or he'd never get by them.

83

At nine o'clock, Bobby went to the ████████ and had the Watch Officer call William and the DCOS. The DCOS arrived first and wanted to know what was going on, but Bobby excused himself to go to the bathroom and lingered there long enough that William had arrived by the time he got back. The three of them went into the conference room and sat down around the table.

"Something's wrong with LXMALIBU," Bobby said.

"Well, that's a surprise," said the DCOS.

"The General grabbed him earlier tonight. By the throat. Pushed him up against a wall and said, 'You little spy, I'll have your neck.' Tom got out of his grasp—he's a quick kid—and got out the back door with the General running after him. When he got home, there were police hovering around the building he lives in. He came back to my place—snuck in over the back fence, because he was afraid the police might be there, too—and told me what had happened."

"Shit," William muttered.

"Why would the General suddenly make an accusation like that?" the DCOS asked.

"I don't know. I mean, he knew Tom worked for me."

"That would be a hell of a conclusion to jump to based on that."

"I know."

"I wonder if he didn't have some kind of evidence?"

"Like what?"

"Like some hard evidence."

"Like what?"

"You tell me."

Bobby sat still, tried to look increasingly nervous, then nodded slowly. "Okay," he said.

"Okay what?" said William.

Bobby paused, rubbed his forehead, then said, "I had him plant a bug in the General's study."

"Oh my God," said William. "The ALD-1."

"I thought . . . I mean, I was getting all this great stuff . . . it was so useful to policymakers . . . but nothing much more was coming over the last month. I wanted to keep it going. For the sake of the intel."

"How could you do this?" said William.

"For the sake of the intel my ass," said the DCOS.

"What?" said Bobby.

"That's right, what?" said the DCOS.

Bobby squirmed, then spoke again. "Okay, fine. Maybe there was some element of . . . you know, I fucked up with TDTRACER. Here's a chance to set some of it right. To do something really useful on this tour to make it worthwhile. I mean, I knew the intel was there. Tom was telling me that the General was having all these incredible talks in his study, with half the leaders of the country. How simple is it to bug that? And here's Tom, he's in there every few nights, he's totally trusted, he's smart and can follow directions. You should see the garden this kid is planting. At my house. And how fast he's learned to write. He's a whiz. So a simple operation like placing the ALD, I have no doubt that he can handle it."

"Did you ever think the General might sweep his house?" the DCOS said.

"It's a ▮▮▮▮▮. I don't think the ▮▮▮▮▮▮▮▮▮▮▮▮▮▮▮▮▮▮▮. Even so, he's obviously not a security-conscious guy. Blabbing around in his study like that with everyone around. I mean . . . I still can't figure out how the hell he found it. Or how he connected it with Tom. That's the thing, I was covered even there, because why the hell would he suspect Tom?"

"Like you said, because he worked for you," said the DCOS, looking like he might jump out of his chair and grab Bobby's throat.

Bobby bent over the table and put his head in his hands. "I just didn't think . . . I didn't think he'd get caught. I still don't really think he was caught. I—"

"We've got to get this kid out of here," said William.

Bobby looked up. William's voice was calm, but he looked grief-stricken.

"What, exfil him?" said Bobby. "To where? He's just a kid."

"We could end up as child killers here," William said. "On the nightly news, for Christ's sake."

"Couldn't we just . . . I don't know . . . ," said Bobby.

"You're not in this discussion anymore," said the DCOS. "Or this Station."

"We should get him out, don't you think?" William asked the DCOS.

"I don't know, William. The whole thing's insane."

"Well, the kid's in danger. I mean, he's not a recruited agent, but they think he is, and we have been using his intel . . . it's my fault, I never should have—"

"Where is he now?" the DCOS asked.

Bobby said, "I told him to stay away from his building, and away from my house, and I'd meet him at a spot I've got inside the woods at ███████████████ the day after tomorrow to tell him what to do."

"What time?"

"Two o'clock."

84

The next morning, William met Bobby in the garage and took him in an ██████ car down ███ and then outside of ████ on the ████████ highway. They were quiet the whole time, although Bobby wasn't sure if it was a tradecraft decision or just that neither of them knew what to say.

They parked on the side of the road and walked into the ████████████████ Preserve. There were a few young men walking around tending to the ████████, but they were used to Westerners and didn't pay any attention to them. William led him onto a path that ran through the woods for a few minutes and then out along the side of a deep gorge. Bobby imagined William pushing him over the side, and even though he knew it was ridiculous, he kept an extra few inches away from him as they walked. (I've had similar fantasies with some frequency—I wonder if this is a persistent fear among Agency officers, that the place is in fact the sinister organization that the paranoids fear and might turn on you if you do something wrong.) After a few minutes, William reached into his pocket to check his ██ █████████████████████████████ Bobby knew they were there to talk.

"I'm worried about you here, Bobby," William said.

"I'm worried about you. I've made you look terrible. I'm so sorry."

"I'll be fine. This shitstorm should work itself out like any other shitstorm. And what's the worst they can do to me? Retire me early? So what, I can stay home and read books."

"Didn't you want to go on to COS Paris or something like that?" Bobby asked.

"That's not for me. Maybe ███████, then see if I had a shot at Chief/██. That was the plan. But at this point, I don't care that much. I'm fifty-seven years old. I'm getting tired. But you . . . you've royally screwed yourself. I want to find a way to get you out of it, but I don't think there's a way to do it."

"You shouldn't be worried about me here. I screwed myself."

"That's certainly true. Which keeps bringing me back to the question. Why did you do this to yourself?"

"I don't know, William. I love this job. Or at least I loved it. And I felt so screwed from TDTRACER."

"You weren't."

"Well, I thought I was."

Bobby felt like William was buying it.

They walked quietly for a few minutes. The path wound away from the gorge and back into thick woods. Groups of █████ were making their strange chirping sound. William stopped and faced Bobby.

"Obviously you're going to have to go home," he said.

He put an arm on Bobby's shoulder and squeezed it. Bobby's mouth opened, and it felt like the truth was about to gush out of him. But he stopped himself. He gave William a resigned smile and wondered if there would ever be a way to make up for this.

85

Back at the Station, the DCOS wanted to stick Bobby on the next plane out, but William said he was the only one who knew Tom and they needed him to help plan the exfil. The three of them went into the conference room, where they put together a preliminary action plan. It called for everything to be finished in seventy-two hours.

Next, they had a heated argument about who would go to the meeting in █████████████████. Bobby insisted that he should do it, but the DCOS argued that he could no longer be trusted, and in any case, since no one even knew exactly how blown he was, he shouldn't be out on the street working an exfil anyway.

William finally sided with the DCOS. They decided the DCOS himself would handle the meeting, and █████████████████████████ ███.

Bobby had prepared Tom for this, but he'd actually expected Craig or one of the other young C/Os to go. He was worried about the grilling Tom might get from the DCOS.

The next morning, the DCOS spent an hour in the conference room planning his SDR, then went to the meeting. He ██████████ █████████████████ and didn't get back to the Station until early that evening. He told William and Bobby that Tom was scared out of his mind. Bobby tried to look stricken, but he knew it meant that Tom had done well.

There were ████████████████████████████████ ██████████████████████. Craig was assigned to ████████ ███████████████████. Bobby had foreseen that he'd be the one. He had handled himself all right at the LIGHTHOUSE turnover—

better than Bobby had, in fact. But Bobby still didn't like or trust him. He was overconfident and not that smart. Putting Tom's fate in his hands was one of the hardest parts of the whole thing.

86

The op began Monday morning at six o'clock. If everything went well, Tom would be in ███████████████████████████
██
████████████████████████████

Craig and two ████████████████████████████████
██
██
██
██████████████████
██
██
████████████████████████████

They should have breezed right through. But a border guard asked Craig ██████████████████████████████████████
██
██
████████████████████████████████████ which still could have been salvaged, but then bad luck kicked in, and ████
██
██████████████████

The two ██████████ were arrested, and Tom was detained. The Station knew within an hour ████████████████████████
██████████████████████████████ Bobby insisted that the border guards would know the General was after Tom and they'd hand him over to the ████. He wanted them to ████████████████
████████████████████████████████. William and the DCOS

were both worried, but the Station hadn't picked up any signs of the General having initiated a manhunt for Tom, and they thought there was a fairly decent chance the connection wouldn't be made. After all, the ███████████████████ bureaucracy was a mess, and this was the kind of thing even the CIA and FBI screwed up all the time.

The cables that had gone back and forth to Headquarters over the previous few hours, getting calmer and calmer as things went downhill, ended with the DCOS writing,

███████████████████████████████████
███████████████████████████████████

and Headquarters responding,

HQS FOLLOWING DEVELOPMENTS WITH INTEREST.

87

Nobody met Bobby at Dulles—he'd half expected Security guys with handcuffs to be waiting at the gate. At Headquarters, DC/█ talked about what a promising young officer he'd been, and asked him what the hell he'd been thinking planting a listening device without authorization. He said Bobby would be debriefed over the next several days, then dismissal proceedings would be initiated against him unless he wanted to resign. Bobby said he wouldn't quit, that he still thought he had something to offer the Agency, but really he just wanted to stay around Headquarters as long as he could to keep closer to any developments.

The next day, during a break in his debriefing, Bobby was sitting in an empty waiting room in Security when a clean-cut man in his mid-twenties walked in the door. He looked at Bobby and said, "Goldstein?"

"Yes," Bobby said.

The man came over and sat next to him.

"I'm Todd," he said. "From logistics. Did some work on that exfil in ███. COS ███ asked me to find you and let you know the boy was released."

Bobby leaned his head back and rested it on the wall behind him so the tears flooding his eyes wouldn't spill out.

"The two ███████?" he asked.

"Still in custody, expected to get prison sentences."

The man left, and when Bobby sat up straight the tears rolled down his cheeks. He wiped them away with his hand and tried to think. Tom had obviously stuck to the cover story he'd given him, claiming that ████████████████████████████ ████████████████████████████ But ██████████████ ████████████.

Bobby told his debriefer he needed a break and went up to ██. C/██'s secretary smiled sympathetically, but wasn't going to let him in. The best he could do was ten minutes with DC/██. Bobby told him he realized that he'd shown terrible judgment, but that Tom shouldn't pay the price for it. He begged the Deputy Chief to find him and try another exfil.

But the Deputy Chief said another exfil was impossible. If Tom was caught a second time, there wasn't a cover story in the world that would keep him out of trouble. And they'd never find him anyway. The DCOS had told Tom to go into hiding if anything went wrong, and to move to another city if he could. By sticking to his cover story and not implicating the Agency, Tom had shown himself to be a smart and capable young man. As long as he disappeared effectively, the Agency would be all right, and so would he.

This was the one thing Bobby hadn't really prepared for. Early on, he'd considered finding some way to enlist the General's help, or even asking NRLIGHTHOUSE to take Tom in if things went wrong. But there weren't any good options, and the truth was, he hadn't been that worried about it. Exfils virtually never failed, even from countries a hundred times more difficult than ██████████████████.

██████ The only thing he'd done was bury five hundred dollars in the ████████████████████ and tell Tom to dig it up if anything went wrong.

Now Tom was probably following the DCOS's instructions and trying to resettle himself in ████████ or ████████. He'd have nobody there, nobody anywhere. At least in ██████ he'd had the General, and a job, and probably a few friends in that godforsaken building he'd lived in.

Bobby had just wanted to give him a better life.

To take care of him. To see him into adulthood.

That had been the plan.

88

Actually firing Bobby was a surprisingly lengthy process. They stuck him on the ████████ while he waited, and since his clearances had been downgraded instead of suspended, he could still ████████ ██. C/HR/█ came by at least once a day to talk or take him out to lunch. Bobby thought he'd probably been assigned to see to it that he didn't leave with any kind of an ax to grind.

Since C/HR was trying to keep him happy, Bobby managed to C/O out of him who his replacement was, and he went to see her. Bobby asked her, if she got assigned his house and Tom ever showed up there, to give him more money and see if there was anything she could do for him. If she didn't get the house, he asked her to find out who did and convince them to do the same. But by the time Bobby's administrative review, dismissal, and outprocessing were completed, she had been in-country three weeks, had been assigned Bobby's house, and had sent a secure e-mail saying that she hadn't seen Tom.

In his final days at Headquarters, Bobby kept having a fantasy in which he moved to a ████████ neighborhood in Cincinnati or Toledo or some other lousy city. He pictured himself living in a little apartment on the second floor over a restaurant, immersed in the culture, doing penance for Ralph and Tom by staying there for the rest of his life, friendless and broke.

But it was just a fantasy. After he left Washington, he borrowed some money from his parents and bought the house in New Hampshire. He moved up there, got his teaching job, and settled in. He e-mailed William a few times over the next year, still following cover rules by pretending William was with ████ and asking only obliquely about Tom. William's responses were less guarded. He wrote that they'd given him a low-level desk job at Headquarters until his retirement. He said that nothing more had ever been heard of Tom. And he said that even after everything that had happened, he wanted Bobby to know that he thought of him like a son.

PART FOUR

1

That was Bobby's story. It had taken him the entire night to tell it to me. He'd looked right at me most of the time, intent and gesticulating, almost like he was trying to sell me something. But near the end, his hands had stopped moving, and he described Tom's failed exfiltration more to the room than to me.

I had a million questions I wanted to ask, but I didn't say anything. Bobby sat perfectly still, staring at nothing a few feet to my side.

"I ought to let you get some sleep," he finally said. He tapped his fingers on the table, then stood up abruptly. "So, four. That's how many lives I wrecked. Ralph's, his mother's, his sister's, and Tom's."

"Tom sounds like a kid with a lot of wits about him. I'm sure he's okay."

I stood up, and Bobby walked me out to my car. He'd already turned back toward the house when he said, "After you get some sleep, come back for dinner, if you want."

2

The woman who ran the B and B gave me an odd smile when I came in, probably wondering what someone did in Beekridge when they were out all night. I made a cup of tea at the sideboard in the alcove, then went to my room and undressed. I wasn't tired, and I sat on the edge of the bed drinking my tea.

I thought again about James McDunne, the instructor at the Farm who had told me losing an agent was like losing a member of your family. It had been at the officers' club late one night near the end of my training. McDunne had been telling me about some of the operations he'd run in the Eastern Bloc in the 1970s. One of his agents had been a ██████ colonel, which sounds a lot less important today than it would have seemed at the time. The colonel had called for an ████████ meeting late one night, and when McDunne was on his way there, he got lucky and caught the tip of a surveillance net five miles out. He'd broken off and gone to an all-night bar, then back home. The next day an █████████████ had the colonel being interrogated by the ████████████, the ██████████, and the ████████. Two days later he was shot.

I had grimaced along with McDunne as he told me the story, trying to show him that I understood how terrible he felt. But as I thought about it now, I realized there was something else there. McDunne had been bragging. Or maybe that wasn't quite it—he wasn't a bad guy. But he was proud of the story. I couldn't quite put my finger on why, but he was proud of it.

I thought about another day in training, during a minicourse on counterterrorism techniques. The lecturer had passed around pictures of the aftermath of a Hezbollah bombing in ██████████. One was a close-up of a large piece of flesh hanging from a tree branch above the blast site. You couldn't tell exactly what part of the body it was from, although it was recognizably human. I'd been riveted by the picture, and only passed it on to the person next to me when I knew it would seem strange if I kept it any longer.

I stretched out on the bed and stared out the window at a string of mountains in the distance. I'd lost my bearings, and I wasn't sure if Bobby's mountain was one of them or if it was on the other side of the B and B. I thought about going outside and trying to orient myself by the time and the sun's position in the sky, which I'd learned how to do at SOTC. But instead, I kicked my shoes off and got under the covers.

I remembered Bobby's bewildered expression as he told me about Ralph's sister getting shot. For a few seconds, I pictured her in some dungeon in █████, a rifle held up against her head. Just thinking about it made me feel sick. I could only imagine what it was like for Bobby to live with that every day.

The next thing I knew, I was looking out the same window at a blue-black sky that seemed to be getting blacker every few seconds. I could just barely make out the traced line of the mountaintops. I wasn't sure how long I'd been asleep, but my mouth tasted terrible. I sat up on the bed, and for a strange second I felt like Daisy was sitting there next to me. She was in her underwear, with no bra on, and she was staring at the almost black window with a slightly confused look on her face.

The moment passed and I stood up. I pressed a hot washcloth to my face, got dressed, and went back to Bobby.

3

He was stirring a pot on the stove when I walked in.

"Would you believe I got into cooking this shit?" he said without turning around.

I saw ▮▮▮▮ and ▮▮▮▮ on the counter, and realized I was smelling ▮▮▮▮▮▮▮.

"Did you learn this from Ralph?" I said.

"No, no, I just cooked with him that one time. I didn't even know how to cook back then. But I got interested. And even in the middle of New Hampshire now you can get ▮▮▮▮▮▮▮▮▮."

I came over to the counter and he handed me a wooden spoon. I took over stirring the ▮▮▮▮ and he opened a package of ▮▮▮▮▮▮ and boiled more water. He became completely absorbed in cutting ▮▮▮▮▮▮▮▮. A silent half hour later, we sat down at the table.

"This is much better than Ralph's," he said. "I don't know why that guy couldn't cook, with all he knew about food. Maybe the ▮▮▮▮ ingredients in ▮▮▮▮ were just shitty."

I hadn't been sure if I should bring Ralph up again—when Bobby finished his story the previous night, I had the sense that he was done talking about him. But now he'd given me an opening, and I raced into it.

"Did you ever see him again?" I asked.

Bobby's hands kept twirling his ████████ but his face immediately hardened.

"I went to see him a few nights after I got back to the States. They'd moved him to ██████ by then. Not a bad place. They'd stuffed it with Ikea, gotten him a TV and a stereo. A used Honda. But he barely knew how to drive, and he was totally freaked out by the Beltway. He didn't go to his English classes because he was too scared in traffic. And he didn't know a soul. Omar had left, so all he had now was a relocation officer checking in on him once a month.

"I went to see him two or three times a week until I got fired. Should have gone more, but with everything that was going on with Tom, I just didn't. I don't think he liked seeing me anyway. He'd just sit there and look sad. Or he'd say, 'Bobby, what I do? What I do?' This was at first. Later, he started begging me for help. Literally, begging. He had ███████████████████████, which meant he wasn't going to last that long without more money. It wasn't that the guy was unemployable, but what was he gonna do, go work in a super-market? His English wasn't good enough for translation or a travel agency or anything. I talked to Deputy Chief ██, I literally cornered the ADDO in the fucking elevator one day, I told them I'd made him a bad deal. But it was a no-go. It was the standard deal. The problem was he was caught so soon after I recruited him he didn't have any-thing in his ██████████. And also the standard deal isn't that fuck-ing great, if you're a mess like he was.

"So finally, he realized I wasn't getting him any more money. That the boat he was in was the one he was in. And he starts telling me I'm no good, saying angry little things like that. And finally—this was after I got fired—I already had the plan to move up here, but I wasn't sure I could leave him. And I go to his apartment one night, and he answers the door, and he just says, 'No you. No again. Never.' And he shuts the door. Didn't even slam it. Just shut it."

Bobby stopped talking. He shifted in his seat, then took a few bites of his food. He was clearly about to change the subject when I said, "That was it?"

He bit his lip and stared down at the table. Then he looked at me and narrowed his eyes a little bit, as if he were trying to decide whether or not he could trust me.

"There was one more time. About two years later. I'd gone . . . I went to ████. A sort of last-ditch, crackpot effort to find Tom. Not that I had anything to do with him if I found him. There was no way for me to get him out of the country. I just wanted to give him some money, say I was sorry. So I went to █████, spent a week in █████. Nobody knew I was there, I don't think. I mean, you never know. I went to his old building, of course he was gone. One guy I found remembered him but had no idea where he'd gone. I spent three days looking around the ████████, in case he was still there somewhere. I checked the ███ and ████████████. Nothing. I spent the rest of the week staking out the General's. Hiding in the fucking woods again. It was a long shot, because Tom couldn't really go back there after the failed exfil. The General would have heard about it at some point and wondered why the hell he was trying to sneak out of the country. But with kids, you never knew. So I went each night when I thought he'd be leaving, if he was working there again. Used a ████████████████ ████████████████████████████████████. I never saw anything.

"The second I got back here, I literally dropped my bags, got in the car, and drove down to Virginia at about ninety miles an hour. I didn't even know what I was doing. I was half jet-lagged to death. I hadn't thought about this, hadn't planned it. I was just like a homing pigeon all of a sudden, heading toward Ralph. Driving and driving for hours. Never got pulled over, even though I should have been. When I finally got there, I parked across the street—it was three in the morning—I was about to storm in. Throw my arms around him. Beg him to forgive me. But instead, I sat there in the car. Eventually it's morning. I see his door opening. I don't even really know for sure if he still lives there. He could have moved. But the door opens, and out comes Ralph. With a wife and kid. I mean, I assume that's what it is. It's a ███████ woman, a little younger than him, and she's got a baby in one of those . . . baby things around her shoulder. They're going out, the mother and the baby, and I see them talking. Saying good-bye. And Ralph smiles this smile, like . . . he looks happy. For that second. And the woman and baby drive off, still in that little Honda, and I'm ready to burst in there again, but now I'm thinking . . . don't ruin it. He looks a little better. Just leave him alone. I sit there another hour, and I can't decide. But that's what I do. I leave him alone.

"I'm halfway back to New Hampshire when it starts to occur to me. It just . . . at first I'm just asking myself . . . do you really recover from that? From what happened to him? His sister getting blown away in front of him? With him watching? I don't know. And I'm not saying he was recovered, by the way. But he . . . he really looked happy there. And the . . . the doubt is sown, I guess. I start thinking about it. Is it possible . . . is there some way it's possible that the whole thing was a . . . put-on? That his sister didn't get killed? I knew it was crazy, but I just couldn't shake it out of my mind."

"My god, are you about to tell me the whole thing was bullshit?" I said.

"Let's spin it out. Let's say he made me from the start. And he figures, here's my chance. I can get to the States on this. Get out of god-forsaken ████, with his low-pay job in the Foreign Ministry, no real future. So he follows along with me, then after our fifth meeting . . . it's a little soon, I think he should've waited, but maybe he couldn't, maybe he actually gets called back to ███████ for something, so he swings into action. Calls for the emergency meeting, tells me his sister, who maybe doesn't even exist, or maybe she does, got taken. Then he goes back to █████, gets a ticket to America, gets on the plane—they don't always do a visa check on that end, but maybe he has a cheap forgery in case he needs it—he shreds his ticket and passport on the plane. I see him doing it in the bathroom, then flushing them down the toilet. That's what I'd do. He gets off the plane at JFK, no passport, no visa, and his letter from the ████. That would be the only trick, the letter from the ████. But fake stationery, ███████ forgers on a computer—I don't know how carefully the

Agency checked it. It obviously looked real, and nobody was doubting him. Or it's not even forged, the stationery, let's say he's got a friend, a cousin or something, who works at the ████ with access to the stationery. They get him one lousy sheet of it. Types it up. That could even get by Documents and Papers, I think."

"There was no independent verification of his story?" I asked.

"One thing. The ████ had taken a woman into custody—we knew that from another source, a ██████████████████████—but was it TRACER's sister? Maybe it was somebody else. Or maybe the source was led. That happens all the time. 'Did you take a woman into custody?' and they say yes, just to make the C/O happy. To earn their keep. Maybe they didn't even take a woman into custody at all."

Bobby was staring right at me, the way he had when I'd first arrived at his house.

"Then once he's in the States, all he has to do is slowly start hating me," he said. "To make it all feel real."

He started chewing on one of his fingernails.

"Do you really think it happened that way?" I said.

"No. Not really. Or maybe. I . . . something's wrong with the whole thing. With TRACER. It just feels a little wrong. So maybe it's this. Sound a little far-fetched?"

"A little."

"But isn't this all totally far-fetched? I mean, the other way, too? What actually happened, if that's what happened? Isn't that just as far-fetched? This whole fucking business is far-fetched."

He had a point.

"I don't know," Bobby said, shaking his head. "On balance, it's much more likely it all happened. But maybe, just maybe, the whole thing was bullshit."

"So you still don't know. That must drive you nuts."

"I lie awake thinking about it, still, after all these years. Over and over again. The same things. Figuring some kind of answer's going to come, even though I know it won't. Believe me, I don't sleep well."

He tried to smile, but what came out on his face was something worn and tired.

"I guess you can't really confront him about it," I said.

"No. 'Sorry I got your sister killed. And by the way, I think you made it up.'"

"You ever ask William about it?"

"We'd fallen out of touch by then."

"It's hard to keep in touch with Agency people after you go."

"It wasn't that. He tried to stay in touch. I just felt so fucking bad every time we talked, after the way I screwed him. I stopped answering his calls after a while."

We were quiet for a few seconds, then I said, "I wish I could help."

"I wish I could be helped."

When we finished eating, Bobby brought over an apple pie. He talked listlessly for a few minutes about the different apple varieties in New Hampshire, and I half listened.

We were standing side by side, doing the dishes over the sink, when I said, "Maybe I should go see him."

"Who?"

"TRACER."

"You want to see him? Why?"

"Maybe I could tease something out of him. I don't know. Observe something useful. When was the last time you saw him?"

"Four years ago."

"Maybe there's something new. Some kind of new evidence, or clue. I might be able to figure something out."

"I appreciate your asking, but what are you going to say? You're a friend of Bobby Goldstein's? He doesn't want to have anything to do with me."

"I'll say I'm from the Agency. Just stopping by to see how he's doing. I could even say I'm an R.O. It's been four years, I'll bet he hasn't seen one of them in a long time."

"He'll be on his guard if you say you're from the Agency. You wouldn't get anything out of him."

"Probably not. But I'd like to meet him anyway. After everything you said, it'd be interesting to get a take on him. And I'll at least be able to tell you how he's doing, which is probably pretty well now.

And who knows, maybe I'll figure something out. Unless you don't want to know, which I would fully understand."

"No, no, I want to know. Maybe I could sleep a little again if I knew."

"So let me have a look."

"It's very kind of you to offer. Really. But I can't ask you to get involved in this."

"Why not? And you didn't ask, I volunteered."

"Don't you have to go back to Chicago?"

"I'm on vacation for another four days. I could drive down tomorrow, see him the next day, call and let you know what happened. Then head home. I haven't got anything else to do."

"You actually want to do this?"

"Sure."

4

My normally clunky Dart was practically humming down the highway. I had the window open and the radio blasting, and for the first few hundred miles it felt like I was back in college. By mid–New York State, though, I was thinking about William. I'd already given up five or six times on figuring out if he had some sort of master plan for sending me to Bobby, but with the hours passing and things too peaceful, I was at it again.

Was this trip itself why he had sent me? Was I supposed to be in a car on my way to Virginia right now? I spun it twenty different ways but couldn't make that make sense. If, for example, he knew TRACER had lied about everything, and he wanted to communicate that to Bobby, he could just call and tell him. Maybe something else was going on with TRACER that he wanted me to find out and tell Bobby, but again, it was hard to imagine this being a sensible way to communicate anything to him. Was it possible that something new had happened in ▮▮▮▮, some piece of intel had appeared or disappeared, and TRACER or the General or Bobby held the key to it? A key that I was part of uncovering for William?

I tried starting earlier. What if Daisy was a plant? By William. Why? To get me fired so that William could send me to Bobby. Why would he do that? In order to have Bobby send me to TRACER, where I was heading now. And why would William want me to go to TRACER? That's where I got stuck again.

Maybe I had to go back even earlier. All the way back to when I got hired. Maybe I was hired so that I could get fired so that William could have Bobby send me to TRACER . . .

This was all a thousand times more complicated than actual operations ever were.

But what about Bobby? That was real. Did he need me to go on this mission to Ralph for some reason? Was that why he'd agreed to meet me in the first place? Why he'd told me so much? I doubted that. It was my idea to go. Not that he couldn't have elicited it out of me, but it didn't feel like that. Or did it feel like that? I ran our final conversation over and over in my head until I realized I wouldn't get anywhere, then I went back to the music and the highway.

5

I was fifty miles from Virginia when I started to feel it. The pre-op flutter. I'd gotten it every time I'd done an SDR in ▮▮▮▮. It was, of course, different this time. The guy I was going to see came pre-screwed. He was in no additional danger from me. And I was in the U.S. Either nobody was following me, or if they were, I hardly even cared. What could they do? I was going to see a guy. I probably had a legal right to do so. Even if I didn't, it was hard to imagine it was any kind of serious crime. More a bureaucratic infraction in a bureaucracy I was no longer a part of.

But as I got close to the Virginia border I turned down the music and closed the window. I checked for surveillance as best you can on a highway. If an Agency or FBI team were on me, they'd probably use at least an ███████████████████████. I wouldn't have a chance anyway.

The evening rush was just starting to thin out when I hit the Beltway. I slowed down and watched the traffic spinning around me, lights popping on every few seconds as the night got darker. I picked up Bobby's directions from the seat next to me and memorized the last leg.

6

A woman in a housecoat opened the door. From the way she looked at me, I suddenly wondered if there was something wrong with my appearance. But when I asked for Ralph, she turned friendly.

"The ████████ man? He left a long time ago."

"I'm an old friend. I didn't know he'd moved. Do you happen to know if he's listed?"

"Hold on."

She came back a few minutes later with a piece of paper.

"You tell him Susan and Dave are taking very good care of his old apartment."

He'd moved about ten miles farther west, deep into an area that was still developing when I'd lived in Washington. As I drove down 66, I was surprised by how quickly and thoroughly the transformation had been completed. The remaining open fields were all gone now, replaced with apartment complexes, schools, and malls. The sense that the country was nearby was completely gone.

I turned off the highway at Manassas, got lost in a swirl of circular streets, and finally found the right block. One side of the street was lined with identical detached houses, each with a yard and a driveway.

On the other side of the street was a new but still shabby-looking town house development. Ralph's town house was near the end of the block. I drove past it, turned the corner, and slid into a dark spot between street lamps.

It seemed like a long time between when I rang the bell and when Ralph opened the door. When he saw me, his lower jaw quivered for a fraction of a second. He wasn't far from what I'd pictured, though he had pocks on his cheeks that Bobby hadn't mentioned and a bit of a belly that had probably developed in America.

"I work at the place you were involved with here in Washington," I said.

He nodded, as if he already knew this. Then he opened the door wider, and I followed him into the apartment. A little entryway led directly into the living room, where he brought me over to a red vinyl couch.

"Maybe you will drink tea?"

He disappeared into the kitchen. The living room had dark wood furniture and ███████████████ on the wall, and generally had an █████ feel, even though the couch must have been the same one from Ikea the Agency had bought him when he'd arrived.

He came back a few minutes later with a ████ tea service on a chipped ████ tray.

"I know you are coming," he said.

I started to say five different things, but caught myself and stayed quiet. Ralph seemed unwilling to sit next to me on the couch, and instead pulled over a heavy wooden chair, ████████████████████ ██████.

"I know," he said.

I took a sip of tea.

"Please," he said, looking away, "I did not want to do wrong things, but nobody help me. Nobody. You will not help. What can I do, please?"

It struck me that his English had probably improved. For all its unevenness, there was a confidence in it that Bobby hadn't described.

"She is old woman," Ralph went on. "Poor old woman. Yes? What do I do?"

I looked him right in the eye, and I could see that he was forcing himself not to look away.

"You must not return her. After what happens."

I opened my mouth to talk, then stopped myself one more time.

"Her daughter dies for you. You must not return her."

"When did she get here?"

"It is seven weeks. I know you are coming."

"Shall I call you Ralph or ███████?"

I barely kept myself from grimacing at my use of the word "shall."

"Ralph or ███████. Both okay."

"Okay. ███████. How did you get her here?"

"Four year I work. First, restaurant. Seven day. I cook ██████████████ for the people. Then in ████████████, when English is better. I save money. Every day. This is how."

"But how did you get her out of █████?"

"You can buy your person there."

"They weren't watching her?"

"So much time is gone. She go at night. Easy to ████████ Harbor. But I pay more because police find her, big trouble. He bring her ██████████ then here. I work every day. For her. Please. Old woman. Now with son. You must not return."

"Nobody's going to return her," I said.

"Please."

"Nobody's returning her. It's okay. I promise."

My words didn't seem to affect him. He continued to beg me not to have his mother sent back to ██████. Eventually, after I'd given my word over and over again, he stopped talking. Then he went into the other room and came back with a small wooden box.

Just as he was about to open it, I heard the lock slide in the front door. I whipped around as if someone might be coming in to shoot me. Instead, a woman in her thirties walked in, certainly the wife Bobby had seen that morning in front of the other house. Behind her, an old woman with a deeply creased face was carrying a shopping bag.

The two women came over and started to talk to Ralph in ████████. Soon, it was just the mother talking, and she kept looking back and forth between him and me. The ███████ words rattled out, flat at first, then full of emotion. Eventually, her voice grew extremely agitated, and then she started shouting. Ralph spoke back calmly at first, but then he started shouting, too.

I stood up and started to think of what I should say in order to get myself out of there. Then Ralph's mother turned and rushed at me. Before I could react, I felt her fingernails slash across my cheek, and I managed to turn my head just before one of them went into my eye. She started swinging both arms, and I got my hands up to partially block the slicing nails, but I didn't really know how to defend myself against an eighty-year-old ███████ woman. Her arms were so thin and bony that I was afraid they'd snap if I grabbed them. And her body was so slight that any kind of push or shove seemed like it would send her flying across the room.

Then her flailing arms were moving away from me. Ralph had grabbed her from behind and was pulling her backward. He was shouting in ███████, and she was kicking her legs and trying to get away from him. After he'd dragged her a few feet across the carpet, he started crying. She was still screaming at me, and Ralph was obviously begging her to stop. She seemed to calm down for a moment, and he started talking gently into her ear. But then she looked over at the wooden box on the coffee table and she went crazy again, shouting and trying to break free from his grasp.

Ralph kept whispering and crying into her ear, and finally, her whole body seemed to slow down. She stopped struggling, and he let go of her. She looked at me, still enraged, but with all the emotion concentrated in her face now.

She walked toward me, slowly. She stopped at the coffee table, picked up the wooden box, and started speaking to me in ███████. I listened to the motion of her words, up down, up down, and then shooting out in an even stream before starting to fluctuate again. I turned to Ralph, but he looked away, obviously not wanting to translate.

His mother nodded down at the couch to indicate that I should sit, and I did. She remained standing and opened the box. She pulled out a photograph, pointed it at me, and said something in ███████. Then she stared at the picture, closed her eyes, and handed it to me.

It was a plain girl, ████████, probably in her mid-twenties. She had a small round chin and soft-looking, pink-white cheeks. Her mouth was closed, and her face was almost expressionless.

Ralph's mother took the picture back and placed it on the coffee table. Then she took another picture out of the box, held it up for me to look at, and laid it down next to the first one. She repeated this process again and again until there were fifteen or twenty pictures of the girl spread out on the table.

Then she started speaking to me again, slowly and quietly. At first, I looked back at her, but eventually I started focusing on the pictures. They were mostly black-and-white, though a few were in a kind of overly saturated color. There was a close-up of the girl as a stern-faced baby, and a formal-looking portrait of her as a teenager wearing a boxish, flower-print dress. In several of the pictures, there was an older boy with her, obviously Ralph. Even as a boy, he was thin and didn't fill out his clothes. In one picture, the two of them stood ███████████ ████████████████████ he had a mischievous grin and a happy twinkle in his eye, while she looked as serious as in all of the other pictures.

Ralph's mother stopped talking. I looked up at her, then back at Ralph, who was slouched against the wall next to his wife now.

"She's beautiful," was what I said.

Ralph's mother started crying quietly. Our eyes met, then she turned and walked out of the room. Ralph's wife followed her.

"Please," Ralph said, the word broken in half by a stifled sob.

"It's okay," I said.

"Please, do not return her," he said. "I ask you, for her. Sister. This thing only. I am sorry, mother is strong. Not want to hurt you. I am sorry."

"She didn't hurt me," I said.

"I am sorry. Please, do not return her."

"I won't, Ralph. I promise. It's okay."

"Not want to hurt you. Anybody. Very kind woman. Because of what happens, crazy sometime. Please. Please, no."

."Ralph, I promise."

"Promise," he repeated, like he was saying it to himself.

7

It seemed like I was driving in circles again, but eventually I turned off a dark residential street onto a busy commercial strip. A few miles down the road, I pulled into a Denny's.

The bustling restaurant was somehow moodless, which felt right. I sat in a booth against the wall and stared out the window at an intersection. While I was waiting for my food, my phone rang, and I looked down and saw that it was Bobby. I didn't answer.

I ate a waffle with bacon, not a combination that I'd usually get. After I finished, I listened to the message. I could tell he was nervous even before he started talking. "It's Bobby, I just wanted to see if you'd been there yet. Curious about what you found. How Ralph is. Anyway, you're probably not there yet, or maybe you're still there. I'm here. Call me when you get a chance."

I felt awful. I knew the truth about Ralph's sister now, and even though Bobby had said the truth would be better than not knowing, it was going to be a terrible blow. He'd sounded almost unhinged in his message, and it was clear to me that he was far worse off in general than I'd realized when I first met him. Maybe this would push him the rest of the way over whatever cliff he was holding on to.

I decided that, at the very least, I couldn't tell him over the phone. It just didn't seem right. It meant another long drive, but I didn't care. I even wanted a long drive before having to face him.

8

I spent the night at a motel next to the Denny's. I slept surprisingly well under the scratchy comforter and woke up alert at five o'clock. I grabbed coffee at the Denny's, got on 66 to the Beltway, and was speeding up an almost empty 95 while it was still dark.

Everything was quiet and peaceful for the first few hours, but then I started thinking about what I'd say to Bobby, and how I'd say it. I must have gone over ten different speeches to him in my head, and practiced and refined each one until it was as smooth and easy to swallow as possible.

I was going ninety whenever the traffic allowed it, and I finally got pulled over in Connecticut. The cop asked why I was going so fast, and I said, "I have to talk to somebody."

9

The sun was down but the sky was still light blue when I parked across from Bobby's house. I knew he'd be wondering why I hadn't called him back yet, and I was anxious for him to see me and realize I'd driven all this way for him.

I opened the screen door and walked into the kitchen. Bobby was standing over the sink in an undershirt, washing dishes. He looked startled when he saw me, but he instantly wiped the surprise from his face and replaced it with a welcoming look.

"What are you doing here?"

"I'm answering your call."

"Why didn't you just call me?"

"I don't know. I thought I should see you."

Out of the corner of my eye I noticed a backpack on the floor by the refrigerator. I glanced quickly at it. The top part, over the front pocket, was covered with buttons. There was one with a peace sign on it, and another one with a picture of John Lennon. The rest were too small to make out.

Bobby moved over to the table and pulled a plaid shirt off the back of a chair. "Let's get out of here," he said. "Too much time sitting around this fucking kitchen."

Before I could say anything he was out the door, and I was behind him. He walked over to his car, and I went around to the passenger side and got in.

"There's a great coffee shop in Briarside, a few towns over," he said. "Let's check it out."

We couldn't have gone more than a quarter mile down the mountain road before I felt it. The speed was wrong. He wasn't necessarily going too fast or too slow, but he was going at a rate recognizable as someone going slower than they wanted to so they wouldn't be seen as going too fast. I started picking up on other things, too—there was something slightly off in the hang of his elbows, and his gaze was too sharply focused out the window. It was unmistakable. He was driving like someone who's trying not to be alerting.

At the bottom of the mountain, he took the turn onto the main road preposterously slowly, then seemed to realize it and started going too fast. I looked at his face and saw the blasé expression that he was using to go along with his excessive speed, like he was some sort of prince tooling around the streets of his kingdom in a convertible. If there were any doubt in my mind as to whether or not I was imagining all of this, now it was erased.

The road butted up against a rock-face to the left and overlooked a valley to the right. After several miles it curved into a heavily wooded area. It was dark under the canopy of trees and suddenly felt very secluded.

A few minutes into the woods, Bobby pulled to the side of the road, jerked the gearshift into park, and put his face in his hands.

"Tell me," he said.

Could I have misread all of his nervousness? Was he driving strangely because he was worried I had bad news about Ralph? I tried to remember all the things I'd gone over in my head to say to him, but everything had disappeared.

"I think it was bullshit," was what came out of my mouth.

"What?"

"I think he made it all up. There were just a lot of indications. When I asked about his sister, he seemed surprised, in the exact way of someone who doesn't know what you're talking about. He caught on, but it took a few seconds. And his mother was there with him. That's good news, I guess. He smuggled her over. But she didn't seem upset about anything. She didn't seem like a mother who had lost her daughter."

"You're lying," Bobby said.

"What?" I said. "What are you talking about?"

"I was in the business longer than you. You come to realize any good news is a lie."

"I—"

"It's okay," Bobby said.

I waited a minute, then said, "I'm sorry."

"But his mother? Is that true?"

"Yes. He got her over."

"That's good."

"That's good for them. Very good."

"But the sister?"

"She was real."

There was a brief pause. "Yeah, I know. I know." He nodded. "She was real."

"I'm afraid so," I said.

Bobby put his face back in his hands. "How did you know?"

"I saw pictures. Of him and her. The sister. The mother, too, with her."

A huge, unexpected sob burst out of Bobby. Tears started rushing down his face, and he shot the back of his hand up to wipe them away. Almost as soon as the crying started, it stopped. He sniffled a few times, took a deep breath, then stared out the windshield.

Finally, he turned and stared at me. I stared right back, fighting the desire to look away. He probably wasn't sure if I'd seen the backpack. But the way I was looking at him now, flat and affectless, should have clearly told him that I had. I was sure that he was reading it right, but he wouldn't let himself crack.

"Bobby, I saw it," I said.

"Saw what?"

"The backpack."

"The backpack? What, the one in the kitchen? That's my neighbor's kid's. So what?"

"Don't insult me, Bobby."

He looked away. I couldn't tell if he was going to cry again, or shout at me, or start the car and drive away. Part of me even thought he was going to hit me. But instead, he started talking.

"They did get stopped at the border. That first-tour, Craig, who I thought was such an idiot, ███████████████████████ ██. It was pretty fucking smart. The next day, Tom was at the embassy in ████████. The day after that he was in Washington. I timed it so that I'd be back from my tour three weeks later. I couldn't have it coincide exactly, it would be too obvious. So when Tom got there, a secretary named Serena took him home. I knew it would be her. She was just sweet like that, loved kids, would do anything for anybody. It was just temporary, while they figured out what to do with him. And I knew they'd be having the discussions in the Chief's office, they had to: 'Why don't we have Bobby take him?' 'Do you think Bobby might want him? He got us into this whole fucking mess.'

"When I got back, I played it like I didn't want him. DC/██, who generally wanted to rip my throat out, asked me what I thought we should do with him, I said I had no idea. And then, after a few days, I go to Serena's house. Tom seemed to know what to do . . . or maybe it was because it was what he wanted . . . but he got all happy when

I got there. He rushes over to me. What are they gonna do? They see the kid loves me. I think Serena and her husband, their kids were grown up a long time ago . . . they like Tom. I think they want him. But they see this, what are they gonna do? Of course she says I should take him. I acted all reluctant. Like, 'Well, it's just a big step. Suddenly having a kid.' I had a funny feeling Serena was slightly suspicious. Like she wasn't buying the whole thing. But she didn't say anything. And that was it. I got him. The Agency got him citizenship papers—real, not forged. I got fired. Here we are."

"What about Ralph?"

"That was all how I said it."

"Did you want me to go there? Was that your idea, that I thought I thought of?"

"I don't know. I'm so fucked up about that. I thought of it, but I wasn't going to push. Then you suggested it. I thought it was time for somebody to have a look. I really thought he might be lying."

I let everything sink in for a minute, then I said, "Where was Tom all week?"

"Spring break. With a friend's family in Vermont."

I pictured Bobby moving everything out of the kitchen—Tom's jackets from the hook on the wall by the door, his magazines from the bench in the corner—stuffing everything into the back bedrooms. We'd spent all our time in the kitchen, and he'd never offered to show me the rest of the house.

"Look, I didn't know what the fuck was going on when you got here. You said William sent you, but I didn't know. Were you from the Agency? I couldn't figure out why they'd be back up my ass now. Maybe trying to get the truth about Tom, maybe something had happened, opened it back up again. Then I thought you might be from the ███████ government, somebody they'd hired. Then I started thinking you were from the press. That you'd figured something out about something, but I didn't know what you knew. He's not eighteen yet. I still worry about him being sent back. I wanted to throw you off the trail, get you away from him, in case you didn't know he was here. I figured I'd bluff. If you knew I was bullshitting, that Tom was here, you'd catch me, and I'd just explain I was afraid you were going to fuck me. Which is basically what I'm doing now. Of course, the whole time I wondered if you knew I was lying."

"William did send me," I said. "I think. I got your address in the mail, I'm pretty sure it was from him. But I still don't know why. Best I can figure, he thought we'd be friends."

Bobby shrugged, indicating that could be the explanation or not, and as usual in this business, we'd never know.

We stared out the windshield for a little while, then I said, "So Tom's fine?"

"He's fantastic. Just the greatest kid in the world. Took him a little while to adjust—he was probably the only kid ever who had to be stopped from doing too many chores. But you should see him now. He's into mountain biking. Walks around with his headphones on. Great at math. He's also a budding peace activist."

"Yeah, I saw that button on his backpack."

"He's got it on a T-shirt, too." Bobby made a peace sign with his fingers. "By the way, I'm sorry about the driving," he said. "I didn't know if you'd seen the pack. He's on his way home from a friend's, I had to get you out of there fast. But I didn't want to seem like I was going too fast. Then I realized I was going too slow."

"You must have done a shitty fucking SDR in your day. Very alerting."

"I'm out of practice. And besides, you don't usually have the surveillant there in the car."

"I should have called before coming back."

"It's all right. I'm actually glad you know. Come on, I'll introduce you."

Bobby started the car and turned around. We drove back through the woods then alongside the valley. We were halfway up his mountain when he said, "He was spying on me the whole time, by the way."

"What?"

"Yeah. Un-fucking-believable, right? We'd been living up here for a year before I even found out about it. I was a real mess back then, very torn up about everything that had happened. Tom's an observant kid, obviously he can see that something's wrong with me. So one day he says, 'Why are you sad?' I tell him it's nothing, not to worry about it. But he keeps on me. He wants to know. So I finally tell him, 'Well, all that stuff I used to do in ███, some of it didn't work out too well.' 'Like what?' he asks. And I figure he's got to live with me, he might as well know, so I tell him, 'I got somebody killed.' And he says, without missing a beat, 'Was it the ███ man who came for dinner?' I say, 'What makes you think that?' And he says, 'Tell me, please.' So I say, 'No, it was his sister.' And Tom just starts crying. He says, 'It is my fault, it is my fault.' It turns out the General and some friend of his gave him ████████ a week—that's about three bucks—to keep an eye on me. Tell them when I came and went. Who was over. What he heard. So of course he told them all about that night with Ralph. And now he thinks that's why Ralph's sister got killed. I tell him he's got it all wrong, the ███ would never tell the ███████ about that, even if they somehow figured out it was more than an innocent dinner. Why would they help the ██████? But that doesn't mean anything to him. He just keeps saying, 'It is my fault, it is my fault.' And I keep telling him it's not. After about an hour, I finally get him to at least say that he believes me. But then he starts going on about how he betrayed me. How I was so good to him, and he did this to me. He's bawling his eyes out, begging me to forgive him, saying he wants to go back to ██████. I can't calm him down. He's practically hyperventilating. I keep telling him it's okay. That he was just a kid. That it was a different life, entirely."

POSTSCRIPT

I've always been able to read people well, in the sense that I could figure out what they needed to hear in this situation or that situation. And I've always been able to sit down with someone—anyone, really—and within a few minutes establish some kind of rapport. But in terms of understanding what goes on deep inside people when they're deciding to do the various things they do, I'm really not the person to ask. Psychology is not my strong suit.

So I can't completely explain everything that happened when I got back to Chicago. For one thing, when classes resumed for the rest of the spring, I started teaching Professor Lang's strategic delineation system to my students. The SDS is based on the idea that countries can best be understood as analogous to individuals, with clearly defined sets of friends, enemies, and what he called "co-optables." Lang's writing is dry, but my class loved it. I found, however, that I no longer agreed with the theory. I didn't disagree with it, either. I just wanted to discuss it with my students and argue about it and see where we went. I liked it when they got worked up and declared, "That is *so* true," or "How can he *say* that?" I liked their passion, even though I felt like I'd lost some of my own.

Things were different in my apartment, too. What had been the slightly depressing smallness of the space seemed sort of cozy now. I rearranged the furniture and bought a media center for the TV and stereo. I started thinking I might stay there for a while.

And then a few weeks after I got back, I met a woman named Cynthia at a basketball game. We were playing Hooper Union, our main rival in the Independent School League. Cynthia was the fifth grade gradehead at Hooper and taught middle school English and Social Studies. She was kind, and a little odd, and I liked being around her. At the same time, I couldn't shake the feeling that something was missing. Cynthia wasn't worldly at all. She didn't follow the news. She was a rabid Chicago White Sox fan. Part of me found this attractive—a relief, really. But it also made me think more and more about Daisy, who knew the world, and had struggled in it, and had a take-it-for-granted sophistication that was much more important to me than I'd realized.

Still, as the weeks went by, I could feel Daisy turning from a person into a memory for me. Cynthia was real, Daisy was not. Cynthia was there, using my toothbrush, and Daisy was God knew where. I imagined her sometimes, lying in a bed in a small apartment in Istanbul, or Caracas, or wherever she was posted after ████, and wondering whatever happened to me, and probably thinking I was a huge jerk. I pictured her there and, even more than missing her, I hoped, passionately, for the best for her.

About two months after I got back from Bobby's, the phone rang in my apartment one night when Cynthia was over. When I picked up and William said hello, I asked Cynthia to wait at the Warsaw for me. I could tell she didn't like it, but I wasn't sure what else to do since the whole subject of where I'd worked before hadn't been dealt with yet. Or, more precisely, since I was supposed to maintain my cover, I hadn't told her the truth about it.

"William, my God," I said when I got back on the phone, "how great to hear from you."

"It's been a long time. I wanted to check in on you and see how you're doing."

"I'm good, I'm good. Doing well. How about you?"

"Doing fairly well, thank you. What are you up to these days?"

"I'm teaching. High school history."

"I would think you'd be good at that."

"I'm not bad. At least most days. Some days I want to strangle the kids, though."

"I'm sure, I'm sure. Kids can be difficult."

"They can."

"So your adjustment back to civilian life sounds like it's going well?"

"Pretty well."

"And what about your ████ lady friend? Have you two been in touch?"

I was genuinely excited to hear from William, and I wanted to talk to him normally, but I could feel that the transitions were too seamless, that he was carrying me somewhere.

"No. I wanted to write her, but I decided it was too risky."

"I thought you were pretty serious about her."

"I was, but what could I do? The end is the end."

"Anybody new?"

"Something, but I don't know. I don't think it's quite right."

"Have to keep looking then."

"William, how the hell did you guys know about me and her anyway?"

The "how the hell" was supposed to inject a note of casualness into the conversation, to gloss over the fact that I was asking for classified information I was no longer cleared for, and on a nonsecure line to boot.

"Does it really matter?" William asked.

"Well . . . yes."

"We picked it up." This meant it was from an intercept. "Their guys"—meaning ████ Security—"had the whole story. Maybe they were doing some routine check on her and turned it up, maybe she reported it. We didn't know."

"She promised me she wouldn't report it. She wanted to keep it secret, too."

"Probably not that, then. Who knows. It could have been anything."

I exhaled audibly, sending a message of resignation and upset at the same time. I was actually feeling both of those things, but I was also exaggerating the feeling to make him think that was where my head was at, when in fact I was after something else—I wanted to know why he'd sent me to Bobby. I didn't want to make the first move, though. And I was right not to, because after what I thought was a slight hesitation, the next thing William said was, "So did you ever wind up meeting Bobby Goldstein?"

So he had sent the postcards.

"Yeah, I did," I said.

"He hasn't wanted to have anything to do with me since he moved up there. Won't answer my calls, won't answer my e-mails. That's why I couldn't just ask him to get together with you. Ex-Agency officers can't resist a mystery, though."

It was quiet for a few seconds. I pictured William sitting on the couch in his living room. It was where he'd sat when we had breakfast with my friends the morning I'd left for ███████.

"The sister was real," I said, testing to see if that was what he was after.

"What sister?"

"TRACER's."

"Was there ever any question about that?"

"Some, yeah. From Bobby."

"I didn't know that. What was the issue?"

"Just Bobby hoping it had been a scam. So he wouldn't have killed anybody, I guess."

"I see," said William.

I waited for him to ask me about Tom, and when he didn't, I said, "And the boy."

"Nice kid," William said. "He was never a real source, of course. Did Bobby tell you that?"

"You knew?"

"I put the pieces together later."

So he wasn't looking for information on that, either.

There was another long silence. I was about to give up and ask William about his wife when he said, "So what did you think of Bobby?"

"He's a great guy. I'm glad I met him."

"Not just great, but the best, I thought. You and him."

"Thanks," I stammered, almost certain that he really meant it.

And then he let me know why he'd sent me to Bobby.

"So you see what you missed. What can end up on your conscience here. There are a lot of C/Os . . . it's not that they don't care, but they can take it. They can lose an agent and feel terrible and get up the next morning and go to work. I don't think you're built for that, Mark. Any more than Bobby was. So you shouldn't feel too badly about the way things turned out. At the end of the day, this isn't where you belonged."

I sat on the couch for a few minutes, then went to meet Cynthia at the Warsaw. On my way over, I realized she might not be there. I had asked her to leave my apartment in such a strange and offensive way that she might have just gone home. But as I crossed Clark Street, I could see her through the window of the near-empty bakery, sitting at a table waiting for me.

I sat down across from her and put my head in my hands.

"You're not gonna fucking believe . . . ," I said, then I stopped.

"What is it?" Cynthia asked.

"I just . . . I just . . ."

I was this close to telling her everything.

In late fall, the Association of Trial Lawyers had its annual meeting in Chicago. Lenny had come to this every year since he'd graduated from law school. I knew that he liked to stay at the Hilton, and the second morning of the conference, I went and waited in the lobby. I missed him in the morning, but around lunchtime I saw him heading toward the elevator.

When I touched his shoulder, he jumped.

"Jesus," he said. "You scared me."

I smiled. "How's things?" I said. "Can we get a drink?"

He frowned but followed me to the hotel bar. I ordered a Heineken, which was what we'd both drunk in college, and he ordered a Bass.

"So I'm back," I said.

"I gather."

"No, really back. I quit the ███████████████. I'm living in Chicago again."

"And now you want to be friends again?" Lenny said.

"I didn't think we ever stopped being friends."

"Well, we did."

We sipped our beers quietly for a few minutes.

Finally, Lenny said, "Were you really in the CIA?"

I wasn't a hundred percent sure why the Agency asked me to maintain my cover—maybe something I'd worked on was considered especially sensitive, or maybe they thought they could be embarrassed by what had happened with me and Daisy.

"No," I said.

"I didn't think so," said Lenny.

"You didn't? You were always teasing me about it. You told everyone within a hundred yards that I worked at the CIA."

"I was just kidding."

"Well, it was fucking annoying," I said.

"Is that why you stopped calling me?"

"Not really," I said, feeling a little bit confused about it myself. "Look, I'm sorry. I was a jerk. I got caught up in a different life, and I was a jerk. But you're my oldest friend. Can't we just start over?"

"I'm your oldest friend?"

"Well, not really. But I like you a lot."

We both smiled, then went back to our drinks.

It was one of those Chicago nights where a freezing rain, halfway between water and ice, is lashing against the sidewalks, the bus stops, the people on the street scrunched into their coats—it was so bad I didn't even want to go out to the Warsaw. So I'd made tea, and I was sitting on the couch grading papers. When the buzzer rang, I figured it was a deliveryman ringing the wrong apartment.

"Hello?" I said.

The intercom barely worked, and I heard a series of sharp crackles and then what sounded like "Daisy."

"What?" I called into the intercom. "Daisy?"

More crackles, and then, "Daisy, Daisy."

I looked over at my boots sitting by the door, then went quickly down the stairs in my socks. Was Daisy going to be there? That seemed impossible. What word sounded like "Daisy"? "Delivery"? It was probably a delivery.

I opened the door and she was standing there shivering in a thin, wet coat. She had what looked like the beginnings of icicles in her hair.

"Jesus," I said.

When I didn't step aside, although it obviously offended her sense of manners, she pushed her way past me into the vestibule. I closed the door, and we stood there staring at each other. I didn't know if I should hug her, or dry her off, or yell, or apologize. I finally tried to manage a smile, but it felt weak on my face, maybe not even noticeable.

I led her upstairs, then sent her into the bathroom with a T-shirt and a pair of sweatpants. She came back out a few minutes later, no longer shaking, her hair still wet but less disordered now. The usual slight stiffness in her bearing was gone, somehow counteracted by the baggy clothes. She'd left her glasses in the bathroom, too, and for the first time, she looked young to me.

I handed her a cup of tea. She looked at me and I nodded toward the couch, but when she sat there, I somehow sat down in a chair instead of next to her. I watched her register this, then take a sip of tea and lean back.

"Maybe you will forgive me," she said.

"For what?"

I tensed, not sure I wanted to know that she'd given me up.

"When you left . . . I ruin everything."

"How?"

"██████, who I believed was my friend. I had to tell, didn't I? I could not keep my mouth closed. Like one of those people who gossip who I hate so much. I had to be exactly like them, didn't I? And the next day, not two days but one day after, that is how long before she tells them. So I am called by Security. They sit across from me, at the table, it is impossible to deny it because they simply tell me ██████ has told them I have told her. And why did I not immediately report our contact? They want to know this. Am I a spy? They ask me. And after a long time, when they see I am crying enough tears, they laugh at me. Because they see I am innocent. And they say to me now, 'Do not worry, this happens quite frequently, it is okay not to report it, we just have to be very tough with you to make sure nothing is wrong. We will take care of you in our report.' And they look me up, they look me down. And they do take care of me in this report, because I have no more trouble. After, I want to call you, but I am afraid. When I finally get the courage one week after, I call and you are gone. Gone without anything behind you. No phone number to call in America, no address, no one in your house. Not a piece of you. I see it is my fault. I told that terrible woman, and it was the same as if I tell Security myself. And . . . I thought you might be dead, then. And later, at last, I meet someone from your ████████, they tell me you have gone home. They do not know why. So at least I have not killed you, yes? But your job—your career—I have ruined it. And I am sure we will never see each other again. That you will never want to see me again. I did not even believe it would be you here tonight."

"Who else would it be?"

"Anybody. Anybody can open that door."

"What do you mean?"

"It could be anybody. How do I know who lives here?"

"You didn't know I lived here?"

"Of course not. I only received the card. No name, no telephone number. Only the address. I thought it was from you, because I know no one else in the city of Chicago. But I am not certain. And I cannot understand why you do not write your name. There is no secret about us anymore."

"You got a card?"

"A postcard. It is not from you?"

I shook my head.

"Then who?"

"It doesn't matter."

She stood up abruptly. "I should not have come here."

"No, no, sit down. Please."

She hesitated.

"Please," I said.

She sat back down. I looked away from her for the first time since she'd started speaking, and stared at the window.

"Daisy . . . you understand what I was doing?"

"What you were doing?"

"Who I worked for?"

"You are one of those people. Like Security."

"Sort of."

Her chest heaved like she might start sobbing, but instead she sighed.

"You understand I wanted to recruit you, to be a spy?" I went on.

"Yes, well . . . I wondered about this. Even before the Security, yes. I was starting to understand."

"So, I . . ." I was suddenly focused on the street lamp outside the window, and I had to shake myself to come back and look at her.

"Daisy, I'm sorry."

She looked angry, but she shrugged.

"I have told myself your feelings for me were real. Perhaps I am a little girl in this way."

"No, not a little girl. They were real. I promise. They . . . are."

"And this thing you did . . . you do it no more?"

"No more."

The ending with Cynthia wasn't so bad, as far as these things go. I told her that an old girlfriend had reappeared, and that I'd realized I was still in love with her. It was the truth. She was upset, but she didn't cry or yell, and I didn't get the feeling it would take her that long to get over me.

She did say one thing, though, that I couldn't stop thinking about later. She told me she never felt like we really got to know each other. Maybe this was just something you said during a breakup, but I had a nagging sense that it might be true. And what worried me even more was that if Cynthia and I had never really gotten to know each other, maybe Daisy and I didn't know each other, either. What if she was going to be totally different now, outside the obviously unusual context in which our relationship had developed? What if it turned out that I didn't love her as much as I thought I did? I had a slightly uneasy feeling about it, like somehow a piece of the CIA had followed me home and would be staying forever.

I went out to see Bobby and Tom in the spring. On the last day of my trip, we hiked a four-thousand-foot peak called Mt. Hayes. At the top, while we were eating lunch, I said I was thinking about writing some articles for the Chicago alternative weekly about various experiences I was having as a teacher. Tom said, "You should write about me. I'm a good story." Bobby didn't like the idea, but Tom kept pushing it. He seemed to think it would help him get girls when he went to college. By the end of the day, Bobby had given in. One condition, agreed upon by all: it would go in my desk drawer until Tom turned eighteen.

And so, in it goes. In a few years, it will come out. I'll send it to the Agency's Publications Review Board. We'll see what they do with it.

As for me, I was sitting with Daisy in the Warsaw recently, eating stefankas. She was reading a new ███████████ novel with a half-naked woman on the cover. I was reading a paper one of my students had written on the final stages of the Vietnam War. As his passion and conviction leapt from the page, it suddenly occurred to me that I was done with the world. Not in a bad way. In a historical way. Wars, politics, people doing all sorts of things to other people. Me trying to be a part of it all. That's what I was done with.

And maybe with lying. Hopefully there would be no more lying.

I don't know what comes next. Daisy has her own apartment, but I suppose she'll move in soon. Or I'll move in with her, since her apartment is much bigger than mine. At least for now, I'll keep teaching. It's an exhausting, stressful, low-paying job, but about half the time I like it. I'm never sure if what goes on in my classroom is actually learning, or teaching, or just the transmission of some degree of curiosity about the world from me to my students. But whatever it is, it seems worthwhile.

Central Intelligence Agency

Washington, D.C. 20505

PUBLICATIONS REVIEW BOARD

October 14, 2006

Dear Mr. Ruttenberg,

The post-review copy of your memoir *An Ordinary Spy* is attached. The PRB has determined that your text contains classified information on multiple pages. You are required to delete the redacted material prior to allowing any other readers to see this manuscript.

We have determined that material in your manuscript is classified based on the following criteria:

1) Reveals the location of specific CIA activities which, if publicly known, would cause substantial harm to U.S. relations with a foreign country.
2) Reveals details about specific CIA agents which could compromise their identities.
3) Reveals nationalities of specific CIA agents which could cause substantial harm to U.S. relations with their countries of origin.
4) Reveals Agency proprietary cover arrangements.
5) Reveals sources and methods used in intelligence collection.

Please note that any subsequent additions or changes to the manuscript require resubmission to the PRB for review. Prior to publication, a final galley manuscript must be submitted to the PRB for approval.

The PRB requests that all authors include the following disclaimer in their manuscripts:

The final draft of this text was submitted to the Central Intelligence Agency's Publications Review Board. The purpose of the Board's review of the manuscript is to ensure that there is no currently classified material in the text. The review should not be construed to constitute an official release of information, confirmation of its accuracy, or an endorsement of the author's views. The Board has no charge to censor the text by deleting or amending information or positions that may be unfavorable to the Agency or the U.S. Government.

Thank you for your cooperation with the review process.

Sincerely,

Elaine R. Tull

Douglas A. Burnett
Chairman, Publications Review Board

ACKNOWLEDGMENTS

Thanks to Leslie Falk, David McCormick, Colin Dickerman, Bruce Feiler, Julia Rothwax, Rosa Weisberg, and Lois Weisberg.
And to █████████████████████████ and ████████ ████████████████, who trusted me with their story.

A NOTE ON THE AUTHOR

Joseph Weisberg is the author of the critically acclaimed *10th Grade*, which was a 2002 *New York Times* Notable Book. A former CIA officer, he grew up in Chicago and currently lives in New York City.